Each and Every Summer

Consistently Inconsistent
One Motion More
Two Different Sides

Consistently Inconsistent

TWO DIFFERENT SIDES

L A TAVARES

Two Different Sides
ISBN # 978-1-83943-735-9
©Copyright L. A Tavares 2021
Cover Art by Louisa Maggio ©Copyright August 2021
Interior text design by Claire Siemaszkiewicz
Totally Bound Publishing

TWO DIFFERENT SIDES

Dedication

Kati,

Once again, because without you I wouldn't be writing this dedication at all.

Blake's story exists because you asked for it. We wouldn't be turning these pages if you hadn't inspired me to write them.

This was the dream.

Rock on. I love you. And, most importantly, Happy Birthday.

Acknowledgements

Since One Motion More published, I've received such an incredible outpouring of love and encouragement that I couldn't possibly thank everyone properly. If you've read my pages or invested yourself in one of my characters, just know you've changed my life with your support.

To my editor, Jamie… Your patience truly is a virtue. I write the stories but you make them readable, and for your talents and knowledge, I thank you for standing by me and trying to mold me into a better creator.

In 2018 I stumbled across a band on Twitter, and there were certain similarities I couldn't ignore. They reminded me so much of the "then" version of Consistently Inconsistent in this book. As a thank you for writing the music that fueled so many of my late-night writing sessions, I added their name into one of the concert scenes in this story as a hat tip to their amazing work. First and Forever, keep doing what you do best. I can't wait to see what big things come next for you.

To 'Favorite Uncle' Russell, I could write an entire story all of its own right here in the acknowledgments and it wouldn't be nearly enough. You always were one of the best supporting characters in Brad's and my own story and for that, I'm eternally grateful. Until we meet again.

Chapter One

Now

It was about damn time I took things into my own hands.

I've loved her for too long and have nothing to show for it. For years I've admired her from afar and she's given me none of her time and even less of her heart, yet she holds mine in her hands. She always has.

Touring and being on the road is exactly what I always wanted, but I wouldn't have any of it without her — in more ways than she even knows.

Now, I stand outside the doors of The Rock Room, ready to give the performance of a lifetime without ever stepping on the stage at all.

The doors creak as I push them open and strut across the venue floor. My steps echo and my heart rate quickens. She's on the stage walking back and forth in heeled knee-high boots. Her blonde hair falls in curls down her back.

"Kelly!" My voice echoes as it leaves my throat and bounces off the walls of the empty venue. She looks at me and her mouth parts, but I don't give her time to speak. I have to get this out. If I don't say the words now, I never will. "I have loved you since the first time I saw you. I've never been able to give my heart to anyone else because it has always only been yours. I've wasted a lot of time trying to get your attention and the truth is, I'll keeping wasting it if you ask me to. I will wait for you, but I'm hoping you won't make me."

There is a long pause. She's completely still—unmoving and holding her breath. I swallow, hoping she speaks because...I've got nothing else.

"Blake," she says, my name echoing through the venue. "Can we...can we do this later? We're auditioning musicians for the house band..." She lifts her hand and points to the seats where bodies fill the spaces that I'd assumed were vacant. I rub my hand at the back of my neck while my cheeks flush something fierce. With no other option, I turn on my heel, leaving without the girl but with my fill of embarrassment for the next few years.

I slam the doors open and stomp through a two-day-old puddle in the alley behind The Rock Room, but the doors reopen and she runs out behind me, her boots hitting the water as she heads toward me.

"Blake."

"No, it's fine. I don't know what I was thinking—"

"Do you *ever* stop talking?" She grabs the collar of my leather jacket, pushes my body against the cold brick wall, then pulls me toward her—against her—and places her mouth on mine in a kiss that was more than worth the wait.

"I'll come by tonight," she says through the kiss. "I have to go back to work."

"Mmm, you should quit." I keep her close to me.

"Not a chance." She steps away, adjusting her clothes and hair before giving me a smile over her shoulder and heading back inside. I slide down the brick wall and sit in the alleyway. Though the ground is wet and cold, this all feels too good to be true—a dream.

* * * *

Hours later, I'm still convinced I made up the whole event—fabricated it to fulfill some decade-plus-long unrequited love quest I've been on since my preteen years. But I sit here, playing new riffs and exciting patterns on my guitar that I'll never remember later because my mind is occupied with thoughts of only her. There is a knock at the door. I ditch my instrument and head to answer with my expectation bar low. With my luck, it will be a package to be signed for or my band mate and best friend, Xander, dropping by without notice.

The knob clicks as I open the door, slowly and cautiously, preparing for the worst but hoping for the best.

"Where were we?" Kelly speaks in a velvet tone and she waltzes in the house like she's been here a million times. She slides off her jacket and drops it to the floor, turning toward me and pressing me against the door as I close it.

Soon she is lying in my bed and arches her back as I slide off what little clothing she has left. I can hear her inviting, requesting breath in my ears as I lean forward over her with my chest touching hers.

She's the very picture of alluring—her body bare and lit by only the moonlight peeking through the windows. Goosebumps appear at the surface of her skin, following the trail of my fingers.

My gaze falls to her ribcage, where a tattoo of song lyrics is scripted into her skin. I press my lips to the inked words.

"I like this." I run my thumb over the black script.

"You should. They are from one of *your* songs."

"How long have you had it for?" I ask between kisses.

"Since high school."

I think for a moment that all the years I spent watching her from afar, she was watching me too.

"I've always wondered about these." She lightly glides her fingertips over the right side of my chest and shoulder, touching the pictures embedded into my skin. "What's the story?"

"I was young, stupid and best friends with Xander." I laugh but she's still staring at the design, tracing the image with both her hand and her eyes. "Seriously, Kelly. There's no story."

The image is a half-sleeve that extends over my shoulder and to my chest. The collage features a pair of dice, a shamrock and one-hundred-dollar bills twisted to look less like money and more like roses. At its center sits five cards meant to be a royal flush, all hearts in suit. The ten card starts the piece and a Jack sits next to it. At the other end there is an Ace and a stern-looking King. A fifth card ties the flush together. Well, it would...if it were filled in.

"Why'd you leave this card blank?" Kelly pushes the spot with her finger tip. "Ten, Jack, King, Ace. You're missing a Queen."

I push my hair back off my forehead and sigh. She's not going to like the answer to this question.

"I read about this tattoo in a magazine once," she admits. A pink color blushes at her cheek.

"So, you already know then." I lean in and kiss her in an attempt to distract her, but my efforts fail, and she continues to press for an answer.

"I know what the magazine says. I want to know if you tell a different story."

I give up and roll off her, collapsing in a heap.

"In the article I read you said you didn't fill it in because there is — and I quote — no *one* Queen." Her lip curls at the corner and she raises one eyebrow.

That part of the story is somewhat but not all true. At the time I was young, single and carefree. I had developed quite the reputation and nothing anyone said bothered me. If they photographed me in some trash tabloid every day with a different woman? So be it. I wasn't sorry for how I had lived my life.

But I'm older now. I'm changing, hopefully for the better. I gave them the answer that magazine *wanted*. They printed the words they thought would sell.

I roll to one side and look at her then run my fingers through her mess of blonde hair. "It's not that I couldn't commit to only one Queen, Kelly." I graze her neck with my lips, and she tilts her head back. I pull my body up over hers and look into her perfect eyes. "I just hadn't found her yet."

A short while later in the pitch-dark hours, she breathes even, slow-paced breaths as she sleeps next to me. My phone buzzes wildly on the bedside table and I answer it, groggily, rubbing the tired from my eyes.

"Xander?" I say once I hear the voice, and Kelly wakes too, wide-eyed and wondering.

"Yeah," I say, "I'll be there. Just give me a few minutes."

"Is everything okay? Is Natalie okay?" She jolts to an upright position, covering herself with the sheet.

"Yeah, yeah. Natalie is fine." I stand from the bed then hop into my jeans, after I pick them up off the floor. I swallow hard. She's not going to take this well. "Xander got arrested."

Her eyes widen and she doesn't need to ask the question for me to know she wants more answers.

"He went to Julian's house. Mariah was there. I don't know all the details, but he's in real trouble this time, I think."

"He...went to Julian's house?" Her voice sways closer to anger than worry. "Do me a favor, Blake?"

"Anything," I say, sitting at the edge of the bed beside her.

"Let me go pick him up."

Chapter Two

I had imagined Kelly and my beginning going much differently. After our first night together, I expected that coveted honeymoon phase where everything is simple and right, but that's not what I got. I haven't even heard from her in days.

"Are you avoiding me?" I slide onto a stool at the bar in The Rock Room. She wouldn't come to me, so I went to her.

"Not avoiding you," she says, but her eyes – dare I say it? – *avoid* mine.

"I don't get it. *Xander* shows up to someone's house and busts through the door. *Xander* threatens someone. *Xander* gets a black eye, a bloody nose and an overnight in a cell and somehow *I'm* the one in the doghouse?" I run my fingers through the roots of my hair and leave my head resting in my hand, my elbow against the bar top.

She finishes pouring the beers from the tap and slides them to two customers sitting near me, then comes around the bar, takes my hand and leads me away from them.

"This isn't *just* about what happened with Xander." She bites at her manicured nails and still won't look directly at me. She rocks back and forth on her heels.

I place my fingers at her jaw and turn her face so she's staring at me. She rests her cheek in my hand where her skin is soft against my rugged palms. I trace where her hairline meets her neck with the tips of my fingers.

"Blake…" she says, and I can tell the next words off her tongue aren't going to be promising. "I'm just not… I'm just not looking for anything serious."

The words cut through me as easy as scissors through paper.

"I thought…"

"I know. I know." She bites her lip. "Everything you said was beautiful. And I thought I wanted it too. But you guys are just *so* complicated."

She walks away, taking the last word with her. By myself, standing in the middle of The Rock Room with my heart in my hands, I sway back and forth in the same spot I was standing just a few days ago. And just like that, the dream is over.

* * * *

Days turn into weeks where I am *oh so lucky* enough to watch Xander get everything he has ever wanted. He got down on one knee and proposed to his girl, who said yes, and they start their life together, all while it's his antics that lost me the girl I've been chasing after for years.

Makes sense, right? *He* screws up for the millionth time and *I* lose the girl because I am, as they say, guilty by association.

At their engagement dinner, I concentrate mostly on the drink in my hand and the empty glasses on the table, but every once in a while, I take a chance and steal glances across the way to see Kelly sitting with her head in her hand, not enjoying the celebration the way I thought she would. Natalie taps her on the shoulder, and she leans in, fakes the biggest smile she can muster and Xander's mother snaps a picture.

"Blake," Xander's mother says, "Get over here. Take a picture with Xander."

I push back my chair and stand in the corner of the room, leaning into Xander's shoulder as his mom snaps hundreds of pictures. We are used to the media, but Xander's mom is exponentially worse. She always has been.

"Everything okay?" Xander asks once our photoshoot is over. "You seem off."

"Never better." I look around to see where the waitress is with the next round of drinks.

"I'm sure you already expected this, but I'd really like it if you would be my best man." He smiles widely, oozing happiness through the buttoned-up shirt he's wearing. I kind of hate him in this moment.

"I would be honored," I say, knowing that my temporary disdain for my best friend — my brother — is fueled only by alcohol and jealousy. Natalie is perfect for him. Somewhere beneath the liquor-infused anger layer, I am happy for him.

As I sit down, Kelly looks to me and our eyes linger on each other. I turn up the corner of my lip only slightly and she gives a light smile back. She stands from her chair and walks by me, saying nothing, but running her fingers across my back as she passes. I watch as she saunters away. When she reaches the door, she places one hand on the door frame, drops her shoulder and looks back at me before retreating completely. I'm not sure if this is a sign that I'm supposed to follow her, but I do.

She stands in the hall of the hotel outside of the restaurant, pacing back and forth across the hallway.

"Kel?" I ask. She turns to me, slowly, seemingly weighing her options of what to do or say next. She steps toward me, almost in a run, then her body is against me, her lips finding mine and kissing me with a desire that leaves me both confused and wanting more.

"I thought you said you didn't want anything serious?" I back away from her for a moment.

"I don't," she responds as she pulls me into the nearest restroom and locks the door behind us.

* * * *

Then

There are boxes covering every inch of the rundown, one-bedroom apartment when I walk in. In the corner, a bucket is in its usual spot catching drips where the roof leaks through a yellow-colored circle on the ceiling. Mother is throwing things carelessly into boxes, not bothering to sort or wrap anything. It's not like we owned anything valuable anyway.

"Mom?" I kick aside some packaging paper at my feet. "What's going on?"

"What does it look like I'm doing, Blake?" she snaps, throwing plates from a cabinet into a box. I wish she wouldn't toss them like that. We can't afford to buy new ones.

"It looks like you're packing up. Did you find a better apartment?" I ask, excited to finally be rid of the dripping ceiling and constant mildew smell.

"Yeah." She continues to pack the kitchen items. "In Massachusetts, just a short way outside of Boston."

"We're *moving* moving? Again?" My throat dries, and all the moisture that once belonged to my mouth migrates to my eyes to form tears I try to blink back. "I just finally got used to *this* school. I finally made friends."

She throws a bowl to the ground and it shatters over the yellowing laminate floor. "Damn it, Blake. We *can't* stay here. Go pack up your room. *Now.*"

That's that. No explanation, no back story. Just me packing up 'my room' which was nothing more than one small bookshelf and a plastic tote by the living room couch I've been sleeping on since we moved there seven months ago. I wasn't ready to start over, but maybe the next place would give me a space of my own. I'm not holding my breath, though.

* * * *

Now

The band members sit on Xander's balcony looking over the cityscape and singing along to older songs Xander plays from his collection of original vinyls. It's relaxed and easy, just like old times. We're quieter now, drinking a normal amount instead of over-indulging and talking about our futures instead of reliving our pasts. Time to face the music. We're getting old.

"So, what's with you and Kelly?" Xander asks as Dom drums against the banister in tune to the song flowing through the air.

"That's something you would need to ask her." I take a sip of my drink. "Then fill me in, too, if you would be so kind."

He laughs, but it's true. I have no idea what she wants. I've left the ball one hundred percent in her court. We play by her rules. When she wants me, she calls. When she doesn't want me, I don't hear from her.

It's not exactly what I pictured, but I don't know how else to move forward with her.

"How did you make Natalie see that you're not the man you once were? I mean, you were, and are more fucked up than the rest of us combined, and she still trusts you."

He glares at me but considers his answer.

"I'm the last person — literally, the last person — who can give advice on that. I probably didn't deserve the happy ending that I got. I was lucky she was willing to give me so many chances. But I had to work every minute of every day to earn them. I still do."

"I guess I just have to do everything I can to show her I mean business — that I'm not out there screwing around anymore."

"It's a start," he says. "My suggestions would include — avoid New York and be clear she's not sleeping with Dom or Theo."

I look their direction with an arched eyebrow and Theo adds, "I don't kiss and tell." I throw a guitar pick at him and we all laugh aloud, echoing sound. It's nice that we've gotten to a point that we can laugh about things that used to make us cringe. Growing up isn't so bad, I guess.

* * * *

For months, Kelly falls asleep next to me in my bed, but I know when I wake up in the morning, she will be gone, just like all the nights before this one. This is all I get from her…physical contact. But we don't talk. She doesn't let me in. Some men would argue I have nothing to complain about – and I'm not, necessarily – but I want to be with her completely and not just behind closed doors.

"How about dinner?" I play with her hair near her temple.

"Dinner? It's two o'clock in the morning."

"Not right now," I say with a laugh. "Later this week some time. We're leaving for the tour in a few weeks, and I'd like to take you out a few times before we go."

Kelly sits up and pulls her shirt over her upper body, then stands and steps into her jeans.

"Where are you going?" I swing my legs over the edge of the bed.

"Home." She walks to the door frame. "Goodnight, Blake," she adds, looking over her shoulder.

She leaves the room, heading toward the kitchen, and I follow closely behind at a jog.

"What is this, Kelly?" I don't hide my frustration. "What the hell is it that we are doing here?"

"We're having fun." She shrugs and shakes her head. "Or at least we were."

"This isn't fun for me, Kelly. I want to be with you…more than this. I don't know how else to say it."

She's silent and answerless for a brief moment. I can't make her stay, but I don't want her to leave.

"I can't do that, Blake – "

"And why not?" I raise my voice to a higher volume.

"Because you're leaving!" she finally yells back. "You are here *now*. You want this *now*. But, Blake, you are literally *known* for having a different girl in every city. The band constantly jokes about you losing count before your very first tour was over and not bothering to learn the names of the women you'd ended up with."

I want to argue back, but I can't. She's not wrong. I rub my hand at the back of my neck, looking at the floor so I don't have to see the look in her eyes as she berates me in my own home.

"I'm sorry, Blake." She places her hand on the door handle and cracks it open. "I like you. I do. I just don't really trust you."

The door clicks as she leaves with no counterargument from me.

* * * *

Then

If anyone ever tells you they *like* being the new kid at school, they're lying and aren't to be trusted. Being the new kid sucks. Being the new kid at your sixth school in eight years over two different countries and multiple states sucks harder. I stand in the hallway, by myself, holding a piece of paper that may as well have been written in hieroglyphics. It makes no sense to me. Then again, school was never my strong suit, right down to the school map and schedule.

"You need help?" a boy in a black jacket and dark jeans asks me. His hair is much too long and he carries a tattered acoustic guitar case at his side.

"Yeah, if you don't mind." In the words that escape my lips, I can hear what is left of the slight South African accent I once had. My years in the States have diminished the sound quite a bit—I've picked up pronunciation and dialogue from each of the diverse regions we have lived in. We usually spent enough time in each area to allow me to inherit pieces of the local accent, creating a unique blend that doesn't belong to any one place in particular but never a long enough time to actually *belong* to any of them.

He places his antique-looking guitar case down next to his worn-out canvas shoes and steps toward me, looking at my class schedule.

"Well, we have the first two classes together, so I can help you with those. Just follow me."

"That sounds good," I mumble. First days have never gone this well for me. My first days have historically consisted of stuck lockers, tripping on untied shoelaces, dropping my books in front of a large crowd or bumping into someone in the lunchroom and wearing their pasta dish for the remainder of the day. This is too easy—too good to be true. I'm sure of it.

"This way, then." He picks up his guitar and heads down the hallway. That's when I realize he doesn't have any books with him. "I'm Alexander, by the way."

"Blake," I say in response, but my voice is distant, my attention elsewhere.

A girl in the hallway spins the lock on her locker about ten yards from us. She wears ripped jeans with her blonde hair dyed to an almost white shade on top with the deepest black coloring the underneath. Her black-and-white canvas sneakers are decorated with writing and drawings covering every inch of the fabric. Her notebooks are covered in stickers of music notes and band names. She has headphones in, listening loud enough that the entire hallway could hear the music. The headphones were useless, really. She would have been better off playing the tracks out loud.

"Alexander?" she says, raising her voice an octave as if she's surprised to see him. He waves to her and she removes a headphone. "I hardly recognized you without your braces and band uniform." She raises an eyebrow and lets out a giggle, returning her headphone to her ear. Alexander rolls his eyes and treks onward.

"Band and braces?" I ask, my eyes widening. He turns and faces me, his eyes narrowed in a way that says we are never to bring it up again. I swallow hard and he turns away, continuing our path to our first class.

"Hey, Alexander?" I ask, quickening my pace to match his. He looks at me over his shoulder and places black sunglasses over his eyes, even though we are indoors. "Who was that?" My voice is hushed.

"Kelly Montoy." He offers no other information except her name.

Chapter Three

Now

The school is almost entirely unlit except for one illuminated exit sign at the opposite end of the hallway and a blinking smoke detector overhead. Kelly's heels *click clack* as we walk, breaking up the otherwise-silent soundtrack.

"What are we doing here?" Her voice is a whisper, as if we're going to get in trouble for being in the hallways of our old school – and maybe we will, but it's a risk I'm willing to take.

"Come here." I take her hand and lead her onward.

"Where are you taking me?" She giggles and follows closely behind.

"Back in time." My voice is smooth and playful as I chauffeur her around the corner and flick on the lights in the hallway above her old locker.

She runs her fingers across the faded maroon metal and spins the lock. She smiles then her eyes find mine.

They turn to a confused glance when she realizes I've left her side.

"That is where you were standing the first time I ever saw you," I say, shoving my hands in my pockets and rocking back and forth on the balls of my feet about thirty feet from her. "And I was all the way over here."

She leans her shoulder into the locker and stares at me, trying to see the point.

"That's how it has always been with us, Kelly. You were always too many steps away from me—always across the room, always in a different crowd, always out of reach."

I start walking toward her, slowly, speaking with each step I take to close the gap between us.

"But if I could go back, if I could do it all again, I wouldn't have waited so long to talk to you."

I lean into the locker next to hers and she looks up at me.

"This time, I'd like to introduce myself—not as the guy you think you know or the guy you see on TV and on tour. I want you to know the new me." I put one hand out. "Hi, I'm Blake Mathews."

A shy smile crosses her lips. She places her hand in mine and shakes it.

"I'm Kelly Montoy," she says, playing into the script exactly the way I had hoped she would.

* * * *

Then

My mother didn't understand why I wanted to play an instrument the first time I came home asking if she would rent me a guitar—she didn't understand a lot of things—but she had also never seen Kelly Montoy before. I was surprised when my mom handed over a large wad of cash and told me to purchase – not rent – a new guitar. I didn't know we had that kind of money, but I figured she was just trying to do something nice. She'd said, '*Why not, son? We're having a good week.*' I never knew what that meant, but I never dared to ask.

Alexander's eyes bulged out of his head like a cartoon character the first time he saw my new guitar.

"It is *beautiful*." He ran his fingers down the strings. "Why'd you buy this one?"

"I don't know. I just thought it looked cool," I admit, though truthfully my knowledge of the instrument is nonexistent.

"Are you taking lessons?" He raises an eyebrow my direction.

"I figured you could teach me." I rub my hand at my neck. I'm certain my mother's '*good week*' couldn't cover both the instrument and lessons – and I didn't want to push my luck.

He looks at the guitar and back at me again.

"I mean, I can try…" he says. "But I would have to teach myself first. I've never actually played a bass guitar before."

"*Bass* guitar?" I repeat the words slowly and carefully. I look at my guitar then at his, recognizing mine has two less strings and a different body style. He claps his hand at my shoulder and lets out a light laugh.

My guitar and new-found interest in playing weren't the only things that changed. Over time, Kelly ditched her drastic hair colors and unique style in favor of brighter, more trendy clothes that fit her new life as we moved into high school. She changed. She got popular. Me? I stayed exactly the same. I am still the kid with the odd accent who strums a guitar with his only friend on the stairs outside the school, playing the music that I picked up to impress the girl who still, to this day, has never found the time to look my direction. She gave up on her love of music, but I didn't. I fell in love with the music the minute I started playing a few simple notes. I picked up the skill relatively fast. I think, maybe, it was in me all along. It just took a young crush and a talented best friend to make it come alive.

A few painfully awkward preteen years after the first time I saw her, she was in the hallway, bent over a table sorting through papers and stopping every few moments to jot something down. I pace back and forth behind her, trying to decide if I should say hello or not, but each time I work up the courage to say anything at all, I swallow it down again. She turns around and sees me standing there, and I really have no idea what to say. I feign an interest in the bulletin board nearest me, accidentally taking down half the paper advertisements and quickly trying to tack them back into place.

"Did you need to sign up?" She points to the flyer in my hand.

"Sign up?" My voice fails me and cracks violently mid-question.

"For the talent show," she says, raising an eyebrow and smirking a half smile that forms a dimple at the corner of her lips. She taps the paper on the table with the tip of a pink glittery pen.

"Right..." I say, "the talent show." The hallway suddenly seems miles long and eerily silent apart from my awkward answers echoing against the lockers.

"Yes," I finally reply, clearing my throat and trying to sound confident. "I need to sign up for the talent show."

She smiles and walks around the table, smoothing her skirt before taking a seat and reaching for the sign-up page.

"Name?" she asks, and I fall apart at the seams, disintegrating into the old, scuffed hallway flooring. I had known her name for years. I knew her favorite song. It was the first one I ever taught myself to play. I knew everything there was to know about Kelly Montoy, and she had no idea who I was at all — not even my name.

"Umm...Blake," I say, and she jots my name down in large, bubbly writing.

"Is it just you, 'Umm...Blake', or will you be performing with others?"

Another question I don't know the answer to. Just as I'm about to respond, the hallway doors swing open and their squeaking hinges echo through the nearly vacant space. One long-haired student walks toward us, his boots letting out a piercing screech as he shuffles across the tile. Alexander's perfectly timed entrance gives me an idea.

"It's a band," I say, too quickly, and I hope she doesn't know I'm lying.

"You're in a band?"

For a second, I think she might be impressed. Before I can answer, the bell rings and hundreds of students fill the space around us.

"See you at rehearsal then, *Umm...Blake*." She waves as she picks up the sign-up sheet and steps in to tread the rush of students.

* * * *

Now

The opening of a show, historically, was my favorite part. The house lights are down and the crowd is antsy after being warmed up by our phenomenally talented opening acts. The venue plays dramatic music to prep our entrance to the stage. It never gets old, the way we walk out onto the stage cloaked in a pitch-black darkness then the spotlights illuminate us. Then, the crowd erupts in a collective cry that shakes the walls of the building and I pick up my guitar from its holder to play us into the same song we have opened every concert with for more than thirteen years.

Xander's voice joins the music I play – perfect, in sync. A natural chemistry that has existed since the first time we decided to play together in our much, *much* younger days on a vastly smaller stage. I love opening a show. Like I said, it used to be my favorite part.

But now?

Now I like the ending.

When we close a show, when the stage cannons explode rainbow confetti over the heads of the thousands of fans who showed up to see us perform, the strobe lights flash and cast dancing shadows across the walls of the building we play in – and none of it is as glorious as stepping off the stage where Kelly Montoy waits in the wings. She throws her arms around me and I pick her up, swinging her around in a dramatic twirl that matches the pace of the music that plays us off the stage. In those repeated moments, each time I exit the stage and take part in the post-show routine we've created, all the applause in the world can't match the way she cheers me on.

We've worked hard to get to where we are today – and I don't mean the band.

She's exactly what I have been wanting my entire life. The fame, the music – that was my second dream. She was the real dream-come-true.

"Do you think you could introduce me to the bass player?" Kelly says in a flirting tone as I reach her in the wings, wrapping her in my arms and spinning her around the way I have after every show she has attended since we've made ourselves officially an item.

"Ahh," I say between kisses, "he's very much taken."

"That's too bad." Her fingers play with the hair that falls against the nape of my neck. "I think I might love him."

I kiss her long and hard, and my tongue finds hers. I've been working all night, singing songs about love and forever, and still none of the words we sang could mean as much as this kiss we share.

"I think he might love her too," I say when we part, and she smiles up at me with a brilliant smile and flushed cheeks.

Xander joins us in the wings and Kelly reaches up to hug him.

"Great show." She kisses his cheek. "Natalie is in the back somewhere, probably reading a book or doing crossword puzzles. You know, usual things to be doing at a rock concert. Are you and she coming out for drinks tonight?"

"No, I think she and I are just going to head back to the hotel to spend some time together before the band hits the road again. Thank you so much for coming. It's been an awesome weekend having you both here."

He walks to the backstage area and disappears from view.

"Xander? Not going out for drinks? Is he pregnant?" she asks and we both laugh, because it's true. Xander drinks whiskey like water and wasn't one to turn down a drink historically, but he's changed a lot over the last year or two.

"They're so…" I start but can't find the words as I pull at adjectives to describe our best friends, "married." She laughs and nods an enthusiastic yes.

Later, Kelly and I sit in a quiet bar in God-knows-where, Minnesota, sipping drinks and enjoying the few hours we have left together before she and Natalie head back to Boston and the band goes back out on tour without them.

This tour is different. Our lead singer is a married man. It's been about a year since I'd brought Kelly back to the school and convinced her to give me a chance. Kelly and I are serious now after years of rejection and being on different pages, then a handful of months as a *friends-with-benefits* type affair. Things were finally falling into place for us – and I wouldn't have it any other way – things were just *different.*

We play shows and we go back to the tour bus or hotels without any pit stops for parties or VIP rooms. We prefer quiet meals at hole-in-the-wall, family-owned restaurants over lavish five-star restaurants. What is happening to us? Another side effect of growing up, I guess.

One major change was the difficulty of goodbyes. They were exceptionally harder. I love being on the road, but I had never had anyone waiting for me at home.

"I'll miss you," she says at the entrance to the airport, her bag in hand. "Enjoy the rest of the trip. Have fun – but not too much." She may be partially joking, but I know there is a part of her that worries about what goes on during these road trips when the girlfriends and wives aren't around. She doesn't have to worry. I'm not that guy anymore.

Chapter Four

The crowd in Denver is one of the largest we've ever played for – and the loudest. Their collective volume yelling over our instruments and mics almost rivals our tone. I can barely hear Xander's vocals over them but it's electric. They're a boisterous, vibrant crowd that's always ready to rock.

As if it were rehearsed, I run toward the edge of the stage, guitar and all, and jump into the crowd, turning in time for them to catch me at my back and legs as I surf along their fingertips. It's one of the few crowds I know I can count on to make it a successful mission – and I take full advantage every time.

Later, Xander and I sit on stage under soft blue light with only acoustic guitars, singing stripped versions of some of our older songs as the crowd sways back and forth using their cell phone lights like candles to the sky. We usually sit on stools at center stage, but not for this crowd. In Denver, our favorite city to play in, apart from our hometown, we sit at the edge of the stage, almost in the crowd, singing to them and letting them sing to us, becoming a part of the crowd while they become a part of the show.

Backstage afterward, Xander changes his shirt and tosses me a bottle of water.

"Theo got us table service at that bar we went to last year. It's been a while since we had a night out. It should be fun," he says, assuming I'm in.

"I think I'm going to call it a night. Go to the hotel, call Kelly and turn in."

"Everything okay, Blake?"

The question shouldn't annoy me, but it does. For the majority of our careers, all the news, drama and bad nights circulated around Xander. He was full of off-nights and poor choices, but I didn't get on his case nearly as much as he's been on mine lately.

"I'm fine."

He shrugs it off and leaves the venue.

* * * *

The sun beats against the glass of the tour bus windows when the band arrives the next morning. Once we are all aboard, the tour bus leaves the parking lot headed to Salt Lake City for our next set of shows. Theo and Dom are blaring some brand-new band's single through the tour bus while Xander I sit at the back in our usual spot by the liquor shelf. He's wearing his sunglasses, as he so often does while sitting back with his feet up, bobbing his head to the music.

"What're you playing?" He looks at my tablet as he hands me a drink.

"Just this online poker game." I scrutinize my virtual cards, unsure if I should chance it, but I do. I take a sip of my drink, place it on the table between us and pump my fist at my winning hand.

Xander shifts positions and leans in next to me. "Is that…? That's not real money, is it, Blake?"

I glance at the current bet and overall winnings box at the top of the screen. I haven't lost in so long that I haven't really paid any attention.

"Umm…not all of it." I feel fractionally self-conscious and turn the screen out of his view. It's not a lie. Some of it is credits.

"Did you play all night? Is that why you didn't come out last night?" he presses.

"You sound like Mom." I purposely don't look up from the screen. "Only she's not quite as whiney."

"Just be careful." The tone of his voice is heavy with concern.

"It's nothing, man. Just a game to pass the time."

"I know, but with your family history…" he starts, but I change seats, cutting off his sentence.

* * * *

Then

In the middle of the night I get up to get a drink and flick the lights on, but nothing happens. I think, maybe, the bulb is out, but then I notice the house is considerably cooler on this already-freezing winter night. Optimistically, I try the hallway light instead, but it too remains dead. Perhaps we're in a power outage, though the weather doesn't seem threatening.

I drag my hands across the old, peeling wallpaper in the hallway until I find the kitchen and light the candle on the stove top. Its flickering flame is enough to give me a small amount of light to get a glass and fill it with water from the sink. As the water runs from the faucet, I look out of the window and realize my mother's car isn't there. I'm alone – again.

The temperature continues to drop and the cold sets in through my socks and sends a shiver up my spine. In the light the candle provides, I see the mile-high pile of bills stamped with 'final notice' and overdue warning stamps and I know this isn't the run-of-the-mill power outage. The lights aren't coming back on.

Neither is the heat.

I bundle up as best I can and leave the close-to-freezing house, knowing there is only one other place I can go.

I tap on Alexander's window and he opens it.

"What're you doing? And how did you get up here?" he says, looking out of the window, trying to mentally recreate my path across the roof to the second-story window.

"Power is out at my house. A car knocked down a telephone pole nearby," I lie. "Mind if I crash for the night? It's freakin' cold, man."

"Yeah, yeah, come in." He grabs my arm and pulls me through the window. "Why didn't you come to the door?"

"Oh, it's late. I just didn't want to wake your mother." More lies.

"Yeah, okay," he says. "Let me find you a pillow and blanket."

* * * *

Now

I *can't* lose.

Our sold-out show in Salt Lake City went off without any issues and the crowd was amazing. We started small in Utah, but every time we go there, the crowd grows and grows and finally, we sold out not only one but two back-to-back shows in Salt Lake.

Next stop, Vegas.

I throw the dice to the table and the other players clap and cheer loudly. I've been at the same table for hours, hardly losing anything at all. People hand me drinks left and right, and I am having the most fun I've had in a long time. Turning a few hundred dollars into a few thousand dollars? It's too easy. This feeling rivals even being on stage, and I thought that was the best high I would ever experience.

My phone vibrates in my pocket. *Eight a.m.*

Eight a.m.? How did that happen? I guess it's true what they say… Time flies when you're having fun.

A slew of texts and missed calls fill my phone screen. Kelly. Xander. Cooper. They've been looking for me for hours.

Starting with Kelly, I dial her number as I head to a coffee cart one hallway down from the tables on the casino floor.

I can hear it now, her voice frantic on the other end, yelling at me and asking where the hell I have been.

"Did you have fun?" Her voice is unexpectedly calm on the other end. I feel like this is a trick question with only one right answer—and since I'm on a roll, I'd bet I give the wrong one.

"I'm sorry. I lost track of time."

"It's okay," she says. "It's Vegas. Xander called last night and told me you guys were out for the night and not to wait up for a call. I'm glad, Blake. You deserve some fun."

Xander. I didn't even tell him where I was going. I've been ignoring his calls.

"Yeah, it was fun." I swallow hard as my chest tightens and guilt over my *AWOL* status sets in.

"Blake?" she says, bringing me back to the conversation.

"Mmm-hmm?"

"I said I miss you."

"Oh, yeah. I miss you too, Kelly."

Chapter Five

My eyes are so heavy with fatigue that I can barely keep them open. My head and arms feel heavy while my chest is weighed down partially from guilt and partly from being so tired. My top lids meet the bottom ones longer than expected, my head falling forward until I jolt myself awake.

Everything seems fuzzy. I'm standing on stage where the lights are flashing and the music plays loudly. Xander looks back at me and I keep playing. The room spins around me. The crowd spirals around me like a spinning carnival ride.

This isn't dream. It's a nightmare.

I imagine myself messing up, then breaking a string as my fingers fumble across the frets, struggling to play notes I used to be able to play in my sleep. Now I can't play them because of lack of sleep.

The set list is in front of me taped to the floor and I run my gaze down it. I pick the chords to open a song we've played a million times, skipping over a handful of songs on the list. Xander plays it cool, jumping into the out-of-turn song I started playing and adjusting as needed, but he turns over his shoulder and glares at me. I turn my head and see Cooper toss a clipboard clear across the wing like a frisbee, yelling something at someone out of sight.

And I realize…it's not a dream at all.

"What the fuck was that, Blake?" Xander hisses through clenched teeth, backstage after the show.

"Easy, Xander, I've got this." Cooper steps between us. "What the fuck was that, Blake?" He reiterates.

"I'm sorry," I say, but I know it's not enough.

"We turned your mics and amps off," Cooper says, answering so many of the questions I have with that one statement. "But we shouldn't have had to. Damn it, Mathews." His eyes are downcast as he walks away, leaving only me and Xander backstage. I'm not in the clear with Cooper. His lectures are lengthy and in depth. He is simply walking away to practice his monologue before returning to me to ensure that I hear the message loud and clear.

"You need to get your shit together, Blake," Xander says, pacing back and forth backstage.

"At least I stayed on stage and made it all the way through *my* worst performance." Immediately, I wish I hadn't said that.

"You do not get to compare what I *went through* to what you are doing to *yourself.*" His eyes are narrowed, and he points his finger at me as he emphasizes the words.

"Exactly, Xander. This is only about me. When you walked off stage that show, you affected all of us. You spiraled and almost messed shit up for the entire band. At least I'm not taking everyone down with me."

The air is hot between us, heavy with angst, anger and pent-up feelings. I hate myself for saying the things I've said more than he hates me for saying them. This is how I've always been. Instead of backing down or apologizing, I dig the hole deeper and make things worse.

Xander turns on the heel of his boot and heads toward the exit, leaving me alone with my fatigue and bitter thoughts.

At least I still have a pocket full of winnings to keep me company.

"Xander?" I call before he's out of sight. He turns toward me, crossing his arms over his chest. "Why'd you cover for me? With Kelly, I mean?"

He stays quiet for a minute, rubbing his knuckles at his jaw over his facial hair.

"We've always covered for each other, man. That's what brothers do."

* * * *

Then

If you told me this time last year that Alexander and I would be standing around a table at Rina Amell's birthday party, I wouldn't have believed it. Loners like me and Alexander don't get invites from the popular crowd. I have a looming feeling we're going to be on the wrong side of a bad joke, but Alexander seems to think you don't pass up an invite to this kind of party – whatever that's worth. Each of us has a plastic cup filled with beer from the keg, and Rina, Kelly and some jocks in letterman jackets join us at the table. Kelly takes a sip of her drink and leans into the table.

"Julian," Rina says to a broad-shouldered, athletic guy in a backward ball cap. "Truth or dare?"

"Truth," he says. This surprises me. I would have taken him for a 'dare' kind of guy, if you're into the whole 'judge a book by its cover' thing.

"Have you..." she says, pondering her question. "Have you ever smoked pot?"

He shakes his head no. "Nah, I've never touched the stuff. Too much to lose, you know?"

Someone calls Julian's name and he steps away from the table, surrendering his turn, so Kelly takes his place.

"Truth or dare, Alexander?" she calls across the room, batting her long lashes in his direction as she tries to include us in their little game.

"Umm, dare."

She smiles a grin that's filled with flirtation and danger. "I dare you to...remove one article of clothing." Alexander grabs the hem of his shirt, inching it up to show his abdomen, and the girls cheer him on. Just when he is about to pull it off, he pulls it back down and kicks off one shoe. The guys laugh. The girls pout.

"Rina," Alexander says, "truth or dare?"

"Truth."

He thinks on it for a moment.

"Is it true that Principal Wheeler caught you in the auditorium making out with Georgy Harris last week?" he asks, and I'm shocked twice. Once, because he hardly ever knows any of the gossip, and again because I'm surprised that he would care enough to ask.

"No!" she squeals. "No. I *did* get caught in the auditorium, but it was *not* Georgy Harris. *Never*. My turn. Blake?"

I perk up and my heart rate quickens. "Dare," I say before she can ask the question, though truth probably would have been the less dangerous option.

"Hmm-m." She thinks long and hard. Kelly leans into her ear and whispers an excited idea. Once she hears it, it's like the lightbulb physically goes off above her head. Her eyes light up and a mischievous grin grows across her lips. "Meet us in the front yard. We will be there in a minute." Rina and Kelly scurry off and we wait outside in the yard as instructed.

"What do you think they are going to make you do?" Alexander asks.

"I have no idea, but maybe we can get out of it. We really should be getting back to your house anyway." I try my best to stall, but I know there's no backing out now.

The girls join us in the yard, linked at the elbow, laughing as they skip toward us. Rina has a backpack strung over one shoulder.

"Come on," Rina says. "We're going for a walk."

Two blocks down on a quiet cul-de-sac, a bright blue Prius sits in front of a quaint house with a wraparound porch.

"Whose house is this?" I swallow back the fear that keeps bubbling at the back of my throat.

"Just a grouchy old neighbor." Rina opens the backpack to reveal a few cans of shaving cream and a carton of eggs. "Pick your poison," she says with a concerning amount of excitement in her tone.

"You want me to…what?" My hands shake nervously at my sides.

"I *dare* you to either shaving cream or egg that car." She pushes the bag toward me.

"I…" I look to Alexander for advice or assistance, but he's off lighting a cigarette, paying no attention to me at all. I reach for the shaving cream, take it out and shake the can a few times. I spray a small amount onto the windshield and the girls laugh and clap an encouraging cheer. I draw a less than tasteful design across the back window and Alexander shakes his head, blowing smoke into the wind. *This isn't so bad,* I think. It's just a little shaving cream, after all. I just want to fit in, and if a tiny prank is the key, I'm going to turn it. I press the plunger on the shaving cream canister, but it has run dry.

"Rina, I need a new – " I start, but look up to see that both girls are gone. Alexander strides toward me with his hands in his pockets, laughing at the masterpiece on the car. He takes out his phone to snap a picture of it, but just as he does, the porch light turns on and the door to the home opens. An older gentleman in a bathrobe steps outside.

"I have called the cops!" he yells, and I realize it's not just any grumpy old neighbor.

It's Principal Wheeler.

We run hard and fast away from the house and down the street as our sneakers hit the asphalt in hard, echoing thuds.

I almost stayed home from school when Monday rolled around, only my stomach pain and nausea wasn't illness. It was nerves and guilt.

"Hey," Alexander says, heading out of the doors as I enter them.

"Hey, where are you going?"

"Home," he says. "I got suspended for the week."

My jaw drops and puddles of sweat form in my palms. How did they know? How much trouble am I going to be in?

"Principal Wheeler saw me at his house. He told me if I opted to get a haircut every once in a while, he probably wouldn't have recognized me but 'he'd recognize this mop anywhere'. His words, not mine."

"Alexander…" I start, unsure what to say. "You didn't do anything…"

"You're my best friend, Blake. I will *always* cover for you."

Chapter Six

Now

I sit on a couch in the backstage area of a Phoenix, Arizona, concert venue and wish the cushions would just swallow me whole. Cooper walks in and pulls up a chair, sitting across from me creating a psychiatrist-office-type vibe – me on the couch, him trying to analyze something on a deeper level that doesn't exist.

"How bad is it?" Cooper leans back in the chair and crosses his legs.

"I don't what you're talking about."

"I am toying with the idea of keeping you benched for the show tonight. The boys can do it without you," Cooper says.

"You…can't do that." Maybe he can. I'm not sure.

"The show is *in* a casino, Blake."

Thanks, Xander.

L A Tavares

Cooper wipes the sweat from his brow. "The gambling. How bad is it? How far are you in? How much have you lost?"

I roll my eyes and adjust my position. This is pointless. I just want to get out of here and relax before the show.

"I haven't lost anything," I say, and at the moment, it's the truth. I have been on an upswing for weeks. Purely profit.

"Just respect, then." His lips pull together in a straight line as he says it. "You're winning money — which you make plenty of, by the way, so I know it can't just be about that — but you're losing respect — mine, the band's. You're so distracted thinking about where to take your next risk that you can't concentrate on a conversation. You're staying out all night so many nights in a row that you can't function on stage."

"That was my bad." Sweat soaks through my shirt and I stick to the leather of the couch. "Are we done now?" I add, standing from the cushions.

"Sit. Down," he yells. I've never seen Cooper yell before — not even at Xander — so that's saying something.

"This is the third time I have had this conversation, and there have only been five band members," he starts as I slowly descend back to the couch. "So, what does that say about *me*?"

I'm confused — which is par for the course with me, but more so now. I don't see how any of this has to do with him.

"I thought we did all of our growing up with Julian's issues," he starts, his voice quiet, his eyes on the floor. "Then Xander. And now we are here. I'm starting to think that maybe it's me — that you guys are reaching

47

for something I can't give you. I'm doing everything I can to keep you all in a recording studio and on the road and as successful as I can, but every time I turn around, one of us is failing. I can't figure out if it's you or me."

Nothing that any of us has done has had anything to do with Cooper. Cooper keeps us together and going.

"I'm not sure how much longer I can do this with you guys," he adds. "So, perhaps, it's time for this to be *my* last tour."

"No, Coop, no," I say, my tone defeated. "That's not what we need."

"I don't think I know what you guys need anymore." Cooper leaves me backstage by myself.

* * * *

Then

The yells are so loud that the walls shake, followed by the sound of breaking glass and a loud bang of unknown origin. I pull the blankets up over my head, as if covering myself is going to protect me from what comes next.

A shiver runs down my spine when the house goes noiseless, because the silence is worse than the yelling. It's eerily quiet, the very definition of muted. The nothingness is broken up by footsteps on creaking stair treads, and I hold my breath. There is nowhere to run, nowhere to hide. When there is silence again, I take a chance and peek out from under the covers. The light under the door is blotted out by two large boots then the doorknob spins—slowly, alarmingly. I swallow hard and the door opens. The sound of his footsteps gets closer and closer until I can sense his body looming over my own. The liquor scent on his breath permeates through my blanket and causes me to gag.

He steals the covers from me and tosses them aside into a pile on the floor, then he tosses my body into a heap in the same fashion. It hurts to breathe. My lungs refuse to fill with air, no matter how much I will them to. I squeeze my eyes tight and wish the demons away, but the second blow comes, no matter how much I try to convince myself that this is all just a bad dream.

The first time my mother had this boyfriend here, I tried to fight back, but I've learned in the months he has been visiting that fighting back makes everything worse.

She knows how he is. He shows up. He drinks. He hits anything that moves. She *knows*. But he pays bills, so, in her mind, he's more helpful than harmful.

* * * *

I knock on the door to Alexander's house and his mother answers. *Damn it.* I was hoping she wasn't home.

"Blake?" She presses her hand to her mouth where a gasp escapes her lips. I chose not to look in a mirror, but I can tell by the pain and lack of vision on one side that the eye is swollen shut and a far cry from pretty. "What happened?" She places her fingers at my jaw and lifts my face to hers to get a better look at the damage.

"I…fell…down some stairs. At school. Tripped over a backpack. I wasn't paying attention." I tell the lie in fragmented pieces, trying to come up with something reasonable on the spot.

"Let's get some ice on that." She leads me into the kitchen and pulls out a seat at the countertop, then grabs a bag of frozen peas and gently presses it to my eye. I flinch at the touch. "Alexander should be ready any minute," she adds, and I nod.

Alexander steps into the kitchen and drops his backpack to the floor in a thud.

"What the hell happened to your face?"

"Language, Alexander," his mother snaps.

"I fell down the stairs at home. Clumsy," I rattle off, trying not to look at him.

"I thought you said it was the stairs at school?" Alexander's mother adds, skepticism heavy in her words. Even with one good eye, I can see the look she gives Alexander, silently asking him if he knows anything about my home life that she should be aware of. He shrugs and shakes his head.

He's not lying. He doesn't know anything. No one does. It has bothered Alexander before — why we only ever go to his house, why I never invite him to mine — but I would guess, at this point, he's starting to put all the puzzle pieces together.

* * * *

Now

"Coop? Do you have a minute?" I ask, scratching the roots of my hair. He looks up from the papers in his hand and nods.

"You look...rested," Cooper says. "That's a start."

"You asked me earlier what I've lost, and I said nothing. But that's not necessarily true. Just because I haven't lost anything yet doesn't mean that I won't. I see that now." My voice is quiet. I've never been good at admitting I was wrong. "I was having fun, but I see now that this is all getting out of hand. I don't want to risk anything else. This career is not something I am willing to take a gamble on. So, I'll walk away from betting if you promise not to walk away from this band."

He looks at me, long and hard.

"I've still got a lot left to learn, Coop. You are one of the only people who has ever successfully gotten through to me. If you walk away, who's going to get through to me?"

He nods but doesn't answer. His eyes soften, though, and that's usually a good sign. I turn to leave but hear him call my name once more.

"Blake?" he says, and I lean into the doorway. "Tonight better be the best damn show you have ever played."

"I know. I know. I owe it to you."

"No, Blake. You owe it to *you*."

I take his words and my promise with me as I head to the backstage area to prep for the show. When we take the stage, I'm feeling refreshed and motivated.

The spotlights shine down brightly, breaking through the blue hue that colors the stage. Xander is on fire tonight, dancing and jumping wildly across the floorboards. It's almost a glimpse into the old Xander.

"Xander." I step away from the microphones but keep my fingers moving and the chords echoing as we speak. "Let's do *Way Back When*."

"I haven't sung that in years. Besides, it's not on the set list."

I kick the set list off the stage. "Live a little!" I yell over Dom's drum solo.

"I don't even think I know it anymore," he yells, leaning into my ear so I can hear him.

"I'd bet you do," I say with a wink, and I play the opening notes, slowly, then faster, eventually picking up the correct pace for the song—and the crowd loses their mind with excitement. Their adrenaline high courses right through me and I can see it in Xander's eyes too. He misses the song. He misses who we used to be.

"Arizona," I say into the microphone, "who wants to hear *Way Back When*?"

Their collective pleading cry would break the windows if there were any. It's loud, boisterous and longing.

"That's too bad," I say, stopping the repetitive riff I played. "Xander said no."

An instant 'booooo' rings through the voices of the crowd of thousands. I step to the edge of the stage, joining their boos and engaging in a dramatic thumbs down directed at Xander.

"Hey now, hey now. I didn't say no. I said… Well okay, I said no," he says with a laugh that echoes through the microphone. "Change my mind!" he challenges, and the fans scream. Their spontaneous screeches turn to a unified chant. *Way Back When, Way Back When. Way Back When.*

"Okay, okay, I'm in," he says. "But you guys have to help me. I don't remember how it goes!" he yells to the crowd and turns the mic to them. They fill the venue with the opening lyrics to the song. I play in, matching their pace, and Theo and Dom do the same. It's beautiful—a crowd-led song that we are merely background music to.

We run off stage and Cooper slaps me on the shoulder. "Now that was a *great* damn show."

"Blake?" Xander says through a sip of water. I wonder if he's still mad at me for antics as of late. "You brought me back, man. What do you say we get out there and play a few more old songs? I'm thinking, *Sunday Best*. What do you say?"

Sunday Best is the first song I ever taught myself how to play. The lyrics to it were written on Kelly's notebook the first time I ever saw her. It's the same song we played for the talent show the first time we ever played together.

I think about the building we're in. Just on the other side of these walls, lights flash atop slot machines, colored chips fall on green felt and cards are being dealt across crowded tables.

"I can't think of anything I'd rather be doing right now," I say, and we jog back out onto the stage that is taking me so far back, and yet, so far forward.

* * * *

Then

Alexander still hadn't answered me about the talent show. He sat on the steps picking the intro to *Sunday Best* over and over again. I tapped my foot off the cement stair, waiting for an answer, but the look on his face leaned more toward utterly irritated more so than overwhelmed with joy – though, that was pretty much just his perpetual mood.

"I didn't know what else to say." I cut through the lack of conversation between us. "She asked if I had a band, then you opened the door and I just kind of ran with it."

"That's great, Blake," Alexander says, his voice sarcastic and pointed. "But there's one major problem. I don't *sing*."

"Sure you do!" I try to be as encouraging as possible, though I've only heard a few notes every once in a while when trying to figure out guitar riffs from popular songs we wanted to learn to play ourselves.

"When is the talent show?" he asks through an upward exhale that blows loose pieces of hair away from his forehead.

"Two weeks –"

"Two *weeks*? You expect us to get our shit together in *two weeks*?" he yells, his voice echoing under the overhang. "Have you *met* us?"

"It is one song. Just show up to rehearsal tomorrow and see what happens," I plead.

"And if I don't?" Alexander clicks open the locks on his barely functioning guitar case.

"Then I look like an idiot in front of the entire school...but mostly I look like an idiot in front of Kelly."

"Not your best argument," Alexander says. "Hell, I'd pay to see that."

I shake my head, returning my guitar to its case and he does the same. He slaps his hand on my shoulder and I turn toward him. "I'm kidding. Have I ever let you down before?"

"Uhh-h –"

"Don't answer that. I'll see you at rehearsal tomorrow."

* * * *

Rehearsal is held in the auditorium with students scattered about the stage and seating areas. One group of students stands in the corner doing scales and vocal warm-ups for their a capella piece they plan to perform. Another student walks back and forth, mumbling to himself as he practices the poem he wrote for the show. One kid stands at the front row playing the bagpipes – poorly – and I'm ninety-nine percent sure that he doesn't even go to this school.

Alexander still hasn't made an appearance, and I check my watch nervously for the thousandth time. Kelly takes the stage and calls bagpipe guy's name. His act is so painful I'd consider stubbing my toe and biting my tongue at the same time more comforting, but believe it or not, he's not nearly as terrible as accordion kid.

"I thought this was supposed to be a *talent* show," Alexander says, jumping over the row of seats in the auditorium and taking a seat next to me.

"I thought you might not make it." I don't remove my eyes from Kelly as she skips across the stage.

"I said I would be here – and I'm here. Feeling pretty confident, actually, now that I've seen the competition." He places a pick between his teeth.

"It really isn't a competition. It's just a show."

"That's bull sh – " he starts to say, but Kelly stands at center stage calling the next group. No one responds. I look around to see a familiar-looking, broad-shouldered kid with a backward hat push the door open and leave and excuse myself from Alexander, following the student outside.

"Hey, are you with *Bad Feeling*?"

He turns around to face me, still leaning into the doors to the outside. "Kelly just called a group but no one went up..."

"*Bad Feeling* broke up about"—he looks at his watch—"four minutes ago, give or take."

"Oh." I scratch my head. "What do you play?"

"Football," he says, pointing to the school's team logo on his shirt.

"Yeah...not what I meant. What instrument did you play with *Bad Feeling*?"

"Oh. Guitar. Keyboard. Drums sometimes." My jaw falls slightly open.

"My band just had an opening for *literally* any one of those things if you still want to do the show." He considers the offer but doesn't accept right away. I reach into my pocket and unfold the sheet music to the song Alexander and I had taken and added our own twist to, handing it to him for his consideration.

"This isn't half bad." He looks over the music. "All right, you've got yourself a new band member."

"Great!" I say, too quickly, too loudly. "I mean, well...cool. I'm Blake, by the way."

He reaches a large hand out and I clap my palm against his.

"I'm Julian. Julian Young."

As we head back into the auditorium, Julian stops to talk to one of his countless friends and I practically run to Alexander to share the good news, but he doesn't share my excitement.

"*Julian Young?*" Alexander says in complete disbelief, "Have you lost your damn mind? He literally exists to ruin people's lives. It's his sole purpose on this green Earth."

"He doesn't seem that bad. Besides, he plays three instruments and writes songs. He's really good for the band – "

"We're not a real band, Blake! You are doing all this to impress some girl. It's not like this is all going to end in a best-selling album and an international tour," Alexander says with a scoff, loud enough that it draws attention from the other talent-show contributors.

Kelly's heels click across the wooden stage and she calls my name.

"Can you please, just this once, get over your preexisting impression and give the guy a chance?"

Alexander sighs, but eventually nods and gets on stage, taking his place in front of the microphone.

I was right about one thing. The boy could sing. I'm not terrible, but I'm no lead singer either. Alexander drew the attention of everyone in the room, and Julian? He drips talent. I'll admit that I was skeptical. The closest I had ever come to Julian Young was holding a football roster with his name on it in my hands at the one game I ever went to. I knew his name and I knew he was a talented athlete, but I never would have guessed he was this talented as a musician. I suppose this is why we're taught not to judge books by their covers.

Chapter Seven

Now

The last few weeks of the tour flew by, especially once we started to stray from the set list and began playing with some spontaneity. Every show was different with each one more exciting than the last. We've been missing that over the last few years of touring, perhaps even plateauing slightly, until now. The buzz surrounding our shows has us trending upward again both on the charts and on social media. Just when we were falling into a bit of a rut, our new format skyrocketed us back to the top. It was fun while it lasted, and there are parts of me that can't wait to get back on stage, but right now a much greater part of me is looking forward to something else.

The hired car pulls up to the curb and I step out.

Home.

It feels good to be back. As I climb the stairs to my front door, it swings open on its hinges and Kelly waits on the other side. *Damn*, have I missed her.

I wrap my arms around her and she gently presses her mouth to mine, biting at my lower lip. She pulls me inside, closing the door behind us.

"How many hours do you have until you have to meet the guys for the show tonight?" She kisses me between each word.

"I don't know. Four?" I say, as she pulls my shirt over my head.

"Perfect," she breathes in a whisper. She looks at me with an earnest, flirting glare, then pulls me by the belt loops down the hall to our bedroom.

* * * *

The Rock Room is packed, as it always is when we're in town. Every seat has a body in it and the standing-room-only sections are easily over capacity. We outgrew The Rock Room years ago, but it's where we started. We have to visit at least once every tour. CommOcean is a new, outdoor venue suited for much larger crowds, and typically we play there too, but tonight we are at home on the stage that allowed us to be introduced to all of the other stages across the country.

"Xander!" an excited voice calls. Jana runs across the backstage area and leaps into his arms, all but tackling him to the ground. Jana and Xander have been best friends for years. She's been in his corner since the moment they met, and they've grown their relationship from friendship to family. Natalie kisses Jana on the cheek then signs to her, and Jana signs back in a seamless fashion. I wish I'd picked up on ASL as fast as Jana has. I'm not quite there yet, but I'm working on it. Everyone else in my circle communicates with Natalie so easily, but she and I are still at the texting or pen and paper stage.

Jana stands with Xander and Natalie, having an excited conversation as they fill each other in on all the goings on since they've seen each other last.

Xander is lucky to have so many people to come home to, so many people waiting here when he gets back. I have Kelly, now, but for so many years it was just me. I don't have a Jana to come home to – a neutral party, someone who's not a girlfriend and not a band member.

"Blake," Jana says, waving me over. I join their conversation and she wraps her elbow around mine. She includes me in their tiny family they have built but still, I'm just the add-on—the extra one included because there wasn't anywhere else to go.

* * * *

Then

My mother sits on the porch swing, and though she's unconscious, snoring away with her head lolled against the wooden swing, an open bottle of vodka has been knocked over and spilled on the deck boards while a lit cigarette glows in the ashtray. I'm not worried about it, though. This is pretty typical.

I place my guitar case down inside the door and extinguish the cigarette, cap what's left of the vodka, then wrap my arm under her shoulders.

"Come on, Mom." I take all her weight and carry her into the house. She's dead weight and no help. I can only get her to the couch, but it's better than being outside.

A heap of laundry sits in the corner that piles halfway up the wall. It hasn't been done in weeks and I'm down to my last clean outfit. She'd said she was going to get to it today—and yesterday…and many yesterdays before that.

I place a blanket over her and throw a load of clothes in the drum of the washing machine, but there is no laundry soap to be found. I take a deep breath and look up at the sky like it holds answers or it might start raining laundry detergent, but I'm just not that lucky. Mother snores loudly on the couch. Giving up on the laundry, I head to the kitchen and open the refrigerator and freezer door, but a putrid smell exits and no cold air joins it. The thawed, rotting food suggests the fridge has been down for days but no one noticed. That's what happens when home-cooked meals – or meals at all – are a rarity, if ever.

The next morning when I wake up, I slide down the banister and head to the couch to wake my mother but she's gone, and who knows for how long this time. She usually at least drops me off at school before leaving me to head out on one of her undisclosed adventures. I dial Alexander and his mother answers.

"Good morning…uhhh…Ms.…Mrs. – "

"It's just Debbie, Blake—like I've been saying for years."

"Okay, Debbie. Is Alexander around?"

"No, Blake, I'm sorry. Julian picked him up early this morning. Did you need something?"

"Umm, no that's okay. I'll just walk to school." I look out of the window at the black clouds rolling in.

"Blake, it's supposed to get really bad out there..."

"It's okay, Mrs.—uhh, Debbie. I'll be fine. Thanks again." I quickly hang up the receiver.

I head to the door and reach for my guitar in its usual spot, but it's gone. I think back to last night. Did I leave it somewhere? Did I even bring it home? I don't remember. Already late, I leave the house without my guitar and head down the road as the sky opens up and downpours, leaving me soaked head to toe as puddles fill the road. I pull my jacket up over my head and walk as quickly as I can, but I still have quite a way to go. A car pulls up behind me and I turn to see whose headlights I'm standing in.

Alexander's mother leans her head out of the window and yells to me.

"Get in, Blake. You're going to catch pneumonia out here!"

"Blake?" Alexander's mother asks before I exit the car in front of school. "This is none of my business, but I have to ask. Is...is everything okay? At home I mean?"

My mouth goes dry and I'm not sure what to say.

"Of course... Why do you ask?" I speak too quickly with not enough force in my tone to convince either of us.

"Alexander says you're home alone most of the time. I'm not trying to pry. I'm just...concerned. You walk miles to school and you've been in the same clothes all week. That eye... I just wanted to make sure you are being taken care of." Her eyes are kind and warm, genuine—a look I don't recognize from my own mother.

"I can take care of myself." The words come out with more of a point than I had meant. I know she means well, but my problems are not her problems. I avoid her eyes as I open the car door.

"I know you can, but you shouldn't have to. Alexander and I… Well, our door is open if you need a hand."

I think long and hard for a moment. I'm grateful, but I'm embarrassed too — once for myself and once for my mother. "Thank you again for helping me today, but I'll be fine." I close the car door and she waves through the window, pulling away from the curb.

* * * *

After a few nights of scrounging together something to eat for breakfast and bringing Tupperware to school to ration my lunch and make it last until dinner, I come home to find my mother's car in the driveway.

"Mom?" I call from the entryway.

"In here!" She kisses me on the head as I enter.

"Hey, Mom, where have you been?"

"Working," she responds, throwing ramen noodles into a pot.

"You…you got a job?" I grab a cup from the counter and fill it with tap water.

"Something like that," she says — but offers no explanation.

"Okay, well, I have a project I have to try to catch up on. I'm a little behind in school. I'm going to head upstairs."

"Great!" She obviously missed the part about me falling behind.

"Oh, and Mom?" She looks at me over her shoulder. "Have you seen my guitar? I can't find it anywhere."

She stops stirring for a moment and turns toward me. "Oh, Blake," she says, a feigned hint of sorrow in her words, "I sold it."

"What do you mean you *sold* it?" I screamed, dropping the glass I was drinking from onto the counter. The glass shatters against the old counter top. "Are you kidding me? That guitar is *literally* the only thing I care about."

"Maybe that's the problem, Blake," Mother said. "You were spending too much time around music. Time to experience something new. This is for your own good."

"You know nothing about what is good for me!" I yell in a voice that cracks, and tears stream down my face. I don't try to hide or stop them. I just let them fall. Years of neglect and hurt fuel this moment. It was bound to happen. "You can't even bring home laundry detergent. We haven't had a real meal in months!"

She steps toward me and jabs a finger into my chest as she yells, hard enough to knock me off balance, "I don't need this!" Then she screams, "*Everything* I do, I do for you!"

"Is that what you tell yourself?" My voice is quiet as my chest tightens. "When you leave for days and weeks at a time without so much as a note... When you sell the item that means more to me than anything else I've ever owned... You're only thinking of *me*?"

She glares at me and crosses her arms, but she doesn't say anything.

"I'm going to stay at Alexander's house for a while," I finally say, standing up for myself, maybe for the first time ever.

"No, no, Blake. Please, stay here." She shows emotion for the first time all night. "Blake, you are all I have left."

I look at her, into her eyes that mine are an exact replica of. Then, I look around the house I have been in by myself more than I care to admit.

"That guitar was all *I* had left, Mom—and you sold it."

* * * *

I bang on Alexander's door with only a bag full of dirty laundry, standing in the pouring rain that hadn't let up over the last few days.

"Hi," I say, thankful that the rain might hide the tears I've been crying.

Alexander takes the bag of laundry and claps a hand on my shoulder, leading me into the house where his mother is cooking a delicious-smelling meal with fresh vegetables on the counter. I can't even recall the last time I saw fresh produce.

"Blake," she says, the warm smile she always wears in full bloom, "are you hungry?"

My stomach rumbles loud enough to answer yes for me.

"Everything smells delicious." I smile a grin that matches hers. "Do you think... Do you think I could use the washer and dryer?" A lump of embarrassment forms in my throat.

"No." Her response leaves me confused. A bright red paints my cheeks. "You're a kid, Blake. Go be a kid. Julian is here too. Join your friends. I'll get that load of laundry in after dinner is ready."

* * * *

Now

"We're back..." Xander says into the microphone, but he doesn't even finish the word before the crowd erupts into a noisy volcano of thrill and anticipation. *Chaotic.* It's the only word that suits our hometown crowd. As I look out at the faces that look back at us, many of them are familiar, probably because we've seen them at every show we've performed at this venue for thirteen years.

Xander flirts with the audience, dragging out the introduction and making them wait for the highly anticipated music. I strum a few patterns quietly behind Xander's back and forth with them, and Theo fingers a twinkling, gentle sound on the keyboard as Xander walks back and forth across the stage, telling the group a story about how we wrote the song we plan to open with. They're soaking it up, hanging on to every word he speaks.

"So, ladies and gentlemen, here it is," he says, wrapping up the song's backstory, "written by your very own Blake Mathews." They applaud, I give them a few hard riffs and wave.

"This one's for my mother," I say, the same way I always do. The lyrics aren't kind in nature — a perfect parallel for her, really.

Dom leads us in, a turbulent beat composed between the bass, cymbal and toms that flows together so intricately that one would be convinced he has more than two hands.

Playing in Boston, it's like we blink and the event is over. The atmosphere is so loud, so energetic that the show is complete in what seems like seconds.

Backstage, the power and volume are gone and quiet sets in again. The adrenaline that coursed through me has dissipated, faded into a nothingness that won't rear its exuberant head again until we step back on a stage—and I don't know when that will be.

I miss it already. Crave it, even. And I know it won't be long until I start searching for something to take its place.

"Blake," Xander says, crashing onto the couch next to me. He smiles a large grin that grows deep into his cheeks and shows his teeth. After spending so many years beside the dark, gloomy version of Xander, happiness looks weird on him. "Kelly still has a few hours left here finishing up with the crew and staff. Do you want to join Natalie, Jana and me for food and drinks?"

I brush my hair back off my forehead and take a deep breath. In many ways, I want to go. But in other ways, going out with them is another reminder that I don't really belong anywhere. I never have.

I'm not sure when it all changed, when these feelings started settling in that I don't have the sense of family that it seems everyone around me does. I have Kelly and I'm grateful that I do, but Kelly has two loving parents, a cousin who is more like a sister, a group of friends she can't live without and a band of employees who see her both as a boss and an acquaintance.

Me? I just have the band.

"No, no." I shake my head and put my feet up on the table. "I'll probably just wait here for Kelly."

"Suit yourself." Xander pushes himself away from the couch and wraps his arms around Natalie and Jana's shoulders, one on each side of him.

I leave the venue and walk around the city streets under a black, cloudless sky. The bar fronts are illuminated with signs, and loud music plays from inside while people line up outside, waiting to get in.

There's a hole-in-the-wall bar at the end of the road that only a few people occupy. The bouncer nods as I walk in, allowing me to pass without showing ID. I pull up a bar stool and order a drink.

A young brunette waitress takes the stool next to me. "Up for a game?" she asks, flashing pearly whites behind a smile covered in red lipstick. She holds up a handful of cash and a whiskey cup with five dice in it.

"How do you play?" I ask, turning toward her.

"It's so easy!" Her voice raises an octave. "It's five dollars to play and you get three rolls. Keep any matching numbers on the bar top and reroll the others. If all five dice match at the end of your three rolls, you keep the pot."

"Yeah, I'll give it a shot." I take the cup from her and shake it up, listening to the dice roll around against the sides and clink against the glass.

Two hours pass and I've spent more money playing with dice in a glass than I did on dinner and drinks.

A tall, tanned woman in a tell-all dress and heels leans into the bar next to me, watching my second-to-last roll. The dice shows a one where I needed one more six. *One roll left.*

"That's too bad. Let me give it a try?" she says, picking up the die, blowing on it, and rolling it to the bar top. *Six.*

The few bar patrons cheer and the waitress skips over, handing me the cash prize.

"This is actually yours, I believe." I hand the winnings over to the woman who tossed the winning number. Her hands wrap around mine, pushing the pile back toward my chest.

"I've got a better idea of what you can do with that," she whispers as one eyebrow arches into a suggestive expression. She bites her lip and leans in, whispering the details of her plan in my ear. "So, should we get out of here?"

* * * *

Then

Alexander, Julian and I clicked fast, just like I knew we would. Alexander got over his reservations and we started practicing together, creating music and writing songs. The talent show went so well that people who saw us perform started asking us where else they could see us play. After a few months of practicing and building ourselves, we added two more members – a drummer named Dominic and Theo, a keyboard player. We spent the whole following summer playing small gigs and local events.

We started our social media pages and gained followers faster than we ever thought possible. To think that all of this started to get noticed by a girl who was never going to pay attention to me.

The bass guitar quickly became the first thing I fell in love with, and I was talented, but Julian had this raw, undefined skill that I found myself almost jealous of. He had been playing a lot longer than me, though, and watching him play and hearing his notes only improved my skills. For someone who didn't want to be the lead singer, Alexander was killing it at the microphone. There's something about his voice that's so distinct and so unique, like he has belonged at that microphone all this time.

Besides Julian, none of us owned a damn thing. We used the auditorium to practice so Dom could use the drums that belonged to the school. Alexander was still playing a guitar that his mother had found at the thrift shop years before I met him. That guitar is so old, so faded, that I swear one of these days if he jams too hard, the whole thing will combust into ash in his fingertips. But at least he has one. I'm borrowing one of Julian's older bass guitars since my mother pawned mine.

"Blake?" I hear a voice ask me from the back of the auditorium when the music breaks. I turn to see Kelly peeking her head into the door. She enters the auditorium and walks about halfway down the aisle. I stand still. This must be a dream. Kelly Montoy doesn't talk to me. We haven't spoken since her and Rina Amell convinced me to shaving cream our principal's car last year. Alexander shoves me in her direction and I start walking toward her with my guitar strap over my shoulder, still attached to the amp. I get tangled in the wire, awkwardly stepping out of it and almost falling on my face in front of the band and Kelly. She presses her painted fingertips to her lips and smiles but doesn't laugh – out loud anyway. I hand my guitar to Alexander and trot to the middle of the aisle where she stands.

"Hey, Kelly," I say, finding it hard to breathe with her this close to me.

"Hey, Blake." My name sliding off her lips sounds better than any music I have ever made — or heard, for that matter. "Rina is having a party this weekend."

Shocker. Rina Amell throwing a party isn't exactly breaking news. These wild, out-of-hand ragers were expected at this point. Come Monday, it's all anyone talks about, but Alexander and I avoid them since the last debacle and Julian has stayed behind in solidarity.

"So, yeah, are you busy this weekend?" she asks, batting her brilliantly long lashes and twirling her hair around her finger.

"You...want me to go to the party?" I asked, struggling to form the words. No wonder she never talks to me. I can barely string a sentence together when she's around. "So, what? You and your friends can screw with me and Alexander again?"

"I want you to *play* it." She rolls her eyes as if I should have guessed that.

"Right, right." I run my hand through my hair, excited to be asked to play, but equally disappointed to not just be on the guest list. I don't say anything, and she breaks the silence.

"So, what do you say, Blake? Are you in?"

Chapter Eight

Now

"So, what do you say?" the woman presses. "Are you in?"

I look at the money in one hand and click my phone to life with the other. No new text messages. No word from Kelly. No one looking for me or relying on me at all.

"What's your name?" I shove the winnings deep in my pocket.

"Isabella." The name rolls off her tongue.

"Okay, Isabella. I'm in."

We enter a hired car and slide into the back seat. She ordered the car and input the address. I have no idea where we are going, but I'm not nervous. I'm excited. With any luck, the reward will be worth the risk.

The car drops us off in front of a large, horseshoe-shaped waterfront building. Two men open the door to the lobby and greet Isabella as we enter. In the elevator, she swipes a key card and hits a button labeled PH.

Penthouse.

Still in the clothes I wore for the show, I suddenly feel grossly underdressed. We reach a door at the corner of the building and she swipes a keycard once more.

"Come on in." She holds the door open.

The room is as perfect as a picture, so immaculate I'm sure it must be the model used for tours only. The only indication someone even lives here is the lingering smell of expensive cigars and the presence of liquor bottles, all half-empty – or half-full for the optimists.

"This way." She leads me to a spiral staircase in the corner of the room. As we climb to the top, I hear the mumble of voices, followed by a deep, hearty yet intimidating laugh.

"Boys, room for one more?" Isabella asks, entering an open second floor layout decorated with exactly one table in the middle of a cigar-smoke haze.

The man at the center of the table wears a perfectly fitted suit and an unwelcoming glare.

"Go home, kid," he says through a puff of his cigar. "You can't afford to play on this stage."

Isabella raises her eyebrow and nudges me toward the table in a silent suggestion, telling me to make my move.

"I disagree." I step toward the table and take the money from my pocket. "And you've got an empty seat."

He looks at me once more, analyzing me from the tip of my hair to the bottom of my shoes. His eyes tell me he's unimpressed and ready to have me physically removed from this penthouse suite, but he doesn't.

"Have a seat, boy. And remember the first rule – "

"Don't talk about *Fight Club*?" I ask. He narrows his eyes as his lips turn to a hard line. Apparently, movie references *aren't* his thing.

"No," he says, snuffing out his cigar. "There's no crying in high stakes poker."

Or, perhaps, movie references are.

* * * *

Then

The party was loud and rambunctious before we even got set up. Rina Amell's house was exactly the way I remembered, though it seems the guest list has grown to include the entire school instead of just our grade. Anyone who is anyone is there—which, I suppose, is why we usually aren't.

Julian moves the amps into the space we will be playing in while Alexander tunes his guitar.

Finally set up and ready to play, my eyes find Kelly's in the crowd and I know this may be my one and only chance to really impress her.

"Blake," Alexander says, bringing my attention back to the stage area.

"Yeah?" I ask, but my eyes still in the crowd.

"You going to play us in or just stand there with everyone staring at you?"

I look around and all eyes are on us. The room has quieted a bit, as if everyone is waiting to see what we can do. I strike a few chords, the vibration of the music flows through me, and Alexander steps toward the microphone. His voice fills the space, singing a song about love and where it starts, and even though he is the one speaking, it's like I'm trying to send a message directly to the girl who I started making music for in the first place – and she doesn't even know.

She smiles a real, genuine grin and waves lightly toward the stage, flicking a few perfectly manicured fingers our direction. I keep playing but nod my head toward her. She rocks slightly back and forth to the beat of the music and I take a chance. My favorite line of the song is coming up, so I lean into the microphone, share it with Alexander, and sing the line along with him, harmonizing in a way we hadn't tried before. He slaps a hand against my shoulder and smiles widely. More importantly, so does Kelly.

We play a handful of songs and take a break. Girls I've never met before offer me drinks, and guys who never knew my name suddenly do. Alexander stands off to one side, chugging liquid from a cup surrounded by a handful of excited partygoers. This must be how Julian feels all the time.

Hopping off the makeshift stage, I walk around the room looking for Kelly. Classmates pat my back as I walk around, people complement our music and shout my name as I walk through the crowd of spectators. Tonight is *my* night. Tonight I was *heard,* but I want to be *seen* – by one in person in particular.

Her long blonde hair is visible past the door frame as she stands outside on the porch, talking with her hands and smiling the same small grin she wore when she was watching us perform. I step through the door and just as I do, she steps out of view. I turn to stand on the porch in perfect time to see her lean forward and kiss a guy who's not me.

I started all of this – the guitar playing, the band – to get her attention, and the smile she wore and the wave she gave as we performed told me I was right. She is into musicians. But those intricate gestures, including the kiss she shares now, weren't meant for me.

They were meant for Julian.

* * * *

Now

"Victor," Isabella says, placing a drink down in front of the man in the suit. He nods and waves her off, keeping his concentration fixed on his cards that lay face down on the table, turned up at the corner by his large thumb.

I can't read the look on his face, but I'd guess he can't read the one on mine either.

Isabella rounds the table and hands me a glass filled with amber liquid. I take a sip and stare across the table, waiting to see what Victor has come up with.

"You should've stayed home tonight, boy. But it's too late now." He flips his cards over on the table revealing a full house – three jacks and two eights. It is a gorgeous hand, and it would sting a little, only my hand is better.

The look on his face when I flip over four beautiful queens is the real win, though turning a few hundred dollars into thousands isn't so bad either.

I order a car and smile the whole way home, flipping through the cash that I won by holding a good hand but also by breaking my promise to Cooper. And if I'm being honest, I don't feel guilty. I feel powerful.

All the lights at my house are off when I arrive. I push the door open, careful not to make too much noise. I'm sure Kelly is fast asleep, and I don't want to wake her. I step out of one boot, then the other as quietly as possible but as I turn around, the lights flick on. Kelly stands at the other side of the room, leaning into the doorframe with a look on her face that doesn't exactly say she's excited to see me.

"Kelly." I run my fingers through my hair and leave my hand at the back of my neck.

"Blake." She smiles a wide but somewhat alarming grin. "It's so good to see you! It's been so long." Her voice is twisted and dramatic.

Welp, that settles it. I'm screwed.

"Where were you?" She walks toward me, closing the gap between us.

"Just out," I say. It's the very lamest attempt at an excuse I've ever muttered. It doesn't even deserve to *call* itself an attempt at an excuse.

"Okay." She grabs at the front of my shirt and pulls herself close to me. "Can you call next time?"

She's not mad. She's not upset.

She's perfect.

And for the second time tonight, I'm lucky.

She kisses me and takes my hand, guiding me down the hallway to our room. Then she's in the bed beside me and I run my fingers through her hair as we lay in a lightless, deep-black atmosphere. She rolls over to face me and props herself up on her elbow.

"Tell me something about yourself."

I sit up against the headboard. "You know everything there is to know. You've known me since junior high, and you've been living here for almost a year..."

"That's not what I mean and you know it." She traces her fingertip along the blanket, avoiding eye contact as she repeats the questions she's asked me so many times before. "Where do you come from? And your parents... What about them?"

I roll over and pull the blankets to my chin.

"Someday, Blake Mathews," she says. "Someday you're going to let me all the way in and I'm going to know every side of you."

Her voice is convinced, steadfast—but she's wrong. That day is never going to come.

* * * *

Then

"The difference between an autobiography and a biography, as you know, is that a biography is written *about* a person by an author and an autobiography is written about oneself." Mr. Langar walks up and down the aisles, stopping only to take an origami-folded note out of Rina's hand mid-pass and toss it into the trash. "Today you're going to pick a folded piece of paper from the basket. It's going to read 'A' or 'B'. If you have a 'B', you'll be partnered up with another 'B' and you will write stories about each other, hence, biography. If you have an 'A', you'll be working individually to write a story about yourself to share with the class. Understood?"

The class moans. At least we can all agree on something.

The basket gets handed up and down the rows while each student begrudgingly selects a slip of paper and unfolds it.

"I got a B!" Alexander says, looking over my shoulder as I unfold mine.

"B!" He high-fives me. "Partners?" I ask, and he nods.

"Mr. Varro, Mr. Mathews," Mr. Langar says, unenthused, "as much as I always look forward to seeing what kind of…effort…you two come up with, you won't be working together on this one. And lose the sunglasses, Alexander. This is a classroom."

Alexander slumps into his chair and pushes his glasses onto his head, pinning back his overgrown hair.

"Alexander, you can work with Mr. Young." Alexander sits back up, suddenly excited about the project again. I roll my eyes. "Blake, you can work with"—he looks around the room, scratching at his chin—"ah, Ms. Montoy."

My hands sweat against the desktop while my heart beats like a drum in my chest. Of all the students in this whole class. Suddenly I'm wishing I'd picked 'A' instead of 'B'.

At lunch, Julian, Alexander, Theo, Dom and I occupy a table at the far end of the cafeteria.

"I was looking forward to working with you, Blake," Alexander says through bites of his peanut butter sandwich. "I've always been curious to know your back story."

"Why don't you just ask?" Julian says, taking a bite of the hot pasta he'd purchased.

"Because it's not like he will answer." Alexander crumples up his brown paper bag. "He just changes the subject."

"I don't always change the subject." I throw a chip at Alexander. "So, have you guys heard the new Detriment album? It's supposed to be really great."

Julian and Alexander look at each other then at me. Okay, so I change the subject. I avoid things. But it's none of their damn business.

"Speaking of the project," Julian says, "you must be stoked you got partnered with Kelly."

I swallow my drink the wrong way and cough as he speaks. It surprised me to hear him say that, since the last time I saw them in the same room she was leaning in like he needed mouth-to-mouth resuscitation.

"It doesn't bother you?" I ask. "Aren't you two like…a thing?"

"Umm, no?" Julian asks, and I don't think he's playing dumb.

"You two looked pretty cozy at Rina's party the other night."

There's a long pause between us. Alexander's face says he has no clue what we're talking about.

"You saw that?" Julian wipes his fingers on a napkin. I nod my head.

"She kissed me. That was it. I didn't expect it. When she pulled away, I told her that I was seeing someone." He opens his tiny box of milk and drinks it straight from the carton, ignoring the straw on his lunch tray.

"You're not seeing anyone…" But the words trail off as I put all the pieces together.

"That's your girl, man," Julian says. "I wouldn't do that to you. I know how you feel about her."

Her ears must have been ringing, because no sooner do we mention her than she waltzes up to the table and pulls out a chair like it's the most common thing in the world for her to take a seat between me and Alexander.

"Blake, Alexander." She nods to us as she speaks but flagrantly ignores Julian. "So, Blake, I'm free tomorrow night if you want to get started on the project."

"Sounds good." I try to avoid looking at her, certain that the redness in my cheeks from Julian's earlier comments hasn't yet faded.

"Your house or mine?" she asks, and I choke on my final bite of sandwich. I swallow hard and clear my throat, looking at Alexander for some kind of interjection.

"Julian is coming over tonight, too." Alexander picks up on his cue perfectly. "You're more than welcome to join us, Kelly."

She looks around with narrowed eyes and a confused expression.

"I'm staying with Alexander." *Short, sweet. Too much and yet, not nearly enough.* I'll have to figure out how to string words together and give her *something* though. It is a biography, after all.

* * * *

If I had drawn an 'A' card, my project would have consisted of *all* bullshit instead of *mostly* bullshit, like they usually do. I would have had to make up every detail, beginning to end, because if I had drawn an 'A' card, my real story would look something like this.

My mother was an international flight attendant and met my father on one of her trips into Cape Town. From what I understand, they fell for each other fast, holding on to the excitement and torment of not knowing when they would see each other next, until she learned she was pregnant and moved there.

I don't remember, but I'm pretty sure it was over for them before it started, but they stayed together for me. The fight that ended it all? Well, I missed the beginning, but I walked in with enough time to hear her say, "If you kick me out, my son is coming with me." *He didn't argue or fight to keep me.*

Looking back, things weren't always as bad as they were recently. It's almost like the farther we got away from Cape Town, the further downhill she went until she was over the edge completely. From the time we moved to America until the day I started staying at Alexander's, I was relying on a woman who relied entirely on men, booze and bad decisions.

Not much of an autobiography, really, but pulling a 'B' card wasn't much better. I still hadn't nailed down which lies to tell, and Kelly will be here any second.

Julian and Alexander head upstairs to Alexander's bedroom and Kelly and I sit at the kitchen table. Alexander's mother has made it abundantly clear that there are to be no girls upstairs.

I take two pencils and drum them off the tabletop, trying to decide what I can say to make this project somewhat decent. I'm equally pleased and ticked off by this task. Talking about myself, my background or my history? That's a whole lot of *hell no*, but I am looking forward to getting to know her.

She rips one of the pencils out of my hand, effectively pulling the plug on my intense tabletop drum solo. I stick the other one behind my ear.

"So, where were you born?" she asks with the pencil at the ready to write my answers down.

"Cape Town," I say, and a slight grin crosses her lips.

"I thought you were from Australia." She giggles as she admits the error.

"You're not the first to think that, and you won't be the last."

"What's it like there?" She rests her head in her hand with her elbow on the table.

"Oh, I don't know anymore, really. I haven't been there in years. I've been in five other schools over the last eight or so years, in all different parts of the country."

Her lips part as her eyes widen. "Why?"

"My mother… She's a…flight attendant." I nod, leaning my elbows into the table and clasping my hands together. I mean, it's not a *complete* lie.

"A flight attendant…" She jots down the words as she speaks them in a bubbly handwriting that crosses over the lines of the loose-leaf paper. "And your dad?"

"Oh, I can't tell you that."

Her eyes meet mine and she can't decide if she should laugh or question my answer, so she does both.

"What do you mean?"

"I can't say any more. It's not safe," I whisper. "I've already said too much." I throw my hand to my forehead for dramatic purposes and try on my best poker face, attempting to remain serious when I want to break into a laugh.

She grins and swats a playful hand toward me. "Come on, Blake. We have to get this done."

"I have a better idea," I say, and she bites her lip. "What about if instead of writing our biographies about who we are and where we come from, we write them about where we are going. Say, twenty years from now, we have our dream jobs and exciting lives. I'll give you my story from the perspective of a famous musician – "

"A famous musician, Blake?" She raises an eyebrow. "Do you know how few people actually make it in music?"

"C'mon. It will be fun. I will be a famous musician and you will be a…" I wave my hands, prompting her to complete the sentence.

"CEO—of a *huge* company. Maybe I'll have a husband and a few kids too." She smiles and her eyes light up.

Kelly worries that we would get in trouble for not following directions, but everything turns out better than I could have planned.

I manage my first A. Alexander's mother even puts it on the refrigerator.

Chapter Nine

Now

Xander sits at the bar by himself, staring into his drink. His head is in his hand, his thumb strokes through the facial hair at his chin. From where I stand as I enter, I can see his shoulders are weighted down like they're holding the world. As I inch closer, I can see the fatigue in his eyes and the way he's biting his bottom lip so hard it might bleed. I've seen that look before. Usually we get a helluva song out of it, but the inspiration is never good.

The stool screeches against the tile floor when I pull it out. Xander doesn't even look up, and his drink sits untouched.

"What's going on, man?" I ask, but he just shakes his head. I order a drink and we sit there, silent. I'll sit here until he's ready to talk.

It seems like hours pass by the time he finally downs his drink and speaks.

"Natalie and I have been trying to get pregnant," he says, and I try to work out the issues.

"Do you…not *want* kids?" I scratch my head. Maybe the Mariah drama changed his outlook on the whole father thing, but his lack of enthusiasm is both confusing and alarming. I was under the impression that he wanted to start a family.

"No, no. I do." He gets the attention of the bartender and points to our drinks, suggesting a refill for us both. "It just doesn't look like it's going to happen."

"You've been to the doctors?" He looks at me as if this suggestion were as obvious as unplugging something and plugging it back in.

"A few. We've had a bunch of different specialists' opinions. Our chances just aren't looking so great."

I swallow hard. Comforting people is not my thing. I offer alcohol and perfectly timed sarcasm to lighten the mood. That's usually all I bring to the sympathy table.

"Hey, are you guys busy?" a young woman says, stepping between Xander's and my barstools. She's petite but her outfit and attitude scream that her personality is larger than her small frame. Her hair is shaved into a design at one side, longer on the other. Her skin is covered in tattoos that rival even the number Xander has, and her eyes are lined in a deep black that accentuates her fierce green irises that can't possibly be natural. Neither of us answer.

"I'll take that as a no." She smiles behind her pierced lip. "I'm Stasia." She offers her hand in my direction and I take it.

"I'm Bla —"

"Blake Mathews, I know. And Xander Varro." She sticks out her hand toward him, but his mind is elsewhere and he doesn't return the introduction.

"What can we do for you, Stasia?" Xander keeps his body and eyes straight ahead as he speaks. His distant demeanor doesn't deter her.

"I'm up next. You two want to join me?" She throws her thumb over her shoulder toward the stage set for open mic night. Xander looks at me and I at him as we have a wordless conversation. We've done this for so many years, through so many situations that we nearly always know what the other is saying. Xander shrugs. "Why the hell not?" He downs his drink in one swallow and hops off his bar stool. This surprises me, but I follow suit.

"You sure about this?" I ask him, clapping a hand on his shoulder.

"I'm thinkin' a bit of music and fun is exactly what I need right now." He turns his attention to Stasia and looks at her with inquisitive eyes. "You look familiar. Have we met before?"

"Nope." She shrugs her shoulders and gently shakes her head. "Guess I just have one of those faces." She turns away from him and his eyes linger on her for a moment in a long stare that says he's still trying to figure out who she is or who she reminds him of.

Stasia waltzes across the venue to the backstage area and we follow. She picks up an impressive Gibson Les Paul that looks like it belongs on a pro rock tour and not on the stage of open mic night.

"That's gorgeous." Xander drools over the instrument. "May I?" He points to the guitar and she hands it over with a nod. "Very nice," he says while looking it over, before handing it back begrudgingly.

"Thanks. My father gave it to me as a gift." She tucks a piece of hair behind her ear. "What do you want to play?" She rushes the question, changing the subject before either of us could ask any more about her father or the guitar. "Something of yours, of course," she purrs, and Xander takes a few steps back, picking up one of the guitars that belong to the house band and hands me one as well.

"Whatever one you know best."

She thinks for a moment before playing a perfectly timed, well-executed riff of one of our more difficult songs.

"Yeah, that one works," I say, equally impressed and annoyed that she can do it as well as I can – maybe better. "Let's do it."

The host of open mic night introduces us, and the small crowd gives a moderately increased applause.

"Ladies and gentlemen, thank you for having me. My name is Stasia and these poor gents I conned into performing with me are Blake and Xander."

Xander and I give quick waves and I plug in the house bass guitar. "You playing us in?" I ask her, adjusting the strap on the guitar.

"No, you do it so much better," she says with a wink, and I start us off, playing the intro to one of our more widely recognized songs. Xander joins me and so does Stasia, only – it's new. It's different from anything we've ever done – a new twist on a song Xander and I wrote and mastered. And it's perfect. She's improved it in a way I never would have thought to do.

Xander sings into the microphone but looks back at her over his shoulder and smiles at her new additions to the old song.

We are nearing a portion of the song where I usually lean into the same microphone as Xander and we crank out the lyrics together, but I'm curious to see what Stasia is made of.

"You going up there?" she yells over the music, not missing a beat.

I shake my head no. "This is your show. Let's see what you've got."

Stasia continues to play, rocking across the stage until she reaches Xander's mic. Like they've done it for years, as if it were rehearsed, she leans into the microphone and sings the lyrics to our song in a harmony style I never would have been able to produce, given our differences in vocal ranges.

It's magic.

It's a rarity to find anyone with real, professional-level talent at these open mic nights but she's incredible. It makes me wonder why she isn't performing at a higher level than open mic nights at The Rock Room.

The song comes to a close and Xander high-fives Stasia at the front of the stage. She presses her hand to her mouth, covering her face-filling smile and laughs as the crowd gives us a rowdy applause. I join them at the front of the stage, and we take a quick bow before exiting.

"That was amazing. You guys are great," she says, taking a sip of water backstage.

"You're not so bad yourself." I hand the bass guitar off to a Rock Room employee.

"Thanks." She shrugs her shoulders. "I mean, it's just something I do for fun."

Xander pushes his hair back with his fingers and turns toward her.

"You've got something there. You should run with it—make it less for fun and more for a career."

"You think so?" she asks, carefully returning her Les Paul to its case.

"Absolutely. Thanks for inviting us up. It was fun to do it...just for fun and less for career," he jokes. His phone rings, and he takes the call.

I pick up one of the acoustic guitars at the edge of the backstage area and sit on the couch, strumming a series of chords I've been trying to perfect and transform from idea to song for weeks.

"That's pretty." Stasia sits on the arm of the couch. "What is it?"

"A mess," I say through a laugh. "I don't know. Something is just not right."

She listens, wordlessly analyzing the piece as I play it over and over again.

"Okay, play it one more time." I do as I'm told. "Now, speed it up right...here," she says, and I quicken the strum pattern. "Now let this last note ring...pause...quick pattern there... There you go!"

And just like that, she's done it. It's excellent. All in a few moments she perfected a piece I've been tweaking for weeks. I keep playing and she picks up an acoustic guitar that belongs to the venue and jumps in, only she plays the same notes in a finger picking style while I strum, and the two together are magnetic – opposites meant to find each other to form one piece.

"That's bad-ass," Xander says, rejoining us at the backstage area. "What is it?"

"The same song I've been working on for *weeks*. Stasia reworked it a bit."

"It's damn good."

"Last week you told me it sucked."

"It did suck. It doesn't anymore." Xander and Stasia laugh. I throw a guitar pick at him and join in on the laugh. "I have to take off. Blake, you need a ride?"

This is the most motivated I have felt in a long time, and I'm not ready to put the guitar down and leave the inspiration here behind the stage.

"I think I'm going to keep working on this, if that's okay with you?" I ask, returning my attention to Stasia.

She nods an enthusiastic yes.

* * * *

Then

Forty-five small, round lights cover the yellowing ceiling of the school auditorium. I know this because I'm lying in the aisle of the room between the seats, counting the bulbs instead of trying to come up with new music.

"When did this stop being fun?" Alexander asks, playing the same sub-par riff on his guitar that he's been picking at for the last two excruciating hours. He's just saying what we are all thinking. It was easier when we were covering other people's music instead of making our own. "And where the hell is Blake?"

"Marco?" Theo yells, his voice echoing through the empty auditorium.

"Polo!" I yell back. His footsteps sound closer but he doesn't reach me.

"Where are you?" he says, and the other band members laugh.

"Here." I raise one arm high in the air, reaching toward the lights I had been counting. He enters the row I'm in and stands toe to toe with me, leaning forward and giving me a hand up.

"What were you doing up there?" Dom calls.

"Thinking," I say.

"Try not to hurt yourself," he adds, followed by a well-timed *ba-dum ching* drum roll and cymbal clash.

"Let's go do something more fun than this. Ya know, like homework or a dentist visit," Julian says. He punches a random assortment of keys into Theo's keyboard before jumping off the stage.

"Hey, do that again," Alexander says, the lightbulb above his head suddenly illuminating.

"I have no idea what that was." Julian scratches his head.

"I do," Theo says, returning to his instrument and mimicking the series of sound Julian made, half by accident.

"I have something for that." Dom spins on his stool and beats on the drums, adding a new dimension to the tune.

I pick up the bass guitar I've been borrowing from school since my mother got rid of mine and make a musical contribution. The instruments together, unplanned, unscripted, create this melodic coherence that is something of a miracle — something created from nothing, nonexistent one moment and the cornerstone to our first full set and album the next minute.

Alexander penned most of the lyrics for that song, but it was the first time he hadn't picked up an instrument when we'd put it all together. The best part about playing that song the first few times we played it for a crowd was seeing what Alexander was capable of without a guitar in his hands. Every eye followed each move he made. He put on a tiny show all in itself, dancing across the stage and putting himself into every word, every note. For a guy who didn't even want to *be* a singer, he sure as hell sells the part.

The rehearsal was almost a complete waste of time, but turned into one of the better sessions we've ever had. Upon returning to Alexander's house, he pushes the door open and sets his guitar down. I haven't been home in weeks. My mother doesn't call to check in, doesn't contact Alexander's mother to see if I'm okay or if she can contribute. It's unfortunate, because Alexander and his mother struggle too. He and I share a room, and she sleeps at the other end of the hall. There's always food on the table, and if we need money for school pictures or a field trip, it's available, but she works very hard at two jobs to keep us taken care of — and I can't help but feel guilty about it. She didn't ask for the responsibility of a second teenage boy, but she never complained about it either.

We turn the corner into the kitchen and there's a guitar case sitting on the small table we usually eat at. At first, I assume it's an upgrade for Alexander, but then I realize, it's not just any guitar. It's *my* guitar.

I bring it to the living room where Alexander's mother is pacing back and forth. I hold it up and ask in a small voice, "Did you do this?"

She shakes her head no.

"Your mother left it earlier."

"My mother? Did she say anything else? Did she ask to see me?" My voice is frantic, wondering if maybe this means we're on the upswing again. Maybe things are improving.

"Blake, sweetie," she says with sympathetic tears in her eyes, "your mother isn't coming back."

Chapter Ten

Now

When I bought this couch, I thought it was the most comfortable possible option. And it is – for sitting. For sleeping, not so much.

An unexpected bang – clashing of pots and pans – causes me to jump inches off the sofa and almost fall to the floor. Ripping the blankets off me, I sit up, looking over the back.

Kelly places the blender on the counter and tosses kitchen items around while preparing to make what has to be the *loudest* freakin' breakfast smoothie of all time.

"Good morning!" she yells over the sound of the blender, though nothing in her voice indicates it's actually a 'good' morning.

"Good morning," I whisper back, standing from the couch and heading to the counter. I reach to place my hand at her lower back, but she turns toward the refrigerator and opens the door.

"You came home late last night — or, well, early this morning." As soon as I open my mouth to speak, she restarts the blender over my words.

"Are we going to talk?" I ask, my patience wearing thin.

"I'm not sure, Blake. Are we? Because lately it seems like I do all the talking, and you sit there and disregard everything I say."

"That's not true —"

"Really? Last night I had the night off. I told you I had the night off and that I wanted to spend time with you. And you *agreed.*"

"Well, yeah, but we never really finalized a plan, so I wasn't sure what we were doing."

"Maybe you should have, oh, I don't know, *asked* instead of going out drinking all night." She wipes her hands clean then throws the towel to the table.

"I had a few drinks with Xander and —"

"*Don't* start deciding what lie you are going to feed me next, Blake, because I was with Natalie when Xander got home last night *without* you."

She crosses her arms across her chest and taps her foot. I plead the fifth.

"I'm really tired of all this Blake. I love you, but you're on stage seven months a year and I deal with that. I do. It would be nice if for one night, you could stay *off stage* and spend a night with me while you're here."

"Off stage?" I ask, confused at first but then I realize what direction this is taking.

"I *run* The Rock Room, Blake. You didn't think that your little show would get back to me? You were supposed to be at home with me, not performing with some half-dressed rock star wanna-be. And unless Xander turned into a petite blonde with breasts, he wasn't the one you were having drinks with either."

My heart clenches. She's not mad. She's... *exhausted* — and I don't blame her. I am hardly ever in this house when I'm home. My absence has taken a toll on her.

"I'm going to ask one time and one time only, Blake. If you look me in the eyes and tell me the answer I am hoping for, I promise to never ever ask again..."

Her voice quiets and trails off, and she's looking anywhere but at me. I nod my head and open my ears — something I should have been doing for a while now.

"You are staying out late or not coming home at all. You're distant and uninterested. It doesn't seem like...like you want to be around me anymore."

My gaze follows the grout lines of the floor so I don't have to look in her eyes as she runs down my list of failures.

"Blake?" Her voice trembles like thunder at the start of a storm. I look up and my eyes find hers. "Is there someone else?"

"No, Kel. No. It's not like that." I reach for her hands and take them in mine. I lift her fingers to my lips and kiss her knuckles. She breathes a sigh of relief. "I have a lot on my plate. But there's only you. I promise."

"I am working today and tonight but only until around nine. Will you pick me up? Maybe we can go catch a movie or something?" Her eyes are pleading, like we're at a point where a movie might be a large enough Band-Aid to keep us together.

"Absolutely." I lock my pinky finger into hers. "I promise."

I lie in bed and watch her get ready for work. I don't know why, but something about the way she wraps her hair around the curling iron and applies perfectly even lines to her eyelids makes me feel like I'm watching an artist work. She looks back at me in the reflection and winks then blows me a kiss. I do love her—I always have—but I know I can't keep her happy for long if things don't change. She's not the kind of girl who wants to stay at home by herself waiting for me to come home. She wants to go out, see the world and dance the night away. I know I need to put my needs aside and prioritize some of hers.

I must have fallen asleep, because eventually I wake up, but my eyes don't find her beautiful face in the mirror staring back at me. Instead, there's a note written on the mirror she had previously been looking in.

9 p.m. Don't forget!

My phone rings and I turn it over to see Xander's name across the screen.

Girls are both working tonight. Want to grab a bite to eat or a drink somewhere downtown?

I consider it, but I know that dinner with Xander means drinks. Drinks means losing track of time, and losing track of time means missing my night with Kelly.

Thanks, but I'll pass tonight.

Making my way down the sidewalks through the busy city streets, I take the roads into the heart of the city where there is abundant shopping. I think it's about time I do something nice for Kelly. *Flowers or jewelry maybe?* It's all long overdue.

As I walk down the row of stores looking in windows and deciding what might be the best choice, my phone pings.

7:30 p.m. Same spot as last week.

I close out the message and walk into the nearest store.

What do you say Blake? Are you in?

The second text in a matter of minutes burns bright across my screen. I shouldn't. It's nearing seven o'clock and I need to be picking Kelly up by nine—but I'm tempted. I hate that I'm tempted. I wish it were easier to leave the past in the past, but it's not. Some bad habits are easier to erase than others, and this is a part of me that can't be deleted so easily.

Yeah, count me in.

* * * *

I knock on the door—three times hard and quick, followed by a pause, then one more single knock. The door opens and Isabella stands on the other side. She wears heels that render her taller than me, skin-tight jeans and a top that hugs every inch of her upper body, except for her midriff, which remains bare.

"Blake," she purrs, "you showed." She opens the door wider, and I step through it. "It's good to see you."

"You too, Isabella." My hands sweat and my heart pounds – side effects of the guilt. I said the last time would be the last time – but I've been saying that for years.

I enter the house and walk down the hallway, finding the stairs and ascending them one by one until my feet find flat ground in the smoky loft. I turn the corner and everyone is waiting, sitting around the table with only one seat open – the spot that I have inherited as my usual chair.

"Mathews," Victor says. His hair is slicked back and he wears a fitted suit. "Have a seat." He pulls a cigar out of a pocket of the suit and hands it to me across the table.

Isabella pulls out the remaining chair and I take it.

"Deal me in," I say, pulling out my wallet and tossing hundreds onto the table in front of me.

* * * *

Then

Going to Julian's football game actually meant drinking under the bleachers with a small group of outcasts like me.

I had no home to go to and no mother planning to pick me up anytime soon…or ever. All I had was a cheap bottle of vodka that burned something fierce as it went down, but I welcomed it. It was a pain I could control.

"What are you doing, man?" I hear Alexander's voice say as he enters the area under the bleachers. "Look… I know I'm not always the best decision-maker, but come sit with me and the guys. My mom will kill you if you come home drunk tonight."

"I'm not her problem." I take another swig from the bottle.

"If you don't get your ass on those bleachers right now, *we're* going to have a problem," he threatens as he pushes his hair back off his forehead.

"What are you going to do about it, Alexander?" I hand the bottle off to the brunette next to me whose name I don't remember and step forward toward him, so we're nose to nose.

"Blake, stop. Let's go, okay?" Alexander offers one last chance to walk away before I lose everything, but I don't take it.

I swing at him hard and miss, throwing myself off balance and falling forward. Alexander grabs my arm and the back of my jacket near my neck. "Let's go," he says, leading me toward the exit.

"Get the hell off of me." I rip my arm from his grasp aggressively and walk away, leaving the game and parking lot behind me.

I get as far as the fence at the opposite side of the field when I hear footsteps cross into the parking lot.

"You're leaving?" Kelly asks, clad in her maroon-and-gold cheer uniform.

"Looks like it," I say, not turning to face her. "I never pegged you as one to join the cheerleading team."

"What is that supposed to mean?" she scoffs, and I turn, slowly, wondering if I should face her or walk away.

"You used to wear black, exclusively. You didn't own a pair of jeans that were intact, and you had at *least* fifty bracelets. Every day was a different band T-shirt and those high-top sneakers you wore? The lyrics on them and the art you drew…"

Tell her, Blake. Tell her the music is because of her. Tell her that everything you are is because of her.

"Well…they were bad-ass." That's the best I can do.

"People change." She drags the toe of her bright white cheer sneakers across the asphalt.

"They do." I step in closer to her.

"That doesn't have to be a bad thing," she whispers, tucking a piece of loose hair behind her ear and securing it under the large bow that ties her curled ponytail.

The liquor is fueling all the courage I need to be open and honest with her—maybe even kiss her if she'll allow it. I lean in, bringing my face within inches of hers and she stalls.

"I have to be going." She looks over her shoulder at the field.

I run my hand through my hair and hold my breath. Swing and a miss—for the second time tonight. She heads toward the field and I walk toward the street with no real destination.

"Hey, Blake?" she calls, leaning into the chain link fence.

I look over my shoulder at her as she twirls a curl around her finger.

"I still have them." she says, and my eyebrow twisting is enough to tell her I'm confused. "The high-top sneakers and the bracelets."

I smile, thinking back on the first time I ever saw her and realizing it hadn't been all that long ago at all. The girl I've always known isn't as far away as I thought.

For a while I just walk, unsure of where to go from here, but end up at an address that was always a house but never really much of a home.

The skies open and the rain pours, forming puddles in the mud at the bottom of the stairs. Thunder shakes the walls of the old, run-down house. The shutters threaten to fall from their hinges. A handful of eviction notes wallpaper the front door. I peer into the windows, imaging the spot where our belongings used to fill the space. It's empty now, with no evidence anyone is coming back.

"Hey." Alexander's voice cuts through the sleeting rain. He puts his hands in his pocket and sloshes puddle water around with the toe of his boot. "You know, when my dad left, he gave me a piece of paper with his new address on it and told me to visit whenever I wanted."

I remain facing the house, watching his reflection in the clouded glass of the storm door.

"At least he left you an address," I say. "She left... She left *nothing*!" My scream echoes a deep, threatening tone that rivals even the sound of the thunder overhead. "Nothing..." I whisper, my voice breaking.

"It didn't exist, Blake," Alexander says. "It was a bogus address. One hundred percent bullshit."

As I turn to face him and rub my thumb at my jaw, I step off the porch and tilt my head back so the rain pours over me like the stream from a showerhead, and I throw my hands to the lightening-lit sky. "Why didn't they want us?" I shout it for Alexander to hear, but on another level, I'm yelling it to some higher being too.

"I think it says more about them than it does about us."

"What am I supposed to do, man?" There are tears in my eyes disguised by the downpour. "My mother cut us off from every family member I've ever had. I wouldn't even know how to start looking for my father. I'm sixteen years old with nowhere to go."

"That's not true," he says, stomping through the puddles as he makes his way toward me and slaps his hands on the sopping wet shoulders of my faux leather jacket. "You're staying with us, and we're not taking no for an answer."

"Your mother didn't ask for a teenage boy to be dropped on her doorstep, Alexander."

"She didn't," he says with a laugh, though I don't see what's funny. "She said if it becomes a problem, I was going to have to go because she likes you better." I smile and he wraps his arms around me, patting his palm in between my shoulder blades.

"Let's go home, Blake—where we belong."

The following Monday, I walked into school knowing that I had a best friend who had become a brother, a roof over my head and four walls around me that for the first time in years weren't closing in on me. I place my books in my locker and the bell rings. As I turn to head toward my classroom, I see Kelly closing her locker too. She waves at me, one finger at a time before turning and walking down the hall. As she enters the classroom, I notice something different about her.

She's wearing her high-tops.

Chapter Eleven

Now

My cards *suck.* Black and red numbers and faces stare back at me. None of them have anything in common and the two and the seven I hold offer no chance of a straight. Sweat beads at my brow. I end up folding. I had so much in on the hand, hoping to obtain better cards and banking on the fact that the other players were overconfident in theirs, but here I sit, watching instead of playing, with no chance to win the pot as it grows or get back what I had already thrown into it.

"All right, all right. It's clearly not my night. I've got to get going." I wipe my hands on my jeans and push the chair back.

"Mathews, please," Victor says through a victorious smile, "I'm sure I can ring another few thousand out of you if you stick around a bit longer."

The table laughs, puffing more smoke into the cigar cloud that engulfs them.

Thousands? I had lost count. On one hand, there's more where that came from, but on the other, giving away any fraction of my bank account is an idiotic loss. I shouldn't be here in the first place.

"Sit down, Blake," Isabella says. "It's only ten past ten. We're just getting started."

Ten past ten.

Now I'm really screwed.

I call Kelly's phone, but she doesn't answer. Her voice sounds over the voicemail, but I click out without leaving a message. This calls for an in-person apology. Even then, it might not be enough.

I call for a ride and have them drop me at the door to my house. When I try the doorknob, it doesn't budge. My pockets are empty in more ways than one. Not only is there a deficit where there once was cash, but I don't have my keys. I'm locked out of my own house and I can't even be mad about it. I dial in another number and the phone rings on the other side.

"I've been instructed not to speak you until the end of time," Xander says, picking up the phone.

"By Natalie or Kelly?" I run my hand through the roots of my hair.

"Both," he says, and I sigh into phone. "Blake, what's going on?"

I shake my head, though he can't see it.

"Nothing," I lie, but he knows me better than anyone. I can lie to almost anyone, but not to him. He knows me too well.

"Well, that's not true. You call me when you're ready to talk." He clicks the phone to a dead quiet and

I sit on the porch steps, deciding what to do next. No house key, no girl.

No luck.

I walk down the road to a bar when I know I should be heading toward Xander and Natalie's apartment, but I can't. I can't see Kelly until I know what I'm going to say—and right now, I don't.

I sit on the bar stool with only my drink to keep me company—the glass half empty. I used to have a drinking buddy in Xander—day, night, good times or bad, he was on the stool beside me, but now he spends most of his free time and days off with Natalie—exactly what I should be doing with Kelly, but I'm not.

"Hey, stranger," a familiar voice says, taking the bar stool next to me with a drink in hand. Stasia smiles at me and signals to the bartender for a drink for me and another round for her. "What's going on?"

"Same shit, different day," I say. I'm actually happy to see her. We had a great time the other night talking music, playing riffs and just hanging out. No pressure. No commitment.

"You want to talk about it?"

It's been a while since I had a friend to talk to—not a band member, not a girlfriend, just a friend.

"Yeah, actually, I do."

Two days later, Kelly still hadn't come home or returned my calls, but eventually I sigh a breath of relief when her name pops up on my phone with one new message.

I'm working tonight. Meet me there.

I waste no time and head to The Rock Room where I find Natalie behind the bar before I find Kelly.

"Where is she?"

Natalie glares at me with her two different colored eyes and turns away, returning her attention to the draft beer spouts.

I take a seat at the bar and twiddle my thumbs. Someone offers to buy me a drink but Natalie refuses to pour it. Kelly is tough, but Natalie…? Well, I don't know how Xander has survived this long, if I'm being honest.

I sit for hours and never see Kelly. Natalie comes to my side of the bar and I catch her attention.

"Can you please just tell her I'm here?" I ask Natalie, and she walks away. Damn, the girl is good.

Another bartender walks by and I take a chance on him instead. "Hey, have you seen Kelly Montoy at all?"

He turns, looks at me and says, "Ah, Blake Mathews. Ms. Montoy told me if I talked to you, I'd be fired." He smiles and I'm annoyed — but impressed as well. She is something extraordinary. "But, between you and me," he adds, leaning in close, "I don't think she was even scheduled today. She was never here."

And now I'm just annoyed.

Fueled by anger and aggravation, I don't even bother to call a car. It's almost a direct path from here to home if I don't detour and take the long way to stop for cigarettes and scratch tickets, which, I do.

The door is unlocked when I enter my house, and Kelly sits on the floor of the living room, painting her toenails an electric red.

"Really?" I ask. "You're going to tell me to show up to your work then ditch me there?"

She doesn't look up from her pedicure. "Oh, I'm sorry, Blake. Does it bother you when someone says they are going to be somewhere then never shows up?"

Damn, she's good. I walked right into that one.

"Kelly, I planned on being there. I did. I even went to the store first to pick up some flowers and a gift."

"I don't want things, Blake. I just want the truth. What the hell have you been up to? Ever since your last tour ended, you've been sneaking around. Your personality is different. You're panicky. I mean, even our sex life is — "

"Just fine, thank you very much."

"Honestly, Blake. Talk to me."

I sit down on the floor across from her and she plunges the top of the nail polish into the bottle, tightening it and putting it aside. She pulls herself closer to me and takes my hands in her own.

I know she deserves the truth. Even more, I know if I don't give her something now, she won't be around long enough to give me a chance later.

"I uhh...I've been gambling." My mouth goes dry. It was easier to say the second time. Rehearsing my confession to Stasia made saying it again simpler. "More than I thought I have, I guess. I mean, I didn't realize how often I was away from home until lately, when it started interfering with us."

"How bad is it, Blake?" She widens her eyes with obvious worry and shifts her position as she asks the question.

"It's not a problem. It started out as fun, and I took it a little too far. I'll work on it. I can give it up," I say, but the way my chest tightens and my stomach rolls says that she might believe the words, but I don't.

"Maybe it's time you get back in the studio." She offers the one thing that could truly keep me away from a poker table.

"You're probably right about that," I say, hopeful that distracting myself with music is enough to keep myself away from racking up anymore gambling losses.

* * * *

Cooper goes over the new material we've submitted and paces back and forth, offering only the occasional 'hmm-m' or 'interesting' under his breath.

He finally puts the papers down and sits across from us, rubbing his fingers at his jaw.

"I just don't think it's different enough from the old stuff," he says. "There's nothing here that really stands out from every other album we've ever done."

"What do you propose we change or add?" Theo asks.

"I don't know. Just something new," Cooper responds.

Dom drums two pens on the table top and Xander snatches them out of his hands, mid-solo.

"Got any lyrics rolling around in that genius head of yours?" he asks Dom.

"I don't do lyrics." Dom steals the pens back and returns to his makeshift beat.

We're silent for a bit, putting our heads together trying to recreate some of our work-in-progress songs with something new and never heard before, but it's tough. Besides, my head is still wrapped around how much money I'd lost last night before I'd called it quits.

"You guys can head out for the day," Cooper says, "but try to find inspiration somewhere. Oh, and Blake...Xander...I saw your little gig in a video online.

No more impromptu shows at The Rock Room or anywhere else. Got it?"

"That's it!" Xander's eyes brighten as the metaphorical light bulb illuminates.

"How are spontaneous free shows going to help us at all?" Dom adds.

"No, no, the girl. Pull up the video."

Cooper pulls it up and clicks the volume up to full blast. The sound is incredible. A female vocal does add a whole new dimension to even our oldest, most overdone songs. The harmonies and ranges we could reach by recording with a female would certainly be a promising way to set this album apart from all the others.

"I'm not necessarily happy about this video...but you're right, Xander. She's good. Better than you, if I dare say so," Cooper adds. Xander rolls his eyes but smiles.

"What do we think? Should we audition some female vocalists? See if we can find a fit? I'll only go for it with the unanimous vote here."

Theo offers an agreeable nod and Xander is in. Of course he is... It was his idea. Dom, for some reason I don't understand, hesitates but comes around after some convincing. I can see it from both sides. This could be great—or it could be a disaster. A female vocalist will give us the chance to try something new, but new doesn't always help. Sometimes too big of a change means losing fans instead of gaining them. It might just be crazy enough to work.

All eyes are on me as I weigh the options until Cooper finally speaks.

"I know it's a gamble, Blake, but what do you say?"

I nod, thinking of all the good that could come of this and ignoring the possible bad outcomes.

"I'm all in."

"We can start auditioning right away," Cooper adds.

"I don't think that's going to be necessary," I say, and all eyes are on me. "Why not just ask Stasia?"

Cooper looks from me to Xander and back again.

"That girl isn't signed somewhere?" Cooper points to the laptop screen. Xander and I shake our heads. "Let's see if she's interested."

* * * *

A few days later, Xander spins on a stool and Dom and I throw grapes to him as he tries to catch them in his mouth. We get older but we don't grow up.

"Gentlemen," Cooper says, walking into the room clapping his hands and demanding our attention, "I come bearing gifts."

We all look up and eye Cooper, but he is empty-handed.

"I give you Stasia Marquette."

She waltzes through the door with the Les Paul in one hand.

"Did you say Marquette?" Xander asks, putting two and two together faster than any of the rest of us. I've heard the last name before. I know I have.

"Like owner of MLA Records Marquette?" he adds, but somewhere in the back of my mind, I can't help but think that's not where I know the name from.

"My father owns it," she adds, "but we're not...close."

I think back to her saying her guitar was a gift but then quickly changing the subject.

I was all for having a female record with us, and Stasia and I get along great. The problem isn't anything to do with music, though. My concern is Kelly. She wasn't super thrilled the first time I sang with Stasia, based solely on her choice of clothing – and right now, she doesn't offer much more for chaste coverage. I'm already in deep with Kelly, and suddenly I'm feeling like I made the wrong bet.

Again.

Chapter Twelve

Kelly sits on the bar top at The Rock Room, and Xander and I sit on the stools at the corner of the bar with Dom and Theo at our sides. Natalie hands a cup of iced water to Dom, then prepares glasses of whiskey and slides them to the rest of us. Kelly intercepts mine, taking the first sip then leaning forward and kissing my lips. It's a perfect, slow kiss, flavored with my favorite liquor and soft lips belonging to my favorite girl.

Things have been good for us. By good, I mean I'm sleeping in the bed instead of the couch and she's not locking me out of the damn house. Baby steps, I suppose. But we haven't told her about our new band arrangement yet, and I'm not sure how she's going to take it.

As if on cue, the *click clack* of high heels echoes through The Rock Room.

"We're closed," Kelly yells, and I turn to see Stasia waltzing across the venue, headed our direction.

"I heard this is where the band members of Consistently Inconsistent hang out." She swings a leg over a stool and makes herself comfortable. "Now the band's all here!" She's smiling but Kelly's not. Her eyes find mine with a darkened glare about them.

Damn it. Couch again.

"I'll take a vodka soda," Stasia says, reaching into her pocketbook instead of looking at Natalie as she orders.

Xander opens his mouth and lifts his hands above the bar, about to fill Natalie in on the drama, but Kelly interjects.

"Like I said, we're closed." She talks and signs simultaneously.

"Everyone else is drinking..." Stasia says, flicking her wrist and pointing to the drinks on the counter.

"They were just leaving." Kelly hops down from the bar top. "And so were you." She wraps her fingers into mine and I stand, walking beside her.

"Anything you forgot to tell me?" Kelly asks.

"So, Cooper invited Stasia to feature on a few tracks for us," I reply, knowing it's what I should have started the night with.

"I see that. She's...charming." Kelly doesn't hide her sarcasm as she says the word. "She's actually very pretty." I can hear it in her voice. She's feeling a little more insecure than she usually lets on.

"She's not you." I bring her hand to my lips and kiss each knuckle.

"Are you coming home tonight?"

"There's no place I'd rather be."

I don't look back at my band mates, new or old, as I leave the venue hand in hand with Kelly. We keep our fingers interlocked the entire way home, talking and laughing as we walk. Our palms never part, like neither of us wants to be the one to let go first. Once we arrive home, though, our hands aren't linked, but our bodies are.

The moonlight glows through the blinds, leaving rows of shadows and light across Kelly's bare skin. She's the definition of flawless. I spent years wanting her, admiring her from afar and every time I see her, still, even though I am hers and she is mine, it feels like the first time, every time.

She drags her fingernails down the skin of my back and pulls me into her. I lean forward, kissing her collarbones, her neck and her ears. I've missed this. I've missed her. So many nights I've spent sitting at tables in smoke-filled rooms, losing money to people I'd hardly consider friends, when I could've been here with her, loving every inch of her and giving all of me over to her gentle touch and…her not-so-gentle touch.

She takes control the way she usually does, flipping me so my back is against the bed, and she positions herself over me, keeping her body close to mine, skin to skin, body to body.

Eventually she collapses on the mattress next to me. I wrap my arm around her abdomen and pull her close, drifting off to the best sleep I've had in a long time and knowing that whatever it was I was out there looking for night after night, I had it all along under my own roof.

When I wake, she's still sleeping. I don't want to leave. There is nothing I want more in this moment than to stay here with her, dreaming right alongside her. But my newly established reputation as 'teetering on unreliable' extends past more than Kelly. The band knows it too, and I made a promise to Cooper that I'd be better. An early arrival to the studio is expected of me, and I know Coop won't accept anything less.

Stasia is already in the sound booth when we all arrive. Cooper is pacing back and forth in front of the music mixer buttons, instructing the gentleman in charge of the controls where to adjust and what to do. Stasia sounds great. Her vocals are perfect and reaching ranges I once thought were myths. This, all of the sudden, is starting to seem like a good idea again.

She waves enthusiastically from behind the microphone in the recording room.

"You guys ready to get in there and lay down some vocals with her?" Cooper asks, and everyone nods.

The look on Cooper's face is one of pure delight, telling us Stasia's presence is exactly what he was looking for when he said, "*something different*".

Stasia is still on the other side of the glass, testing her style on some of our material. The band and Cooper stay on the other side of the window watching as Stasia works her magic in the booth. She's so comfortable there, so natural, that there's no way she's as unexperienced as she lets on. The phrase 'too good to be true' comes to mind, and I find myself wondering if she's being one hundred percent honest about her musical background.

"I want to talk to you all about something." Cooper turns so his back is to the sound booth and he's facing all four of us. "There have to be rules."

None of us respond vocally but our obvious collectively confused expressions are enough for him to continue.

He clears his throat. "No inter-band relationships." It's the least confident lecture Cooper has ever given us.

He barely looks at us as he speaks like a father having *the* sex talk with his sons for the first time.

The band lets out a collective '*ohhhhh*' mixed with a few laughs at Cooper's expense.

"I'm serious." His voice shifts into a more familiar, down to business manner. "I've never had to get involved in your love lives, and I certainly don't want to start now, but this is a good thing we have going. She could be great for this album. Do *not* ruin it—for her or for the rest of us."

Cooper isn't wrong to set the tone for things going forward. He's never had to worry about any relationship drama amongst the band before—and adding a member of the opposite sex could have made some waves five years ago, but now? Xander is happily married. I have eyes for only one woman. Dom doesn't date. He's never brought a love interest around in all the time I've known him. It's not his style – one-night stand or long-term love. Dom avoids both. He's content by himself and has been that way as long as I can remember. Theo's love life is complicated, but it also makes it unlikely that he would be the one to rock the boat while we tread these new waters, but at any rate, he's the first to agree to the new terms.

"It's a good call," Theo says, nodding as he speaks. "This will all be for nothing if it gets ruined over a fling. Treat her like one of the guys. That's what she is now."

"One of the guys," Dom reiterates as he watches her sing into the microphone in the booth.

We all watch Stasia for a while from beyond the glass. Even in recording, she sings like she's performing for a crowd of thousands and not four other band members and some studio staff. She sways back and forth to music only she can hear through the headphones she wears. As she hits big notes, I can practically see her vocal cords getting their exercise under the skin at her throat. Cooper gives Xander and me a bit of direction and insight as to what he wants and sends us into the studio with Stasia to give this experiment a go. It is mostly moments of us screwing around, trying to get used to each other's sounds and contributions, practicing with our new person before laying down a committed track, but Cooper is happy with the outcome regardless.

"Brilliant!" he yells as we exit the booth. "I don't know why we didn't do this years ago. It's fresh, and it's perfect. You, Stasia, you are a very talented girl."

"Thank you." She smiles and it appears she's blushing, but it's hard to tell under the makeup she wears. Cooper is right. Stasia is talented. She is, dare I say it, the female version of Julian Young – superior talents and musically inclined, but with any luck has a better head on her shoulders.

"Coffee?" Xander says through a yawn and the band – all *five* of us – exit the recording studio and head to Chance's on the Corner.

* * * *

Kelly has a shift at The Rock Room and has booked some band that's quickly gaining popularity. She asked me, Xander and the guys – well, guys plus one girl – to come check them out, and we agreed. They don't start until half past eight, so I have time to kill, but Blake Mathews and time to kill is historically a lethal combination.

I sit at the counter shuffling a deck of cards. They fall from one hand to the other in a long cascade of plastic-coated paper, meeting again in a pile in my other hand. My phone rings and I'm hesitant to flip it over. Every time I look, the phone lights up with Isabella's invitations to another hand of poker that I can't afford – and I don't mean financially. But it's not. It's Stasia.

Grab a pizza before The Rock Room?

A second thought didn't cross my mind. Going out with Stasia is a safer bet than any other choice I could make. I typed back an enthusiastic yes and met up with her for dinner and a bit of fun and games at a local arcade. The puck flies toward me and I stop it under the blue plastic air hockey paddle, striking it hard and sending it back across the surface toward Stasia. The puck slides perfectly into the goal slot, lights illuminating overhead in the middle of the arcade.

Stasia lets out a frustrated snarl but slips another payment into the machine and the clocks set to zero.

"What do you say we make this more interesting?" she adds, reaching into her pocket and showing off a crisp one-hundred-dollar bill. She tosses it next to our drinks on the table beside the air hockey surface.

I reach into mine, pulling out enough to match her bet. Staring at the money, I realize that I couldn't say no if I wanted to. When I have the chance to take a risk, I take it every time. But this is hardly a bet. I'd beaten her seven to one. This isn't a bet. It's a sure thing.

I toss the money on top of hers.

"Ladies first." I slide her the puck. She slides it right back and laughs. "All right then," I add, hitting the puck toward her. She hits it back slick and fast, buzzing right past me and into the slot. The lights overhead flash.

I reset the plastic disc and hit it toward her. She returns it in a zig zag motion across the surface and I knock it back toward her. She's stops it with a quick hand, then flicks her wrist back my way. *Clink.*

Two-zero.

"You played me," I say, staring at the ten to three score on the board as she pockets the money.

"I was hoping you would say no," she says in a small voice as she sits on the edge of the air hockey table and hands me back the money I put down. "That was a test. You failed."

"I – " But there are no words worth saying. The only option is to stand there and look like an idiot—which, admittedly, I deserve.

"Blake, you told me you have been gambling. You said you're only doing it for fun, but it's getting in the way of work and love and I *want* to help you. I do. But you have to help yourself too."

"You aren't telling me anything I don't already know." I run my hand through my hair and feel the back of my neck get hot in a mix of frustration and embarrassment. "Why do you care?"

She tilts her head and raises an eyebrow. "Listen... I know we just met. But we have a lot in common. You're easy to talk to. I don't have a lot of friends here yet. I consider you one. Besides, my father ruined our family with his inability to stay away from a poker table."

I nod. She's right. We mesh. For a long time, I have wished I clicked with someone the way Alexander matched with Jana or how Kelly and Natalie meshed. Close friendships, outside the band, weren't something I ever really had.

"Come on." She hops down from the table and puts her hand on my forearm. "I'll buy you dinner."

As we wait for our food, something she had said replays over and over in my head. *'My father ruined our family with his inability to stay away from a poker table.'* She hardly ever talks about her father, but I find myself wanting to know more. The words stuck to me like a dart in a bullseye because for the first time, I know it is a very real possibility that if I don't figure this thing out, my own inability to stay away from tables could ruin my own family – both my band family and any future one I may have with Kelly. But when the opportunity to ask her more arises, I can't ask the question. Maybe, in the end, I don't really want to know the answer. Instead, I change the subject.

"So, why haven't you pursued a career in music?" I ask through a bite of pizza. "I mean, your dad is like…apparently a music god, according the boys. He has some of the most famous musicians of the decade on his label, and you're better than half of them."

"I'm better than more than half of them," she says after a sip of her drink. "But that's part of the problem. I want to make it on my own and not because of who my father is. If I make it in the music world, I want it to be earned, not gifted."

When we started out, I would have taken any gift that was given. I didn't care how we got there I just wanted to get there—but she's entitled to her wrong opinion.

"Besides, you don't know my dad. Signing with him was the biggest gamble of them all, honestly. He's made musicians but he's ruined them too. And everything my dad does comes with strings attached.

He would've owned everything I've ever done. And despite all my efforts, he almost did."

My face twists in confusion and I raise one brow.

Stasia wipes her hands on a napkin and holds up one finger before reaching into her purse for her phone.

"I'll show you this one time then we're never going to bring it up again. It's a part of my past, and truthfully, it kind of hurts to watch it."

"You don't have to..." I start, but I truly have no idea what I'm talking her out of.

"I want to. You guys are taking a chance on me, and it's the best chance I've had in a long time." She shrugs her shoulders and clicks into a video that begins to load. "You all want to know why I haven't pursued a professional career. This is why."

The video completes its download, and the phone comes to life. At first, a dark blackness covers the screen then an instrument plays intermittently. It's different. *Violin, maybe?* Each time the string instrument rings its rich tones, a light flashes and the silhouette of a person holding an instrument between her shoulder and chin illuminates. I was right about the violin. When she stops, the light stops. When she plays again her spotlight returns. Her song and rhythm pick up speed, her sound powering the brightening light in the distance behind her. As she strings together gorgeous yet harsh notes, the light gets closer and brighter. Her shadow starts to grow on the ground as the spotlight grows nearer and the scene starts to take place. She's standing on railroad tracks under the entrance to a tunnel.

The spotlight isn't a spotlight at all but the headlight of an oncoming train.

The train comes close enough that its wheels against the metal tracks overpower the song and the force of the wind from the tunnel sends her hair flying up and out of place—then the scene changes. Stasia's singing on the heavily graffitied staircase of the train station, her voice and incredibly wide ranges echoing through the empty brick stairwell. As the song continues, she switches from violin to guitar and joins another performer with make-shift drums on the platform parallel to the tracks. Passersby throw money into his hat as they walk past.

At the opening to the chorus, she's on the roof of the train station, joined by a drummer and a keyboard player among other musicians who are set to make the rooftop look more like a concert stage. At the opening of the bridge of the song, Stasia is sitting cross-legged on the train station turnstile, singing a fast-paced section of the song.

The song picks up intensity and the drummer, keyboardist and other guitarists can be heard, though not seen. In the video, Stasia plays her guitar on top of the moving train while belting out the lyrics that end the words of the song and as the music fades out, she's stepping through a door on to a train with a destination labeled *Anywhere But Here*.

"It's an incredible video. You are an unbelievable performer. But you already know that." She smiles and nods an agreeable yes. "So, what happened? This is professional-level stuff, Stasia. How has nobody seen this?"

"It didn't work out." For one moment she was willing to give me *some* information but not all. She's still holding back the piece of the story that causes her the most pain. "It was a great video, and it could've been something amazing. I poured everything I had of myself into that song and recording those scenes. But that label went a different direction, and I knew there was something out there better for me."

"I get that." I shrug, trying to see it from her side. "If Cooper hadn't come along, we would've ended up on a label. But we made it without one. We got lucky."

I lift my glass and she taps hers off mine.

"Let's get out of here before we're late for the show and Kelly hates me more than she already does," Stasia says.

"She doesn't *hate* you."

Stasia rolls her eyes.

* * * *

Then

Alexander's mother knocks on our bedroom door and asks us to come downstairs. Neither of us knew why, but we weren't about to start admitting things. We head down the stairs, having a silent argument about who was going to go first.

"Now!" she bellows and we rush down the stairs so as not to make things worse. "Alexander," she says as we turn the corner. *Phew*, it's not me. "Tell me... How does one get a *zero* on a test?"

"Umm-m, they don't answer any questions correctly?" He scratches his head. She slides an awkwardly folded piece of paper in his direction.

"A *zero*, Alexander? And please, *please* tell me if I refold those lines that paper won't turn into an airplane." Her glare narrows and she taps her foot.

"I wouldn't recommend trying," he says, shoving his hands in his pockets and rocking back and forth on his toes. I laugh but swallow it, turning it into a faux cough when her eyes meet mine.

"Blake, yours isn't much better. What is going on with you two?" she asks, her voice finally softening.

"We're just busy, Mom," Alexander whines. "We are good at music. We love music. We're getting paid to do some small shows here and there. School just doesn't seem that important."

He's so wrong. There is a time you are honest with your parents and a time you bite your tongue – that should have been a tongue-biting moment. He had a fifty-fifty chance of choosing correctly and he chose wrong — though, that test we'd taken had been *true* or *false* and he'd failed that too.

"Okay," she says, tapping her fingers on the countertop. "I don't know how else to get through to you, so here it is. You have a history test this coming Thursday. If *either* of you fails, *neither* of you plays your show this weekend. You can study together, help each other out or bring each other down. The choice is yours. But you both pass or you both miss the show."

"But – " we protest, but she raises her hands and walks away.

"That's final," she says as she heads into the next room.

"So, I'll start posting cancellation flyers then?" Lord knows neither of us would pass that test.

Alexander gets this look in his eye and curls his lips into a half smile.

"No." I shake my head hard.

"I didn't even say anything!" he says, feigning innocence.

"I know, but I know that look. If you don't tell me what you're thinking, then I'm not lying when I say I had nothing to do with it."

"It's nothing bad." He shrugs.

"Scouts' honor?" I ask.

"I got kicked out of scouts...twice."

"How do you get kicked out of Boy Scouts?" I ask. "You know what? Never mind. I don't want to know. What's this plan?"

* * * *

We sit in the school library — after about twenty-five minutes of looking for it — and I work on writing song lyrics instead of studying. Off to a good start.

The library door opens, and Kelly walks over to our table, sits down and cracks open her history book. I look at Alexander then back at her.

"Umm, hi?" I say. Kelly doesn't just sit with me and Alexander. "What're you doing?"

She looks at me as if this is the dumbest question in the world.

"Tutoring you?" she says with obvious skepticism. Alexander looks away, his eyes to the ceiling. I could kill him.

Kelly and I haven't really spoken since I'd tried to kiss her and she'd made it abundantly clear that my chances with her were about as good as my chances of passing this test. Nonexistent.

I'll give Alexander credit. It was a good idea. She's brilliant and patient and she teaches us history in a way that I understand, instead of just throwing a book at us and telling us to read it. Unexpectedly, I even kind of enjoy it.

"Okay, I think that's good for today." She closes the book. Alexander and I give her a few 'thank yous' and 'see you tomorrows' as she pushes her chair out and walks away.

"Go talk to her," Alexander says as we stand. "You barely said three words the entire time."

"It was tutoring, not a blind date," I say under my breath, shoving my books into my bag.

"So I'm killing two birds with one stone then," he says, then shoves me hard in her direction as she reaches the door. My books hit the ground with an echoing slam, and she turns to check the commotion.

Walking toward her with my hands in my pockets and my eyes on the floor, I take a deep breath and take another chance.

"So, I really appreciate you doing this for us." I drag my toe across the tile and bite my bottom lip. "I thought maybe I could take you out this weekend…as a thank you. You know, for…this."

She smiles but it's not genuine. It's forced. Sympathetic, even.

"I actually have plans with my cousin this weekend." She leaves the sentence open ended. I'm not sure if it's a no – which is worse than a no.

"That's even better. I'll invite Alexander and we can take you both out somewhere," I offer.

"Oh, umm, I'm not sure Alexander is her type, honestly. But, maybe some other time. See you tomorrow, Blake."

Strike two.

* * * *

Three days with Kelly paid off — well, for my history test anyway. By the look on Alexander's mother's face, one would have thought we'd brought home a winning lottery ticket instead of a couple of Bs on a history test. She sticks them up under faded Red Sox magnets on the fridge and hugs us both.

"I knew you could do it!" Her voices rings through the kitchen. "See? Why do I have to be mean to get through to you two?"

"Tough love," Alexander says. "It works."

"Okay, okay," she says, "I wasn't going to tell you this, but I'm so proud of you – of both of you – that I can't keep it a secret."

Alexander and I look at each other then back at her.

"I have a friend who owns a small – *really* small – recording space."

My muscles clench with excitement. I can feel Alexander's body shift next to mine. *No way.*

"It's nothing special...but he agreed to let you...put down a track or whatever you guys call that."

The words that come out of Alexander's and my mouth are not comprehensible. I'm not sure they are even words. We race up the stairs to the phone to call the rest of the guys and tell them the news.

This can't be real. I repeated those same four words for days, right up until the moment we walked into the studio for the first time and the dream started to take shape into reality.

Watching Alexander in the booth is a thing of pure ecstasy. You'd think he was performing for a crowd of thousands and not singing to a microphone and a wall. Even though we're standing there and I can see it happening, it still feels like a dream. We will walk out of here today with a demo, and I'm just waiting for someone to pinch me awake.

"You boys have a great sound. There's a lot of talent here," a brown-haired man says, removing his headphones as Alexander leaves the booth.

"Thank you." Alexander is out of breath and sweat beads at his brow. "And thank you so much for having us, umm...*sir*."

The man laughs and sticks out his hand. "Gary Cooper," he says, taking Alexander's hand in his own, "but you can just call me Cooper."

* * * *

"We have a single, boys," Alexander says, lifting his drink and the rest of us follow suit. "No band name...but a single!"

We all laugh a sound that echoes across the football field and into the open air, decreasing in volume until it reaches the stars and fades out altogether.

Julian cracks another bottle and fills all our cups, minus Dominic's. Never once has he succumbed to the peer pressure of this group. The football field spins around me in a green blur. I don't need more, but I take it.

The sky is speckled in tiny white lights that glitter against a black backdrop over the school, yet if you go any closer to the city, you can't see them at all. The skyscrapers and abundant light sources blot out the starry sky overhead just miles from where are. What a concept... Sometimes you need darkness to see the light. I can relate to that.

"Okay, band names. Go," Alexander slurs and the guys throw out names. I lay back with my hands behind my head, looking at the star-studded sky. "Light Pollution," I say. It's the first thing I think of as I lie here analyzing the sky. But there are no bites.

Julian throws out a name that none of us catch, no matter how many times we ask him to repeat it.

"I don't think any of you are in the right state of mind to be making such a decision," Dominic adds. He sips Gatorade from a bottle.

"We're out of vodka," Julian says, trying to stand up but stumbling across the white paint on the grass of the field.

"Where are you going?" I ask, sitting up too quickly. The world turns, as does my stomach.

"Locker room," he says, "I'm pretty confident Coach keeps a bottle in his desk."

"Absolutely not," I say, but he's already a bus length away from me before I can do anything about it. The guys follow close behind him, laughing loudly, and making no effort to be discreet.

If you can't beat 'em, join 'em. I run to catch up.

Julian fiddles with the knob. The door doesn't open.

"Locked," he says.

Well, dare I say it, *duh.*

"We should be going anyway – " I start to say, but another voice cuts through mine.

"You won't be going anywhere."

I don't have to turn around to know that voice. I have sat in his office enough times to know that it's Principle Wheeler. This time, he has back-up. A uniformed police officer stands at his side.

Julian's parents come first. He slides into the back of their family's luxury SUV and waves to us from the back window before they pull away from the school. Before long, Theo's grandmother arrives, followed by

Dom's parents. We are the last two unaccounted for, and Alexander's mother isn't answering the phone.

"I can't let you boys go without a parent," the officer says, snapping his phone closed and slipping it back in his pocket.

"My mother works two jobs. She's probably home trying to sleep for a few hours before her next shift."

"C'mon," he says, throwing his head over his shoulder. "Get in. We can take a ride over there."

The back seat of the police car is hard and uncomfortable, both physically and mentally. My stomach turns just thinking about how much trouble we are about to be in. Growing up, though, I was never truly praised as a child, but my mother never necessarily cared enough to scold me, either.

The officer bangs on the door and we stand awkwardly outside awaiting our fate. The light flicks on behind the front door then Debbie opens it, wearing a bathrobe and a sleepy expression. Her exhaustion is knocked out of her abruptly when she puts together the pieces of the puzzle and suddenly she's wide-eyed and furious.

The officer, who, all in all, was much kinder than we deserved, recapped the story as they stood at the door while we stayed at the kitchen counter.

"So only the one boy is yours then?" he asks.

"Blake has been with us for a while," she says. They try to keep their voices hushed, but the house is only so big, so it's easy to hear their conversation.

"Do you have any kind of paperwork like power of attorney or legal guardian forms? Anything that says you're caring for him at this time?"

I know what's happening and so does she. Alexander has never been great at math, but he's solving this equation as fast as the rest of us.

"Please," she says, "this has been hard enough on him. He has nowhere else to go."

For a moment a few mumbles are exchanged then silence before the man says, "That's not a name I've heard in a while."

There is no more back and forth after that. She steps inside and closes the door behind her. The name she spoke, the name he recognized, was my mother's. And the only reason he agreed to let me stay was because as soon as Debbie uttered her name that officer knew I was better off here, regardless if the arrangement had been legally bound.

"Who feels like talking first?" She leans into the counter we sit at. Neither of us respond. "Okay, I will," she says. Suddenly I wish I'd volunteered.

"I got these letters in the mail this morning. The school sent them. It's a notice that says *both* of you are at risk for failing the term if you don't pull off a passing grade on your exams."

I pick at some dirt from the football field under my fingernail so I don't have to look at her. This is only going to go from bad to worse. "I planned on talking to you tonight about these letters and then you were brought home by a cop instead so *thank you* for saving me some time. Now I can yell at you for everything all at once."

It's a one-sided conversation. We stay quiet, getting through the lecture to find out what our inevitable punishment is.

"You two were doing well. You were playing music and making some money to put toward that music. Your grades went up – for like *two-and-a-half seconds.*" She pauses a long, silent moment and takes a breath. "I can't keep up with you two. Just when I think I can let my guard down and trust you both are maturing, you pull stunts like this. Inconsistency is just about the only thing you two *do* consistently."

Alexander and I looked at each other automatically, doing that wordless conversation thing we have perfected over the years. Even though we ended up being grounded for two weeks, we also ended up with a band name that fit us in a way nothing else could.

Chapter Thirteen

Now

Stasia and I enter The Rock Room in a fit of laughter that has morphed from giggling about something dumb to that silent, gasping-for-air-type laugh that comes when you keep piling stupid things on top of the joke that wasn't necessarily that funny in the first place. I take a deep breath and she wipes a tear from the corner of her eye.

"You sound nothing like me." The words are choppy as I'm recovering from the fit of laughter.

"I sound *exactly* like you," she says, botching all her efforts to mimic the words I pronounce slightly different than she does.

My stomach muscles hurt from laughing so hard. It's been a while since I've been so unwound, so...*childish.*

"You're here," Kelly says as we enter the backstage area. Her voice raises in surprise as she says the words.

"You asked me to be…" A confused grimace replaces the smile that I wore seconds ago, "The band should be going on soon, yeah?"

"Not until nine-thirty." She flips through papers on a clipboard, never looking up from her work as she talks.

"You said eight-thirty."

"Yes, I did." She tucks the clipboard under her arm. "I figured you'd be late if you showed up at all, so I gave you a one-hour buffer. But, look on the bright side. At least you won't have to be alone while you wait." Her lips press into a hard line and she returns her gaze to her paperwork. "Stasia," she says with a nod. No 'hello', no 'how are you'. It's the bare minimum of noting Stasia's presence at all.

"Kelly," Stasia responds with a paralleled lack of enthusiasm as Kelly leaves us backstage.

Stasia raises her brow to an arch and holds her hands toward the area Kelly just exited through.

"What?" I say, losing the game of charades she is playing.

"Go after her, you goon," Stasia says, slapping her hand against her thigh with a loud sigh. "She's clearly upset about something. She's your girlfriend. Go fix whatever that something may be."

"I don't think she wants me to follow her."

"She wants you to follow her. Trust me. Now *go*." She steps forward and pushes me toward the door.

"Kelly," I say, quickening my pace to catch up to her. She turns to me but keeps her eyes on her clipboard, immersed in her work the way she always is. I take the clipboard from her and toss it to the ground. She looks up at me, surprised, and I place my fingers at her jaw and my lips on hers.

"What was that for?" she says through a smile.

"I *miss* you."

She looks up at me with confused eyes.

"I haven't gone anywhere," she says, placing her hand against my chest where my heart beats under her fingertips.

"I know, but I have." She braces for impact like bad news is coming in for an impossible-to-avoid collision. I can feel it in the way her body tenses and she holds her breath. "No, no," I say, taking her hand in mine. "I've been distracted. I've been looking for what comes next, when everything I have been looking for has been just a few feet from me the whole time. I don't just want to be *home*. I want to be *present*. I'm going to be better, Kelly...for you."

She places her palm at the back of my neck and pulls me in close to her, leaving her mouth lingering on mine like a pinky promise of the lips.

"I want to show you something," I say when we part, and she nods. I open an app on my phone and punch in the pin to a side bank account I've had for years. "I asked you to take charge of my bank account when you moved in, because, let's face it, Kelly, I suck with money. And since then, you've kept everything going — the house, the bills. It all comes out of the account that you have access to."

"I know." She nods in a slow pattern, trying to follow.

"But this account," I say, handing her the details on the phone's face, "is the dream account. It was Cooper's idea. I'd bet Xander has one too. When he realized how horrendous of decisions he and I made, Cooper suggested we have a bank account for right now — the one the bills get paid out of — and one for someday. The dream account… This account is one we will need in the future when the music isn't there anymore."

"I don't understand." She eyes the numbers on the screen.

"This one, Kelly," I say, tapping the screen. "This one is *our* account. Our 'someday'. We're going to do something with this—a year-long trip of a lifetime, vacation homes, whatever you want…what *we* want. We're going to do it together."

"What's *your* dream?" She puts the phone back in my hand. "Where do you want to go? What do you want to buy?"

I think about it for a moment. I've never thought about it before. When I look into the future, I can't see the whole dream, but I can see one clear part of it.

"I don't care where we go or what we buy, as long as we're doing it together."

She nods and kisses me again, then nuzzles her forehead into my neck and holds herself against me. I'm not sure how long we stand there, but I won't be the one to step away first. I won't *ever* be the one to step away first. If I could have, I would've made that moment last hours, but Kelly's job calls her away and I sit backstage where I watch her work, counting my blessings each time she walks by. The rest of the band shows up and takes the seats around me. We talk, laugh and drink until Kelly pops her head in to the back and tells us she's ready for us.

The band we're here to watch, *First and Forever*, takes the stage and we observe from the wings. They're excellent, with a great following of their own. They remind me a bit of Consistently Inconsistent's early days, all energy and emotion, soaking in the excitement of looking out from the stage and knowing you're on your way to the top.

"Great show, really well done," Xander says, clapping his hands loudly as the band exits the stage and joins us in the wings.

"Thank you so much. You guys are a huge inspiration. You were all we listened to growing up," the lead singer says, sweat dripping from his hair.

"Ouch, now I feel old." Xander says it, but we were all thinking it. "What's the plan going forward? Looks like you're getting some good exposure."

"Yeah, not so bad. We had a call just the other day from MLA records. They're requesting a meeting, so we will see what happens with that."

Stasia turns and walks away so quietly that no one else noticed—but I did.

"Any advice?" another band member adds.

"Follow your gut. If you get contacted by a label that can take you to where you want to be and leave your sound intact, do it. But this is *your* music. Don't get stuck anywhere that tries to take that away from you," I say, and they nod in response.

"We're weighing our options," the lead singer says. "There's a lot of checks in the pro column to staying unsigned, and so far, we're not doing so bad, but we want to explore options and see what is out there for us. Thank you so much again for coming out."

"Looking forward to seeing what you do in the future," Xander says. Their band members exchange handshakes and well wishes with ours and we go our separate ways.

* * * *

Then

Our demos are sailing. Small news outlets in the area have helped us promote our songs and our social media pages are gaining traction faster than we can keep up with. One night, late into the evening hours, Alexander and I sit at the table and do our homework — yes, seriously.

The phone rings and Alexander's mother answers it. She looks over at us every once in a while but offers only the occasional '*mm-hmm*' and '*uh-huh*'. Alexander and I look at each other, trying to figure out what we might have done wrong without starting to admit to anything. She hangs up the phone and doesn't say a word. She returns to the counter and continues preparing dinner. We hold a collective breath for a moment, only she goes on to hum a little tune and not say anything at all. We shrug and return our gaze to our books, then she finally speaks.

"Why don't you two invite Julian, Dominic and Theo to join us for dinner tonight?"

Our faces are a matching set of confused grimaces, but we do as we are told.

"What are we here for?" Dom asks, a bit later when they arrive, but the rest of us know nothing more than he does.

"Not a clue," Alexander and I say in unison.

Alexander's mother comes into the kitchen and takes a seat with us.

"So, there's a record label that has heard some of your songs and they want to meet with you."

We're all silent, absorbing the sentence but not reacting to it.

"Let's try again," Debbie says in slow, drawn-out dramatics. "Record label. Likes your songs. You guys. Meeting."

There are no words. Literally, the sounds that come out of our mouths are not English...or coherent. It's just a mix of excitement and half-formed questions—and for some reason smacking each other hard on the arms and shoulders as an expression of enthusiasm.

For days, time moves backward. No matter what we do to pass the minutes or make the clock move faster, it doesn't. Our seven-hour school days age like years as we wait for our meeting, but we survive the brutal anticipation.

The restaurant chosen for the meeting is one of those dimly lit, prices not listed on the menu, waiters with towels over their arms type atmospheres that I've only ever seen in the movies. Self-consciousness rushes through me as other patrons walk by eyeing our ripped jeans and rugged looks in comparison to the expensive clothes they wear and the designer handbags they carry.

We're seated near the bar area but in a booth. None of us speak—nerves, I think. I tap my foot, nervously shaking my leg, which in turn shakes the table and Julian tells me to quit it. Alexander chugs his third water refill.

"Who did they say they were sending again?" Theo asks.

"Some dude named Charlie Adams." My nervous leg-twitch returns.

I'm unsure what to expect. My thoughts trend toward a man in a suit with slicked back hair and a holier-than-thou attitude. But I'm wrong.

A woman in a black leather jacket and impossibly high heels joins us at our table.

"I'm Charlie Adams," she says, "Artist & Repertoire representative for MLA records. I'm so sorry I'm late."

She reaches across the table, introducing herself to each one of us individually and asking us a bit about ourselves.

"Order whatever you want, boys. MLA is taking care of you today."

Charlie wastes no time, diving right in to what MLA would like to see from us, what they do — and most importantly, why we need them. I'm not sure any of us absorbed even one word of the material she presented. It was like school but fancier and far more confusing.

We dive into our meals like we've never eaten before, leaving nothing spared on the plate.

"So, you'll think that over then?" She flashes teeth that sparkle as she smiles. "Call if you have any questions." She hands over her business card and leaves the table, her heels clicking through the restaurant in an even echo.

We chat among ourselves, repeating everything Charlie said, but not really knowing what to do with the information.

"Mind if I join you for a minute, boys?" a deep voice says. The man drags a chair around, straddling its seat and leaning his elbows against the back of it. Sitting with the chair backward at the end of our table, he looks almost as out of place as we do.

It took me a minute to realize that we knew him. He's Alexander's mom's friend. Greg? George? Gary? Something with a G, I think, but I don't really know.

"Hey, how are you doing, Cooper?" Alexander asks. "Thank you for all your help so far. My mother says you've been distributing our demos to your friends in the industry."

"Oh no, this was all you, boys—hard work and a little bit of luck." He picks up Charlie's business card from the table. "So, MLA, huh?"

"Yeah." I nod. "Kind of surreal."

"I think you can do better." His eyes are on mine. His lips are tightly pressed and matter of fact. I think he might be kidding.

He's not kidding.

"Consistently Inconsistent is already on the fast track to something, and no one has gotten you there but you. You're playing small shows. You're in a recording studio. By my observation, your followers on your pages are growing exponentially every day."

"You're following us?" Alexander asks.

"Yes, of course, Xander," Cooper says.

"Oh, it's actually Alexan—" Alexander's voice trails off and his lip turns to a curled smile. "Xander is fine."

"I think you've got something good going, and MLA is great, for sure. Don't get me wrong. But they would own everything you do. Your sound won't be *your* sound anymore. You can do this without them."

"Well, Cooper," Alexander—or Xander, I suppose— says, "why don't you tell us your thoughts? We will let you buy us dessert."

"Sounds like a plan," Cooper responds through a smile and a laugh.

Chapter Fourteen

Now

The table is set, the candles are lit, and the only thing that can make it more perfect is Kelly's arrival home, which should be any minute.

I pull my chair out and sit, accidentally knocking my fork to the floor as I do so. It bounced under the table to a place I can't reach. I slide off the stool and put all my weight on one knee, grabbing the utensil and returning it to its spot. Just as I'm about to stand, Kelly walks in to find me on one knee beside the romantically decorated table.

Her gaze finds mine and both of our jaws drop, mirror images of the other's surprise. I look at the table, at her then back again.

"Blake…" she says, hanging her coat on the rack.

"This…this isn't what it looks like." I stand and brush myself off.

"Oh, thank God." A sigh of relief escapes her lips.

"*Oh, thank God?*" I repeat. "Tell me how you really feel. Don't hold back this time…"

We both laugh, a loud, full sound that echoes throughout the house and we have to force ourselves to breathe again.

I pull out her chair then my own.

"What is all of this?" The candlelight flickers in the reflection of her eyes.

"I do have something for you. It's just not a ring."

She laughs again, shaking her head back and forth. I lean over and pick up an old, tattered photo album and hand it to her. She takes it but doesn't open it. She glances over the book from under deep black lashes.

"You said you wanted to know everything about me. That's it. That's all I have of them—my parents, that is."

Kelly cracks open the book and runs her fingers over its yellowed pages. She asks about my mother and I tell her everything, leaving out no details—all the way up until she left me with Xander and his mother.

There are times her eyes fill with tears, times she looks at me with a shocked expression as if she doesn't believe all that could have possibly been happening for so many years that she *knew* me but didn't really *know* me.

"Where was this one taken?" She points to a picture of my father and I sitting on a dock, with large rocks and a gorgeous body of water as the backdrop to the picture. We look almost nothing alike. His hair is a bit darker, and his facial structure was different from mine, but we both smiled widely.

"A beach in Cape Town." I curl my lips into a light smile at the memory. "I was five or six in that picture. My mother had been gone for a whole year. At the time

I thought she was working, but now I have no idea what the hell she was really doing. My father, though, was determined to keep me happy, even if it meant going there every single day to watch the penguins waddle around the beach."

She rests her head in her hand and listens as I narrate my trip down memory lane.

"That's all I really remember about living there." I shrug and she nods her head.

When my mother returned from her year-long hiatus, that's when the fighting started. That was the beginning of the brutal end. They screamed and yelled while I sat at the top of the stairs and eavesdropped but missed the peak of the argument.

"If you kick me out, my son is coming with me." My mother's voice echoed from their room up the stairs. Even after that year together, the daily trips to the beach, the penguins, the smiles...he didn't say a word. Then mother and I were on a plane.

"I'm sorry." Her voice is low and quiet.

"Don't be." That's the last thing I want.

"I'm sorry I never knew or noticed. I was always so caught up in trivial high school stuff..."

"Hell, I lived with Xander, and he never knew the details either, really." I push my food around my plate with my fork. "His mother always knew. She read me like a book. She still does. She's extremely perceptive. Xander, not so much."

She laughs but stifles it, covering her mouth with her fingertips.

"This is your mom?" She turns the page of the book toward me, and I nod.

"You haven't seen her since you moved in with Xander?"

I take a sip of my drink and return the glass to the table.

* * * *

Then

Xander hands me a hat and gloves almost identical to the set he's wearing.

"Do you all do this every year?" I ask as he slides on one boot then the other.

"We have a fake tree, too. Some years we've been a little tighter on cash, so we set up this old artificial tree that's sadder than the one in *A Charlie Brown Christmas*. But every year that we can afford something extra at the holidays, we go to the Christmas-tree farm and cut down a real tree. Then we pick a day and watch Christmas movies and listen to music while we decorate."

I have never been more jealous of Xander than I am in this moment. His mother and him are so close, and he's not embarrassed or shy about it.

"How about you? Any traditions?" Xander asks as we head down the stairs.

The only tradition I ever had was waking up, walking around the house and looking in each room, left to wonder if mother was home or not. I was a regular Kevin McCallister in *Home Alone*, only I didn't wish for my family to disappear. That was just the way it always had been.

"Not really." My voice is miles away.

We lock the door and walk to the car with snow crunching under our feet.

"I have always loved stockings," Xander says. "My mom fills them with all kinds of candy and trinkets. I used to wake up before her, and I wasn't allowed to touch any of the gifts—but stockings were fair game."

"Mmhmm-m." The sound of Xander's excitement goes right under my skin. I wish it didn't, but it does. The ghosts of Xander's Christmas past and the ones of my own are two very different spirits.

"You okay?" Xander asks as he opens the SUV's passenger-side door.

"Never merrier." I close the back door behind me after I slide into the car.

We're silent for a while as Debbie drives down the road. I lean my head against the cold window and watch the snow fly past. She pulls over at the gas station and gets out of the car to fill the tank.

"I'm sorry," Xander says in a sullen voice. He leans into the center console, turning to face me. I lift my head from the window and look at him. "I should have realized this must be hard for you— "

"It's fine, Xander."

"No, it's not fine. It's your first Christmas without your mother—"

"Actually, it's not."

My tone doesn't waver, ensuring that my statement is the final word.

By the time we arrive at the tree farm, I still hadn't said a word. When we park, Xander hops out of the car and heads toward the rows of trees. I take my time exiting the vehicle and Debbie walks around the back of the car, cutting off my path.

"I would ask if everything is okay," she says, putting both her hands on my upper arms, "but I already know the answer."

I nod, retaining my silence.

"I'm trying as hard as I can to make things here perfect for you, Blake. I'm really trying. But I don't want to push you out of your comfort zones either. If you don't want to be a part of something, if you need space, just say so. I'm just trying to walk that line between knowing what's enough and knowing what's too much. This is new to me too, you know?"

She squeezes my upper arms then lets go, turning away and walking toward Xander.

Part of something. Of all the words she'd spoken, that's what hit me hardest. She made me part of a tradition, of a family, of a home. She's the one who made me part of something. I jogged toward them, and as I reached them, she put one arm around me and one arm around Xander as we walked onward through the rows of green.

They even let me pick the tree. And later I sit at the bottom of the staircase, staring into the living room. The house is dark, except for the tree. It's perfect—just like in the movies—the tree I always imagined, wished for, wanted.

This is the type of Christmas I dreamed of every single year and never got.

I have it now.

And it's perfect—but it's not.

I make my way to the top of the stairs and fall asleep in a bed that was given to me by someone who is not my mother, under a roof that was not provided to me by my mother, feeling safe and happy—comforts I never could have *gotten* from my mother.

So why do I miss her so much?

When I wake, Xander is gone, and his sheets are strewn over the side of the bed. I shuffle down the stairs and stretch through a yawn that echoes in the stairwell. The cold shoots up through the soles of my feet when I leave the carpeted stairs and stand on the floor in the entry way. Xander sits on the couch with his back to me and Debbie adjusts some ornaments on the tree.

"Good morning, Blake." She smiles a warm grin that twinkles like the lights on the tree.

The mantel catches my attention. Stockings decorate the ledge, perfectly placed with red and white trim.

Three of them.

Mom. Alexander.

Blake.

And my eyes fill with tears. I don't hold them back. I don't try to hide my emotions anymore.

For the first time, I belong somewhere. They gave me a sense of belonging that I'd spent my entire life searching for. Debbie wraps her arms around me.

"Thank you." The words sound muffled against her shoulder.

She steps back to arm's length and nods. "It has been a pleasure having you as part of this family," she says, and as she does, the doorbell rings.

"I'll get that." She walks away and Alexander steps toward me, standing where she stood.

"I spent every Christmas, my entire life, wishing for a Christmas tree and a stocking." I stare at the décor in the living room.

"I spent every Christmas wishing for a brother." Xander grips his fingers into my shoulder.

"Blake?" Debbie rejoins us at the living room.

"Yeah?" I say, suddenly grateful that Xander's hand is on my shoulder, holding me up. Otherwise, I'd have fallen to the floor in shock when my mother joined Debbie at the entrance to the living room.

"Blake," she says, holding her arms out and wearing a large smile like this was a pleasant surprise, a reconnection between two old friends who hadn't seen each other in years. She steps in and wraps her arms around me in the coldest hug I've ever received.

"Well," Debbie says with forced excitement, "I was just about to put dinner on the table. Why don't you join us?"

My mother pulls away but places her hand around my wrist and pulls me toward the kitchen, following Debbie and Xander to the table.

Dinner is quiet. Well, it's quiet for me, Debbie and Xander. My mother hasn't stopped talking since she got here. She details how well she's doing and what she has been up to. She tries to explain why she had to leave, but the story changes every time she reopens her mouth.

"I heard your song." She chews as she speaks. "You boys are great. You're really going to be someone, Blake. I always knew you would be."

Then, I get it. She doesn't miss me or want me. She thinks I might be worth something now, so she came back for me.

"Really something," she continues. "Have you been offered a record deal or anything like that?" She shovels food into her mouth like she hasn't eaten in months.

"Yeah, we turned it down," I say, all business, no fluctuation in my tones.

"You did *what*?" She's furious now, red in the face. "Blake, you've never been the sharpest boy, but this is the dumbest thing you have ever done."

"*Excuse* me." Debbie slams her fork to the table. "You will not come into *my* house and talk about *my* boys in that way."

"You are not his mother," my mother spits back at her. Tension fills the room.

"I'm not…but someone had to be."

"Blake." My mother wipes her mouth and pushes her chair back from the table. "Pack your things. We're leaving."

I don't know what to think or say.

"Now." She narrows her eyes.

"Sweetie, you don't have to go," Debbie adds.

The chair screeches against the tile as I push it back from the table, standing to walk past my mother and out of the door.

"Blake!" Mother yells as she follows me.

"What do you want?" I scream, turning to her with my arms out at my sides and my voice echoing through the night sky. "Why are you here? What could you *possibly* try to take from me that you haven't already taken?" My voice cracks, my throat strained.

"You are *talented*, Blake. And I know people. You could make it big. You don't need to have a band. You don't need Alexander eclipsing you. We could take you to the top."

She sells it all so well that it's almost believable. Of course, she knows people. Of course, we could make it an overnight success. It's a fool-proof plan just like every other one she has ever made in her life.

I turn my back and walk a few steps, distancing myself from the black hole that she is.

"You can't walk away from family!" she yells, her voice cracking as she cries out.

I turn around too fast, almost knocking myself off my feet and stepping in too close to her.

"You walked away!" My voice travels for miles. "I'm not walking away from family, *Mom*. That's the point. *They* are my family. Xander and his mom and the band? That's my family. And I will never, *ever*, quit on them the way you quit on me."

Chapter Fifteen

Now

Steam floats into the cool air off the surface of the hot jacuzzi water as it rises to meet the stars above us. Kelly leans into me, her skin against mine. I press my lips against her temple and leave them there, inhaling the scent of her hair.

She links her fingers into mine and extends her hand, pointing to a star that flies across the sky, leaving a bright tail of light behind it. I wonder what she wishes for as a small grin crawls into her cheeks. I wish that things would always be this way — simple, steadfast.

"Can I ask you something?" She shifts into a different seat, facing me. The cold air sets in, nipping at my skin where her body had been. I nod, though, in my experience, no good conversation ever started with *'Can I ask you something?'*

"I don't want to ask—I don't want to *have to* ask—but I feel like I can't help you or support you if I don't..."

"Just ask the question, Kelly." I tilt my head back and stare at the stars as she beats around the proverbial bush.

"Are you still gambling? When's the last time you played? I guess I don't know what or how to ask."

"I haven't been gambling." I'm annoyed but trying not to show it. I don't want to fight tonight, and my inability to disguise my emotions usually fast-tracks me to the couch. "It's not a problem."

"I read that *'it's not a problem'* is usually a pretty good indication that it is—"

"You...what? Internet searched it? You are turning this into something it's not."

"Can you just answer the question? I'm trying to help you." Her words are pleading. I can't help but think this is because I told her about my past. That's what I didn't want. She doesn't have to save me. I'm not broken. This is why I hide those parts of myself. My past doesn't have to dictate my future. Now she's going to worry in a way she didn't have to when she was ignorant to those parts of my history.

"When's the last time you gambled, Blake?" she asks again with no hesitation in her voice this time.

"Technically, yesterday before The Rock Room." I lower my gaze to meet hers. "Stasia bet against me on an air hockey game. But for real money? Not since I told you about it."

"You... I'm sorry. Stasia and you went out before the show?"

"Well, yeah, but it was good. She really helped me see the problem this is becoming."

"Blake." Her eyes drift into a saddened narrow and she tilts her head to one side. "I don't like to be a self-conscious person. That's not me. But can you really not see how much it bothers me that you have this connection with this girl that you *just* met but don't seem to have that same link with me?"

"Kelly, that's just not true." I slide across the jacuzzi seats and settle in close to her. "I don't look at Stasia the way I look at you. I don't feel anything like that for her. But, Kel, you grew up in this perfect family with two parents. You lived on the same street your entire life. Your parents are *literally* perfect. Stasia is somebody who understands how I grew up. She never knew her mother, and her father was absentee. We're friends. That's it. She's working with the band now — practically one of the guys."

"Okay." She nods. "I trust you. I just wish she wasn't so damn gorgeous. I couldn't blame you if you were attracted to her. Hell, *I* might be attracted to her."

"I'm *not* attracted to her." I place my hand on Kelly's thigh. "She's like…a sister type. Like Xander is with Jana."

Kelly nods then shifts back and sinks down into the hot tub.

I lean in and place my lips at her collarbone, her neck and her ear then wrap my finger into the knotted bikini tie at the nape of her neck and pull it free. She presses her chest against mine and puts her body weight against me, pushing me back into the seat at the other side of the jacuzzi. A wave of water follows our bodies and crashes over the edge.

* * * *

The next morning, I volunteer to pick up coffee from Chance's before our impromptu meeting that Cooper called. The standing ovation I received for being the person that showed up with coffee is almost as good as the one from any performance.

"Morning, gentlemen." I place a cup in front of each band member. Stasia clears her throat.

"And lady," I add. Stasia smiles a victorious grin as she takes her coffee. "Anyone know why we're here?"

The room is all shrugs and head shakes through sips of coffee but there are no answers. We sit for a while, cracking jokes and messing around until Cooper joins us. He sits at the table and opens a folder to a page that looks like a printed-off email.

"Unfortunately, the lead singer of the band *Most Of Us* was involved in an accident this weekend," Cooper says, his voice forlorn.

"Nate Bertrand?" Xander leans into the table. "Is he okay?"

Nate is a good man. We toured with *Most Of Us* a few years back. They are a great group. We had a lot of laughs on that tour, many of them provided by Nate himself. It was like touring with a comedian instead of a musician.

"He should be okay, but it will take him a long while to get there," Cooper says. Xander sinks into his chair and swallows hard. I'm sure news like that isn't easy for him. Not too long ago it was Xander laying in a hospital bed, casted and broken while wondering if his injuries would get in the way of his career.

"They are slated to play three nights in Miami in a few weeks. It's a musical festival-type benefit with about a dozen other bands on the roster." Cooper turns a piece of paper toward us, showing us the list of bands expected to play. "They asked us to take their place while Nate recovers. I wasn't sure what you all wanted to do. We don't do things here without a unanimous vote, so give it a few minutes, think about it and give me a yay or nay."

I look at Xander the way I have since I met him in sixth grade. I always like to know what he is thinking before I give an answer of my own—and he does the same. We have this wordless conversation, composed of head nods and eye narrows, but usually arrive at the same answer.

"Stasia," Cooper says. She offers him her full attention. "Do you think you're ready to take the stage with this lot, or do you want more time just in the studio before going live?"

"I'm ready to go." She is as confident as ever. "If that's what everyone else wants."

Theo and Dom both vote yes and Xander decides he's in.

"I guess I'm in too," I say, and Cooper closes his folder.

"That's that then. I'll let them know." As he heads to the door, I think of one more question.

"Coop?" I say and he turns, leaning into the door frame. "What dates did you say the show is?"

"The twelfth to the fourteenth." His phone rings and he takes the call in the hallway.

Xander pushes himself next to me, the wheels of his chair moving easily across the tile floor. "You fucked up, didn't you?" he asks. I put my foot on the seat of his chair and push him back to where he came from.

He's not wrong, though.

When I arrive home, I recap the meeting and detail the rock and hard place I'm stuck between.

"Blake" — Kelly sighs — "that's our anniversary weekend. We made our hotel reservations like four months ago."

"I know. I know. I'm sorry. I'll make it up to you. I'll call and get us reservations for the following weekend."

"What if they're booked? They're *always* booked."

"I said I promise, right? I'll make it happen." I take her hand to my lips and kiss every knuckle.

"Okay, but I'm going to hold you to it." She goes to her tip-toes to close the distance between us and I lean down to meet her, placing my lips against hers.

* * * *

Then

I can hear Debbie and Xander yelling at each other before I get through the door. It's not loud or aggressive. It's par for the course with them. That's just how they talk to each other. In a way, it's kind of comical. They get along so well, but they get loud with each other too.

"I don't care, Alexander," she yells up the stairs. "I don't care if it's the biggest tour that has ever existed. If you don't *graduate*, you're not *going*."

"It's just *Xander*," he yells, appearing at the top of the stairs.

"Your birth certificate says 'Alexander' and so will your headstone if you don't pass this semester."

I laugh, giving myself away. She looks over her shoulder and smiles at me, but her smile dissipates as she turns back to the staircase and resumes her stance against her stubborn son. I'd never say it out loud, but he gets it from her.

"Maybe Blake can help you," she says. "He's passing all his courses."

Xander flies down the stairs, practically riding the banister.

"You're...*studying*?" He places his hands at my shoulders and shakes me gently. "Traitor!" he yells. I laugh but he doesn't.

"You. Books. *Now*," Debbie says in her most intimidating voice. Xander sits at the table in a heap of disinterest and frustration.

"So," she says, "Blake, who are you asking to prom?"

"He's asking Kelly Montoy." Xander opens a book so the cover slams against the table. I take an apple from the bowl on the counter.

"I am not."

"If you don't ask her, I will." Xander places a pencil above his ear.

"You wouldn't," I say through a bite full of apple and a narrowed glare.

"I would."

"You know what? Go for it."

The following Monday, he accepts the challenge. I shouldn't have said anything. I thought he was kidding. He wasn't.

"Watch me," he says, finalizing the back and forth exchange we carried on all weekend.

He clears his throat as he leaves my locker, straightens out his jacket and walks toward Kelly.

"Kelly." He runs his hand through his hair and gives her *the nod.* My stomach turns. I know how she used to see him. She knew him as the awkward loner version of Alexander Varro. He's becoming something—we all are—but he has changed the most. People know his name and they talk about him everywhere he goes. He got louder as he got more well-known and more arrogant in many ways. I stayed the same.

"Yes, Xander?"

"I was wondering – " He looks over his shoulder to make sure I am still watching. "Do you have a date to prom?"

"I don't." Her mouth grows into a glowing smile.

"Great, that's good. I was wondering if you would go with me."

She laughs. *Laughs.* Then I laugh too, covering my mouth to stifle the sound.

"I can't, Xander. I'm sorry. I – " And I swear, for a moment, her eyes meet mine in a quick, stolen glance that I almost missed. "I'm going with someone."

"But you said – "

"Yeah, sorry about that. I have to get to class."

She walks away, leaving him standing there alone in his stupid leather boots and flashy jacket. He shuffles back toward me with his hands in his pockets.

"Xander?" a voice says, catching us both off-guard. Rina Amell leans into a locker a few doors down from Kelly's. "I don't have a date to prom yet." He looks to me in surprise. I nod and he turns on his heel, walking over to Rina and leaving me behind at our lockers.

Later in the lunchroom, I sit by myself watching as Xander sits at a separate table laughing with Rina Amell and her friends like he belongs there. Maybe he does.

"Blake?"

My gaze leaves Xander's table to find Kelly standing beside me. I shift into a better posture, trying to make myself as presentable as possible.

"I was wondering…" She twirls a piece of hair on her finger. "Do you have a date to prom?"

I panic. My mouth goes so dry I can't speak. This is a joke, just like the night I shaving creamed Principal Wheeler's car. There has to be someone waiting to jump out and laugh at me the minute I fall for this *again*.

"I'm not going." Her smile turns to a tight line.

"Oh, okay then." The air between us is heavy, each of us waiting for the other to say something worth cutting through the awkwardness between us but neither of us do.

She just walks away. I turn to find Xander glaring at me, shrugging his shoulders and mouthing 'What the fuck, man?' from across the room.

Maybe the opportunity was real after all, a train with a promising destination, and I let the doors close, waving it onward without ever trying to get on it, as my reservations kept me cemented to the platform.

Chapter Sixteen

Now

It is hot in Miami. Stepping off the plane, the humidity engulfs us in a cloud of heavy, thick air, the kind that hurts a person's chest when they try to inhale it.

The house *Most Of Us* had rented to share is like a small hotel in itself. It boasts eight bedrooms, waterfront views and beach access, two hot tubs, a private pool and a game room with a full theater attached. Kelly would love it here.

The room I choose has high ceilings, arched doorways and a view prettier than a painting. The balcony is beautiful and serene. I can see myself sitting out here while making music and enjoying the sun. It's the first time I've stepped into a home that made me toy with the idea of leaving Boston.

That's a dream for someday, though. I'm still rooted deeply in Massachusetts for now.

"You settled in there, Blake?" Cooper says after he knocks on the open door.

"Yeah, this is gorgeous. I can't believe the views here."

Cooper joins me at the balcony, leaning into the railing.

"How are you holding up?"

I swallow hard and look away from him. I'd be better if everyone would stop *asking* me how I am doing. It wasn't even a big deal. It was a few hands of poker.

"I'm fine." It's all I can manage. I keep telling everyone that I'm fine. I keep saying it's not a problem and it isn't. But every time someone asks, every time someone keeps tabs on me, I think about it more and more. Then I'm itching to open my computer, join a virtual table and play my way into the next morning. Every time I get a few days away from the last time I played, someone asks how I'm holding up, and I want to run to the nearest casino.

I enjoy it.

Admittedly, my cigarette intake goes up the more my gambling time goes down. I need to occupy my hands and head with something, so I replace one bad habit with another.

"I'm fine," I say again, chewing a fingernail. He claps a hand on my shoulder.

"Let's make this a good weekend, make it through a whole show. A whole weekend with no drama, no news outlets — just a damn good show."

"Oh, Coop," I say, shaking my head as he walks away.

"What?" He turns in the doorway.

"You can't go around saying those kinds of things out loud," I say with an added *tsk tsk*. "We're all screwed now. You've doomed us."

"You're probably right about that with this lot." He nods and leaves me with my thoughts.

"No fair." Stasia's voice echoes as she joins me on the balcony who knows how long later. The views have me losing track of time. She places two glasses, an ice bucket and a bottle of whiskey on the table. "Why do you get the best views in the house?"

Stasia pours two cups of the good stuff and rejoins me, handing me a glass.

"Cooper likes me the best," I say through a half-assed smile. Everyone knows Xander is Cooper's favorite.

"I don't think he likes me very much." She takes a sip of her drink.

"You don't think *anyone* likes you." I turn to the table to refill my glass. "He likes you. He just doesn't know you. Give it time. He's been dealing with the rest of us for thirteen years."

We're silent for a while, watching the sun dip into the earth where the sun meets the water from lounge chairs on the balcony.

Stasia's phone buzzes and she leans over to glance at the screen. A light smile appears at her lips and her cheeks flush a light pink. She doesn't answer the text though. She simply laughs and closes the screen to a black backdrop.

"What's so funny?"

"Nothing," she says, and yet she laughs again. "Just a silly text."

Since she won't give me any real information, I try to take it. I lunge forward fast enough that I spill a drop of my drink and grab her phone. The screen illuminates and I catch a glimpse of the notification before she jumps forward and tears the device out of my hands.

"Who the hell is Arthur?" I scrunch my forehead at her. "You can't date a guy named Arthur."

"You're right. I can't." Her voice gets quieter for a moment. A hint of heartache laces the words. "But not because his name is Arthur." Though I think I hit a nerve with the subject, she seems to have returned to her kidding ways. "Besides, that's not even his real name."

"What is his real name?" I'm genuinely curious, but she doesn't budge.

"It doesn't matter. We can't be together."

"Maybe it won't always be that way."

She looks at me with an eyebrow raised.

"Look at me and Kelly. I never thought it would happen for us. We had everything in the world working against us, but we found a way. You will too."

She smiles a thankful grin and nods—but she still seems unconvinced.

"I didn't realize you were seeing somebody." I'm surprised she's never mentioned this guy. I tell her all about Kelly, but she hardly ever interjects with details of her own love life.

"You've never *asked*," she hisses, exaggerating the word as she reaches for the whiskey bottle, but I pull it away. She plunges her hand into the ice bucket and throws cold water and frozen cubes my direction. I return fire, grabbing ice from the bucket and tossing it at her as she runs to the other side of the balcony. She screeches loudly and runs back toward me, grabbing the bucket. She lifts it high above her head to dump its contents over me, but I put the bottle down and grab her wrists just in time to change the direction of the bucket, pouring it over her instead.

"You're so dead," she whispers, combing her wet hair back off her face.

"It's just a little water," I say, continuing the laughter, though hers is muted.

"That's not what I meant." Stasia points past me and I turn to see Kelly standing in the doorway of the vacation home at the entrance to the balcony.

"I thought I'd surprise you for our anniversary." Her voice was lost somewhere between sad and pissed.

"Surprise." Stasia picks the bottle up from the table and chugs the final drops.

* * * *

Then

Hundreds of balloons float across the ceiling. I sit in a chair at the edge of the dance floor at an empty table. Everyone else is dancing, laughing and having a good time. Xander and Rina have been inseparable for weeks, and now that I think about it, they're nowhere to be found now. Probably in the back of the limo, if I had to guess.

Kelly dances with a group of girls in the middle of the dance floor. The lights catch the gems adhered to her dress, scattering rainbows across the floor like prisms as she dances and sways and twirls.

She's perfect. She laughs, dropping her head back at something a friend did or said and then her eyes find mine and the laughter fades. Her smile disappears.

My date, Carissa – I'm not sure of her last name – joins me at the table, but instead of taking one of ten empty seats, she sits on my lap. I shift uncomfortably underneath her.

"Come dance." She pouts a pink-tinted bottom lip.

"I don't dance." It's not completely true, but I'm not in the mood.

"Then why did you ask me to prom?" She rolls her eyes.

"I didn't," I say, not withholding my annoyance.

"Xander said –"

"Yeah, I know what Xander said. If you'll excuse me, I have to take a p – I have to use the restroom."

She removes herself from my lap, reluctantly, and I head to the main doors.

As I exit and turn toward the bathrooms, I run directly into another body.

"I'm sorry, Kelly." I put my hands at her upper arms and steady her from our collision.

She pushes past me and heads to the door but pauses before re-entering.

"If you didn't want to be my date, you should have said that." Her voice trembles as she speaks. Sadness drapes every word.

"I didn't say that." I step toward her, shortening the distance between us.

"You said you weren't coming to prom." She crosses her arms. "Then you show up with Carissa Kennedy."

Kennedy. Right. That's her last name.

"I didn't want to come!" My voice gains volume. "Xander told Carissa I would, and his mother told me I couldn't back out on her. Trust me, I tried faking sick. I tried cancelling."

She smiles a bit at that but it fades again.

"Why didn't you ask me, Blake?" she asks in a whisper so quiet I almost think I heard her wrong.

"I've never thought I was good enough for you. I didn't want to set myself up for any kind of embarrassment." I step forward, taking her hands in mine. "I wouldn't have wanted to be here with anyone else, Kelly." She steps toward me, only inches away and reaches her face toward mine. I lean forward, mustering up any courage I have ever had to use in this moment. Finally, I might get the kiss I've been dreaming of for so long with the girl who has captured all my attention since I walked into our school all those years ago.

The music stops on the other side of the doors. "Ladies and gentlemen", the deejay says, "your prom king and queen, Miss Kelly Montoy and – "

Some guy who's not me.

"I have to go," she says, pushing the door open and canceling any hope of what might have come next.

"Blake," she says, "meet me on the balcony at Rina's after-party."

And the glimmer of hope sparkles once more.

I dance with Carissa while Kelly shares her dance with the prom king, but both of us keep our eyes on each other across the dance floor, though there are other bodies between us. When the night ends, my group of friends and their dates pile into the limo and Carissa, once again, tries to sit on my lap rather than take a seat. I move at the last second so we're on separate benches. Thankfully, I have the spot nearest the door, because as soon as we arrive and the driver opens it, I'm jumping out and moving as fast as my legs will allow.

Rina's house looks different when you're attending the party and not playing it. Loud music blares through the speakers, couples are draped all over each other at every turn and the house smells like liquor and weed.

I take each step to the upstairs and wonder if she will really be there. I overthink it, I know, but my palms sweat and my neck runs hot. Nothing can go wrong this time. Each time I've had my chance to be with her, something has gotten in the way or I've gotten in the way of myself. Not this time.

I stand on the balcony overlooking the lush greens of the expansive backyard of the Amell house and hear the *click clack* of high heels join me. Hands are at my shoulders, running the length of the tux jacket I wear.

"I saw you come upstairs," she says, the loud music making her words hard to hear. "I figured that meant I should come too."

I turn to face her, ready to pick up where we left off, only it's not Kelly's hands that are on me. It's Carissa's.

I look over Carissa's shoulder to see Kelly standing at the doorway. "I wouldn't have wanted to be here with anyone else, Kelly," she says in a tone that mocks my original sentiment. "You're a liar, Blake. Stay away from me."

Chapter Seventeen

Now

"Stasia," Kelly says, "let's go."

My mind moves like a ping pong ball in a fast-paced match.

"Go...where?" Stasia's words are slow and cautious as she talks to Kelly.

"I'm taking you out."

"Can you be a tad more specific? *'Taking me out'* sounds like it's not going to end well for me." Stasia talks with her hands and rocks back and forth on the balls of her feet.

"Out, out. Shopping, drinks. If you're going to be friends with Blake, then you're going to have to be a friend of mine, too." She shrugs her shoulders, waiting for a response.

Stasia looks at me for advice, but anything I say is going to get me in trouble so I, for once, shut up.

Yeah, that sounds…*super* fun." Stasia adds two thumbs-up for good measure. Kelly walks out of the door. Stasia turns to look at me, her jaw practically on the floor in disbelief. "If I don't make it back, tell Xander he can have my guitar."

"What? What about me?"

"You got me into this mess," she says in a low growl. "You get nothing." She walks away, following the path Kelly took.

I call Xander and suggest we meet up for a drink. Luckily, he agrees.

The bar Xander found is an on-beach tiki-hut-style place full of neon colors and light music. Our dark-colored clothing, jeans and boots contrast against the bright colors, floral shirts and bathing suits everyone else wears.

"What did you do this time?" Xander asks, as the bartender slides his drink across the bar top. "Or *who*, should I say?"

"Oh, nothing like that." I signal to the bartender for a drink. "Kelly came out here to surprise me for our anniversary and Stasia was in my room. Now they're hanging out."

Xander chokes on his drink and slams his hand against his chest as he coughs. "Wow," he says, his cough turning into a laugh. I recap the details of Kelly's arrival.

"I love Kelly. You know that, man, better than anyone. Stasia has turned out to be a great friend. I want them to get along, I do. I just don't see it working out in my favor."

"Honestly, Blake, I don't think you're giving Kelly enough credit. Name another girl – any other girl – who would try to get to know your female friend instead of just pulling the 'it's me or her' card." Xander takes a sip of his drink mid-lecture, then continues to his point. "She's not the jealous type. If you mean it when you say you're just friends with Stasia, Kelly will figure that out too."

"We're just friends," I reiterate. "Besides, Stasia's seeing someone, I think."

Xander takes a sip of his drink and nods to the open wall where the beach meets the bar.

A few hours and multiple drinks later, both girls, Kelly and Stasia, make their way up the beach with their shoes in their hands.

Well, they're both alive and together, so I take it things went *okay-ish*, at least.

Kelly belongs in Miami, honestly. She doesn't stand out like the rest of us. I could picture her living here, standing on the balcony of some extravagant beach home with the sun lightening her already-blonde hair. Now, she walks across the beach under the dim light provided by the moon holding wedge sandals in the crook of one arm and her coral-colored dress flows around her body as she walks. Stasia, by comparison, almost blends in to the darkened world. Black fitted leather pants and a dark gray ripped tank top have her matching the midnight-colored sky overhead.

Kelly stands at the door, a smile on her face when my eyes meet hers. That's a good sign. She nods over her shoulder toward the vacant beach. I leave my cup on the bar top and meet her at the entrance. She laces her fingers in mine and we walk along the edge of the water. There's silence between us but I don't want to break it. I don't want to talk first.

"You were right." Her voice carries out over the open ocean. Where's a tape recorder when you need it?

Hell, I've never been right before, and I'm certain she will never say it again.

About?" I tighten my grip in her fingers.

"Stasia. She's fabulous." Kelly runs her thumb across my hand as we walk. "She's the female version of you. You both have so much in common. I didn't understand it before, but I get it. I really, *really* didn't want to like her, but she's hard not to like."

I keep my thoughts to myself in fear of ruining the moment, but I am happy in a way. I like Stasia and I like spending time with her, but I *love* Kelly, and I want to spend my life with her. Hopefully, with any luck, things can stay civil.

We walk along the beach, leaving our footprints in the sand and our fingers laced in each other's. The public portion of the beach is behind us now. At the entrance to the private beach area that belongs to the vacation house we are renting, I pause to look back on the views.

How would you feel about living in a place like this someday?"

"It's beautiful," she says. "I have no idea what I would do here, but it's beautiful."

"What do you mean?"

"For work. I don't know what I would do if I left The Rock Room. I've been there so long and worked my way up, so I'm not sure what I would do next."

"You wouldn't have to do anything." I take a seat on the sand and pat the ground next to me. She leans down then sits in front of me. Her back rests against my chest and I wrap my arms around her.

But I'd want to. It's just who I am. I like working. I don't enjoy sitting around with nothing to do."

I can't see how anyone would pass up the opportunity to spend their days relaxing by the pool and enjoy a life with no schedule, no deadlines and no one to answer to. But that's not Kelly. She likes being relied on. She likes having something to do.

"Do you remember the project we did all those years ago? We created futures for ourselves."

"Yeah," I say, smiling at the thought. I lean forward and rest my chin on her shoulder. "I was a famous rock star and you were a CEO."

"That was the dream." Her voice is quiet. "But it only came true for one of us, Blake."

I always thought Kelly was happy with where she was and what she was doing. She's never said otherwise.

"I still believe there are doors out there for me to open. I'm not going to spend my days on a beach somewhere until I know I have tried to unlock every single one of them."

I didn't think it was possible to love her any more than I already did but I've never felt more admiration for somebody than I do in this moment. She never backs down from a challenge, never settles and never lets anything get handed to her without earning it for herself. I can't help but feel inspired by her.

She turns so she's facing me and puts her legs over mine, one on each side of my body. In the distance, a live band plays. Their soft tunes echo to where we sit. She puts her hands on my shoulders and sways a bit, like we're slow dancing under the moon's spotlight without really moving at all. As she moves to the far-off beat, I put both my hands at her waist and pull her in closer to me, taking all her bodyweight onto my lap. She places a palm at my neck and her fingers find my hairline as she pulls herself against me, leans in and bites at my bottom lip. In return, I kiss her with a heated passion as warm as the air around us.

She slides her hands down my chest and stops at my waist, where she unclips my belt buckle and undoes the button on my jeans.

A smile presses at one corner of my mouth and my neck grows hot. She leans forward and grabs the hem of my shirt, then pulls it over my head. Her tongue and lips trace every inch of my skin as she works her way down my jawline, my chest, and my abdomen.

"What are you doing?" My tone is playful but yearning. She stops for a moment and looks up at me with glistening, flirtatious eyes and whispers, sounding out every syllable, "Whatever. You. Want."

That is all I need to hear. I laugh, help her up and we're off to our Miami accommodation.

The beach, the shower, the balcony... Kelly is determined to christen every surface of this vacation home. We moved all the lavish pillows and overstuffed comforters from the four-poster canopy bed out onto the balcony. We lay together among the gold fabric under the sparkling stars and explore each other's bodies like it's the first time. We fight time, trying to make it stop, to stay still in this moment where there was no one or nothing else. The world is quiet. Our moments are our own. And for the night, we adopt nocturnal habits where we loved under the light of the moon and find sleep only once the sun rises again.

• • • •

Backstage at the venue, musicians from different bands walk around answering questions from the allowed media and saying hello to old friends whose paths haven't crossed in a while.

"Your girlfriend is the scariest person I know," Stasia says as she tunes her guitar.

"That's because you haven't really met Natalie yet," I add. Xander laughs and shakes his head. Stasia's eyes widen at the words and she looks back and forth between Xander and I, trying to figure out if we're kidding or not.

"I felt like I was on a job interview," she adds as Cooper joins us in the backstage area.

"How are you feeling, Stasia?" he asks, sweat beading at his brow, partially from the Florida heat, but I think he's nervous too. We haven't had a fifth member in a long time.

"I…I don't think I can do this…" She looks at Cooper with alarm in her eyes and terror in her words. "There's just *so* many people."

Cooper places his hand at the back of his neck and exhales loudly. The pacing will start any second. This isn't our first rodeo with a preshow Cooper breakdown.

"Stasia –" he starts and turns toward us with eyes lost somewhere between pissed and empathetic. She bursts out laughing, then Xander does too, clapping a hand on her shoulder. "You were perfect," he says to her between laughs.

"You –" Cooper searches for the words. He nods and bites his lip. "Okay, okay. That was good. You got me."

He walks away and leaves us behind to laugh like school children.

"If he didn't hate me before, he does now." Stasia flips her short wave of hair to the opposite side.

Oh no, he doesn't hate you." I shake my head. "If anything, you just solidified your part in the band. You're one of us now. But he can and will retaliate, so watch your back."

Though she had been joking before, she does seem nervous to take the stage with us for the first time. The house lights are down, and the stage sleeps under a dead black. As we head to the center of the stage, I turn to see that Stasia hasn't stepped forward with the rest of us.

"You okay?" I have to raise my voice over the music the venue is playing.

"Just taking it all in." She peeks through the curtain and assesses the thousands of people on the other side. They chant our name and scream for us to get the show started. She turns toward me and throws one thumb over her shoulder. "Is it always like this?"

"Every damn time."

She inhales deeply and lets it out.

"Are you coming or not?" Dom asks as he jogs toward us. "No reason to be nervous." He winks as he delivers the jab.

"I don't get nervous." She steps past him, leaving the apprehensive version of herself in the wings of the stage. As I make my way out to join the band, I see Dom's hand leave Stasia's lower back. Maybe she did need a gentle push, physically and mentally, after all.

"Mmmmmm." Xander says into the microphone. "Damn, you are a lucky group."

The crowd flirts back, whistling and applauding as they hang on to every word he speaks.

"We have a special show planned for you, Miami. Joining us tonight, for the first time live, Miss Stasia Marquette."

The fans in the crowd give a booming, bold welcome to Stasia as the spotlight falls over her.

"I'm going to let her start us off for our first song." Xander has his lips against the microphone. "Do you know why?"

The crowd yells a 'why' in unison, playing perfectly into the track Xander is laying down for them. "I *said*, do you want to know why, Miami?"

Their response grows to an unmeasurable volume. If we were in a building, the walls would tremble. Instead, their noise fills the sky like a thunderstorm.

"Because she's just that damn good!" He turns and points to her. The house lights drop, leaving only the spotlight that follows Stasia as she strikes the guitar, leading us into the song. The lights brighten again as the rest of the band joins in.

I join Stasia at mid stage, our guitars facing each other so close they could kiss if our strumming hands weren't keeping them apart.

It's clear in that second, in those notes, that this band was meant to have five musicians. We got by without Julian, but having someone as talented as Stasia join us finally gave these love stories we sing the happy ending they deserve.

After the show Kelly meets me backstage. Despite the material of my shirt sticking to my skin from the sweat that soaks me, she throws her arms around my neck. I forgot how much I missed her awaiting embrace at the end of a good show.

I wrap my arm around Kelly, ready to take her back to my room of the vacation home, but Stasia catches my attention on the way out.

A tall, thick man in a black button-down shirt and pants looms over her, saying something I can't hear.

She tries to step past him, and he grabs her wrist. The grimace on her face is a mix of pain and frustration.

"Go check on her." Kelly steps toward the band and Cooper.

"Do we have a problem here?" I step in front of the man, keeping my body beside Stasia's. The man releases his grip on her and she rubs at the area where his hand had been. Xander joins at her other side, crossing his arms over his chest. Dom steps in behind her, placing both his hands at her upper arms.

"I'm fine, guys. Honestly." Her voice is withdrawn and quiet. "He was just leaving."

"Your father isn't going to be happy," the man growls.

"I don't work for him," she says, finding her confidence. The man pulls out his phone, jams it against his ear and stomps away before the situation escalates any further.

"Who was that?" I watch to ensure he exists.

"He works for my dad at MLA," she says. "My father isn't super happy with my choice in bands."

"I'd say we're doing just fine." Xander holds his arms up and looks around the room.

"You rejected his offer then made it big. He hates you. In turn, he's not my biggest fan either these days." She shrugs and walks away. Probably partly because she's embarrassed about the whole scene, but more so because its habit for her to cut conversations about her dad short.

From what we have talked about, she never knew her real mother – some deadbeat who took off when she was born. Her father married again, a stepmother who Stasia adored but her father spent too much time and money rolling dice and got caught up in too many shady affairs to keep her stepmother interested. Losing his wife didn't bring him home much more, though. If anything, his hours away from home increased, both in work and play, leaving a young girl to grow up without a steadfast parental figure.

She'd done all right without parents.

We both had.

Chapter Eighteen

Kelly sits up in our bed with her glasses perched on her nose. She usually wears contacts, but I won't lie, there's something I love about her in glasses. Her hair is wildly knotted at the top of her head. She chews on a pen, clicking through a website on her laptop.

"Maybe I'll go back to school."

"Go back to school then." I click the buttons on a stupid game on my phone.

"I don't know, maybe I won't. Maybe I'll just stay at The Rock Room."

"Stay at The Rock Room then." My voice doesn't fluctuate or change. I click a few more buttons, keeping my eyes on the game in front of me.

"Are you listening to *anything* I'm saying?" She closes the laptop with more force than necessary.

"I am listening. School. Rock Room." She reaches over and grabs my phone out of my hands, sending my virtual race car off the track and into a wall where it goes up in flames. "That was my best time, you know,"

I say, and she laughs. She tries to be serious and attempts to keep a straight face, but she can't.

"Blake, c'mon. I'm trying to talk to you about something." She tries to regain her stern disposition. She would be a garbage poker player. "I want you to help me decide what to do next."

"I've been nothing but supportive. I told you. You want to go back to school? Go back to school. You want to stay at The Rock Room? Stay there. You want to retire at thirty-one and never work again? I'm all for that."

She stands up, walks over to her laundry basket and pulls clothes from the pile. We somehow wash and dry clothes, but they never find their way back to a drawer. It's a perpetual dance. Wear. Dirty. Wash. Dry. Fold. Laundry basket. Wear again. Dirty. Wash. Dry. Laundry basket. Wear again. Repeat.

"I don't just want you to support me, Blake. I don't want you to just agree. I want your opinion. I want you to know what you're supporting."

Sigh. A literal, loud, audible, no-holding-back kind of sigh. I can't say anything right.

"I just want you to be happy." I climb out of the bed and join her on the other side of the room. She runs her fingers down my chest then leans up and presses her mouth to mine. I kiss her lips, down her jaw and at her neck then push against her until we're backing up together, finding the bed and crashing into it.

"I am happy," she whispers. "With you I'm happy. Right now, everything is going well for us. Everything is perfect. But I want that kind of happiness and perfection in other aspects of my life too. I want to love my career like I love you. I want to be as confident in the rest of my future as I am in the one I see with you."

"Okay then." I wipe my hair from my forehead and leave the bed.

"Where are you going?" she says through a light laugh.

I return with a deep-colored lipstick and stand in front of the mirror. "You don't need this, right?" I hold up the tube. She hides her smile behind her hand and laughs a muffled sound.

Drawing a line down the center of the mirror with the lip color, I mark one side 'pro' and one side 'con'.

"Let's do it." I stand at the mirror like a teacher at a blackboard. "Pros and cons of going to school or staying at The Rock Room or whatever. Right here, right now."

She sits and throws ideas at me and I list each sentiment in the columns they belong to, but in the end, we end up exactly where we started – a confused version of Kelly that has plenty of options but not enough confidence in any route to choose it definitively.

Even with the purple lipstick words crossing her perfect reflection, she uses the mirror to get ready for work and leaves for her shift.

The Rock Room has been busier than ever and as a result, Kelly doesn't find her way home very often. I'm alone with no obligation and no responsibilities which for me, tends to be a lethal combination.

Especially since there are multiple unanswered texts from Isabella on my phone. For weeks I've ignored them. There were times when I considered blocking her altogether but I can't. I never was strong enough to commit to fully cutting her off, which, effectively would have shut down the portal to my worst vice. And now her most recent tactic is sending pictures of the ever-growing money piles and the smoky penthouse I've grown so fond of.

My stomach turns and tightens, but I can't explain why. I'm not hungry. The pressure seeps into my chest, making it harder to breathe. I inhale deeply, trying to expand the walls of my lungs, and sweat beads at my brow. I'm not sick. I'm tempted, which is worse. I remember how bad the withdrawal got the first and only time I ever tried to give up cigarettes. This is similar, and I now understand that I have an addictive personality in more ways than one. There's a lingering invite to the Penthouse, and I want to go. The part of me that knows I shouldn't go is overshadowed by the part of me that doesn't care what happens next. It's only one time. This could be my last game.

A loud knock at the door interrupts my reeling thoughts but I don't get up. I don't call out to the person on the other side of the door. I inhale deeply again through my nose and let the breath out. As I do, the door opens. I whip my head around, making the room spin, to see who it is.

"You okay, man?" Xander says, his voice filled with concern. "I knocked. You didn't answer."

"What the hell are you doing here, Xander?" I snap at him, wiping my forehead on my sleeve.

"Picking you up? We're supposed to go do that video blog interview about Stasia's tracks. Cooper and the guys are outside."

I forgot all about that. Truthfully, I don't even remember committing to it. Important things have been slipping through the cracks lately. I can't concentrate. I can't stay organized.

So, are you ready?" Skepticism leaves his voice sounding unlike himself. "Or do you need a few more minutes?"

"I'm not going." My voice is so quiet that I'm not sure if I said the words aloud or if he heard them at all.

"You're what?" He steps in through the doorway, taking cautious steps across the room until he's only a few feet from me. "What the hell is going on, Blake?"

"I said I'm not going!" I yell, standing up and pushing past him, my shoulder hitting his on my way out the door.

He heard me that time.

* * * *

Then

There are about fifty rooms in Rina Amell's house and Kelly isn't in any of them. Half-naked couples scream profanities at me as I whip open doors looking for her. I feel my luck starting to fade. She's gone.

I find the kitchen, fill a cup with liquor from the counter and chug it, refilling it and drinking that too. I rip off my tie and toss it to the counter. There was a chance for her and me — a real chance — and I blew it.

Well, Xander blew it for me.

He sits in the living room in his tux with his sunglasses on, a crowd of people around him and Rina sitting on his lap.

"Hey, man, what's up?" He says in a casual tone as I approach.

"You ruined everything." My voice is a low growl. "I didn't even want to come tonight."

"Then you shouldn't have." Xander slurs his speech. Rina moves her legs off him, and he stands, straightening out his tux. He loses his balance for a moment but regains it.

"All I ever wanted to do was help you — set you up with a pretty girl and get you to prom — "

"I don't need your help." My face grows to a hot red while my jaw is pained from clenching it.

"Now I don't think that's true." The smell of liquor pours off his words. "You'd be sleeping on a fucking park bench if it wasn't for me."

I hit his chest before he even finishes the sentence. He flies backward, tumbling into a table that falls on its side, spilling mixed contents over the hardwood floors. He gets to his feet and springs toward me. Our bodies collide hard as he tackles me to the ground and throws a hard punch that causes my nose to bleed, the crimson flowing across my lips and into my mouth, leaving a gruesome metallic taste.

Dom pulls him off me then I'm standing too, with Julian's assistance.

Xander breaks free of Julian's grasp and steps toward me, but I get one last connection in. My knuckles crack against Xander's jaw.

"Let's go," Julian says as he grabs my arm and drags me out of Rina's house. "You can crash with me tonight."

When we arrive at Julian's, I wash up the best I can in the bathroom sink. The water runs over my hands and I analyze them, unsure if the blood they're covered in is mine or Xander's. I stare at myself in the mirror for a long while, replaying the night in my head. I hardly recognize the person looking back at me. I splash some water on my face and take a few deep breaths before joining Julian in his room.

The leather gaming chair I sit in rocks back and forth as Julian and I pound our thumbs into controllers and play the game on the big screen TV in his room. Our tuxes are still on, though mine is torn in a few places and dried blood decorates the once-white sections. Debbie is going to kill Xander and I. Both of our tuxes are rentals.

Footsteps echo up the stairs, getting closer and closer to the door, but neither Julian nor I flinch.

Xander leans into the doorframe, his tux in worse shape than mine. "You should put some ice on that." I can tell by the soreness when I scrunch my nose that the swelling is getting worse instead of better.

Julian pauses the game and stands, leaving the room. "I'll give you two a minute."

I remain in the gaming chair on the floor, not looking at him and refusing to speak first.

He steps forward, turning to sit on the edge of Julian's bed.

"I didn't mean it." His voice is so small, so quiet that it must be borrowed from someone else. Xander is loud. Everything about him is loud except for the sentence he just uttered.

"What happened tonight, Blake?" He slides down the foot of the bed until he's sitting next to me on the floor. "If you wanted to go to prom with Kelly, why didn't you just say yes when she tried to ask you?"

I just shake my head, not wanting to tell him what's going on in the depths of my thoughts.

"I'm not leaving until you talk, Mathews. You've been dodging my questions for years, and I've allowed that because I thought that's what you needed. But you have to talk to someone, man. You have people. You don't have to do everything alone all the time."

He has given me space. He's never pried too much. I'll give him credit there. He doesn't push, but is always available to listen on the rare occasions I do reveal any part of my past.

"You weren't wrong." I adjust my position so I'm facing him. "Tonight, when you said I would have nowhere else to go, it was true."

"Blake, I shouldn't have said that. I was drinking and angry and stupid – "

"No, just shut up for a second." He quiets and lets me talk. "I like Kelly. I don't think that's a secret at this point, but I'm...I'm not good enough for her, Xander. Can you imagine what people would say about her if she started hanging out with me? She was the *prom queen*. I couldn't even afford to rent a *tie* for tonight, never mind a tux if it weren't for your mother. I am the charity case already, and when Kelly started talking about prom, I couldn't picture myself standing next to her and feeling like I belonged there. I don't. I don't really belong anywhere."

He looks at me long and hard. I can see it in his eyes and the way he parts his lips. I know something is coming, something good, something so *Xander Varro* that it will break through my walls and have a forever impact on the way I feel about myself. That's what he does. He writes intricate songs, creates lyrics and unfolds beautiful sentiments, even when no one asked him to.

"Blake" – he places his hand on my shoulder – "you are the biggest fucking idiot I know."

I'm speechless in a confusion I can't recover from. That is not what I expected – not that he's wrong. I do the only thing I can think of and return the blow.

"You call geography 'map-ology', but *I'm* the idiot?"

He laughs and nods, appreciating the joke.

"Blake, Kelly likes you. She doesn't give a damn where you came from or how you got here or how much of a disaster your mother is. She wanted to go to prom with you because you make her laugh and make her feel seen."

I nod, knowing that at the end of the night that this wasn't Xander's fault at all. I was hiding when I said I wasn't going to prom. I fear getting close to her — to anyone, really.

"What do I do now?"

"Ask her out. Find her, be up front with her. But, if she says yes, plan on scheduling for a date in the way distant future."

I arch my brow and tilt my head. "Why?"

"When mom sees what we did to these tuxes, we're going to be grounded until we die."

• • • •

Now

The ice clinks against the glass as I rotate my cup, swirling the amber liquid around the crystal edges. A gentleman who goes by the name of JX sits under the gun, two positions to my left. He doubles the bet. Victor raises the stakes once more, and the two players to his left fold. I hold a pair in the hole, hoping to strengthen that hand with cards from the community cards. It's a good start, one of the best I've had in a while, so I roll with it. I raise.

Maybe it's luck, maybe it's skill, but everyone says you can't beat Victor – yet here I sit with his money filling my pockets.

I'm on a roll. It's a high I don't want to come down from. The cards in the hands I'm dealt are so perfect that they couldn't be better if the deck was stacked. I've lost track of time and money at this point, but I have no intention of quitting while I'm ahead.

Another hand is dealt, and the outcome is positive – for me, at least. The same can't be said for Victor, JX and the other players.

Toward the end of the hand with only one community card remaining, Victor and I take turns staring the other down and raising the bets.

"I'm tired of losing money to you tonight, kid. Let's make it interesting before we call it a night."

He's scared to play. I *like* that he's scared to play. I feel on top of the world and I love the view from up here.

"How much money are you willing to lose tonight, son?" Victor asks. I weigh my options.

"What did you have in mind?"

"I say, double or nothing." He scratches his chin. "I win this hand, and I'll take back all of the winnings you have over there. You win, I'll double what I've already lost."

"Child's play." Confidence courses through my veins. "Give me a number with a few more zeroes behind it."

Victor waves Isabella over to his side of the table and she leans forward, listening closely to his hushed words. She walks around toward me, her heels clicking against the floor as she nears. She leans in and whispers his offer in my ear.

My heart pounds in my chest. The thing is, I *know* I shouldn't do it, but I don't waste time trying to talk myself out of it.

"You have that kind of money, Mathews?" Victor asks, flicking a flame to life with his Colibri lighter and running it across the end of a cigar.

"Don't you worry about me," I say. "I have it and I intend on keeping it where it is." I think just for one second about how long it took me to build up that dream account. Where I was when I started it, how empty it looked when I opened it and how I *promised* myself it would never be empty again.

The thing is, I'm better at breaking promises than I am at playing poker. He flips his card and suddenly I'm eighteen years old again, starting anew, without even two dimes to rub together.

. . . .

The cushions of the sofa have morphed into a new shape – a permanent crease where my ass has been for the last – I don't even know how long.

I can't move. I can barely breathe. All I can do is sit there, feeling only inches tall and trying to figure out where it all went wrong.

Thinking back on it all hurts. The loss, the game, the winnings prior, losing my cool on Xander and forgetting important dates and times because of the distraction this game provides. It's the worst kind of pain. I think of solutions, ways to rebuild the fund and ideas to recuperate. My first thought – keep gambling and win it back. I've done it before.

Kelly flies through the door with a large smile across her face. At least one of us is having a good night. She grabs my hand and pulls me to our room.

No 'hello'. No 'how was your night.' Nothing.

She drags her hands down the mirror, ruining the pro-con list we created. She turns to me and her eyes are the brightest I have ever seen them.

"Ethan is selling The Rock Room." She takes my hands in her lipstick-stained fingers.

"This…is good news?" I ask, unsure where she is going with this.

She looks away, nervous to say what's on her mind and holding back. She takes a deep breath, and in those seconds where she questions her words, I figure out what she wants.

"I want to buy it."

She confirms my intuition.

"You…want to buy it." The weight on my chest increases exponentially.

"I know it's a lot." She talks in a fast-paced way where her words bump into each other as she spits them out. "But we could do it, Blake! We could own The Rock Room. I already know how to run it and it's already so successful that I feel like we can't lose. It's a sure thing, Blake, a safe bet."

Sharp pains pierce in my stomach as she talks. Nothing is a sure thing, especially in my hands. There are no safe bets.

"I know how hard you worked to save up that money in the account you showed me, and at the end of the day it's your money, so it's your call. You called it the 'dream' account, Blake. Don't you see it? You were going to be the rock star and I was going to be the CEO. This was the dream."

I step away from her. My words, my actions and my calls have crushed Kelly in the past but nothing I have ever done before could hurt her in the way I'm about to

Blake? she whispers. The excitement fades from her voice. I turn toward her, my face twisted into a sorrowful frown. "Oh...Blake...you didn't."

My stomach turns. I'm going to be sick. The thing I find the most disturbing is not that I lost a hefty chunk of everything I have worked for and not that I can't be the one to make her dream come true. It's that she assumed before I said the words that I had drained that account on a bad bet and she was right.

＊ ＊ ＊ ＊

Kelly and I haven't spoken in days. She's made it abundantly clear that it's not about the money – that the money in that account was mine to do what I wanted, when I pleased. She was mad about the lying, the gambling and the inability to say no or to determine when enough was enough. She was mad that I couldn't see a bad idea when it was right in front of me.

I'm still doing fine. My main account is certainly not hurting, but I've seen firsthand how easy it is to lose it. The reality is that I had room to make mistakes before, until I made the biggest one of all time. Now I have no buffer

My caloric intake over the days since Kelly left is composed of mostly coffee and beer. Empty cups and bottles scatter the floor around me as I lean against the couch. I came down here looking for the remote, didn't find it and never made it back up to the couch.

There's a knock at the door that I don't get excited about. It's not Kelly. She wouldn't knock. Otherwise, I don't really care to see who's on the other side.

Stasia opens the door and enters my house, kicking an old pizza box out of her way as she enters.

"Are you kidding me?" She looks around the apartment. Though I can't see her, I know the expression she's wearing is an even mix of surprise and disgust. She makes her way over to me, crossing her legs and sitting on the floor across from me. "You missed my video interview."

I nod my head, knowing that I have a long list of apologizes ahead. Kelly, Stasia, the band – the list goes on.

"How'd it go?" I ask, unsure if I want to know the answer.

"It wasn't the same without you." Her eyes are kind, understanding. "So" — she twiddles her thumbs, dancing around the question — "what the hell happened?"

I give Stasia the details of my crash and burn.

"Can you go back to him? The guy you lost to? Talk him into giving you your money back?"

"Yeah, sure. He's super understanding. I'm sure I'll get all of my money back and make it out alive in one piece." I roll my eyes. I know she's trying to help, but there really isn't a solution to this riddle.

"My father was gambling through my entire childhood. He probably still is. He always said that 'there's always something better than money.' You just have to figure out what this guy wants in exchange for what you lost."

"Probably a kidney, Stasia. These tables are no joke. I'm going to walk out of there a complete joke if I walk out of there at all. They'll probably break my kneecaps for asking."

"You've watched too many movies." She pushes her hair off her face. "Regardless, I don't see you coming up with anything better that doesn't involve gambling."

"Maybe I'll hit the lottery in this lifetime."

"That's *still* gambling." She rolls her eyes. Maybe I am just too far gone.

At the end of the day, I come up with no other solution than the one Stasia offered. I swallow what's left of my pride and head to Victor's to see what kind of deal with the devil I'd have to make to earn back what I lost.

The smoke cloud engulfs me the way it usually does when I enter the penthouse, only this time, the scent is different. It's not just cigars, but cigarettes too. I smell the difference as I inhale and taste the two distinct flavors as I breathe.

"He said you can go up," Isabella says, rejoining me in the doorway. "All the seats are taken, though."

I nod but don't speak. On one hand, I'm glad the table is full—less room for temptation. But I'm frustrated too. I *want* there to be an open spot.

We take each step of the spiral staircase to the loft, as my desire to turn back grows stronger with each forward motion. Victor laughs and the rest of the table follows suit. I step into the room, trying not to draw too much attention to myself. A woman with long, light-brown, almost blonde hair sits in my usual seat, her back toward me.

"Is there something I can do for you, Blake?" Victor asks. His voice is uninterested, teetering on annoyed.

I'm about to say my piece, to take a chance on asking him what my options are when the newcomer turns over her shoulder, looking me over from head to toe. She analyzes every inch of me, but I can't tell what she's thinking.

"Blake," she says, casually, like we do it all the time.

I take a deep breath, wondering if I'll be able to get any words out, but I can only manage one.

"Mother."

I left that penthouse so fast that I almost crashed through the door instead of opening it. There is nothing to say to her and no chance at rekindling a relationship or putting the pieces of our shattered family back together.

And here I thought things couldn't get any worse. I was wrong. *Shocker.*

Chapter Nineteen

When Kelly first moved in, I'll admit, I worried about it. Growing up, mother and I often shared small spaces then I shared a room with Xander. Our success grew practically overnight, and the minute I could afford to be on my own, I took advantage of that and it had been that way since. Kelly knew that I was struggling with the idea of sharing my space. She just didn't know why. Instead of packing up her belongings, moving them here all at once and claiming my address as her own, she did it gradually. First, a toothbrush. Then, a few shirts. A hairdryer. Nothing major or overwhelming.

She bought me a plant. A *plant*. I can barely keep myself alive and she brings me some kind of ridiculous fern.

One morning, I watched her walk around the kitchen like she owned the place, pouring us both coffees and doing tedious things I never think of doing, filling the napkin holder, refilling the sugar shaker. That was when I started counting back the days. When was the last time she had *left?*

As the band prepared to leave on tour, she said, "I'll tend to your plants," and we laughed, both knowing all too well that the damn plant wasn't the only thing that had grown roots there. It wasn't until later I found out she had cancelled her lease at her apartment weeks before that.

Now I don't even remember what 'alone' is like. She's been here so long and done so much for me that I can't find things in my own house and I have no one to ask.

I call her phone, but she doesn't answer and truthfully, I'm glad. The only way to clean up the mess I had made was face-to-face. Since she won't come to me, I'll have to go to her.

The Rock Room is more crowded than I thought it would be for a Sunday night. I didn't check the calendar to see who was on stage that night, but it must be someone decent.

Kelly walks out of the backroom and behind the bar area. I watch from afar, just for a bit, as she walks back and forth, telling the employees what she needs them to do, and they get to it with a smile. She's not afraid to dive in. She serves a customer with a smile on her face, punches some buttons on the register then heads through the door once again. She's only out of sight for a moment, reappearing on stage at the wing when she points at something out of sight, telling the crew how she wants some things adjusted. She crosses her arms and taps her foot as the crew member talks to someone in the microphone of his headset. After a moment or two waiting, Kelly holds out her hand and the crew member hands over his headset. Kelly slides it over her perfectly styled hair. She speaks only for a second but then smiles a victorious grin that says she got her way. I'm not surprised. She hands the headset back and makes her way off the stage again.

She does it all. Every job there is to do in this building, she has done it. She loves bartending — it's why she refuses to give it up — but she's got the management side down to a science too. This is Kelly's business, regardless of if her name is on the title or not.

She belongs to The Rock Room. The Rock Room should belong to her.

And it will.

Whatever I have to do, however I have to make it happen, no matter what promises I have to make, this property will belong to Kelly Montoy.

Her eyes meet mine but as my smile grows, hers fades.

She walks away through the door that separates the main area of the venue from the behind-the-scenes portion of the building. I follow, fighting my way through the crowd to get to her.

She continues to walk away from me, stomping her heeled boots against the tile floor in an effort to keep herself from me. She slams the door to the outside and swings it shut behind her. I catch the door with my body and push it open once more. The cool air in the alleyway bites at my arms and face.

"Kelly," I yell, my voice echoing against the brick walls. She turns to face me but for the first time, I can't read her.

"I can't do this tonight, Blake." She holds herself tight, rubbing her hands at her upper arms.

"When then? You haven't come home, and you won't answer my calls."

"I don't have anything to say yet." Her voice is fatigued and frustrated.

I lean into the brick wall beside me and pull a box of Marlboro Reds from my pocket, sticking one between my teeth and lighting it. I don't know what to say but I don't want to leave either.

I inhale, the red-lit tip of the cigarette brightening against the dark air, then exhale, leaving a ring of smoke to meet the sky and become part of it. Kelly walks toward me, holding her red-painted fingertips toward me. I hand her the cigarette and she takes a drag.

"Are we over?" I ask, forcing out the question I don't want to ask.

"I don't know." She flicks a spray of ashes into the concrete ground.

"Hell of a thing to not know, Kel." My volume raises in frustration.

"Don't push me to make a choice this second," she hisses, tears forming in her eyes. "You won't like my answer."

"Why though, Kelly? Why isn't this something we can work through?"

"I don't want us to be working all the time, Blake. Sometimes, every once in a while, it would be nice if me and you being together just came easy."

She walks away, just enough to put distance between us, facing away from me so I can't see her emotions. My shoulders rise and fall with each breath and my chest tightens.

"That's part of a relationship, Kel. You work for it. You fight for it."

"I don't know that this relationship is worth fighting for." She flicks the fading cigarette to the cold ground and crushes it beneath the toe of her boot, putting out any heat it had left.

Her words are a sharp weapon that cuts through my layers to the deepest part of me.

"The thing is, I dealt with it when you chose gambling over your work. I stood by you when gambling got in the way of your friendships. You chose gambling over *me*, more than once, and I still stuck around." Her turbulent words flow over her trembling bottom lip. "But this time, Blake, you chose gambling over *you*. You let it take over everything. If *you* can't choose you, how am I supposed to?"

"I can change." It's a hollow expression with nothing behind it, like writing a check from an empty bank account. Kelly takes my hands in hers and holds them tight. Everything else is numb except where her skin touches mine.

"I hope that's true, but don't change for me. Change for you. Because if you don't... I'm scared of where you'll end up." She steps backward, removing her hands from mine as the space between us grows. She puts her hand on the door and opens it.

"Kelly... please." My voice cracks under the weight of my emotion. "What do you need from me? Right here, right now. Tell me what I need to do and I'll do it."

The world stops, frozen in this partial second between her opening the door and stepping through it or letting go of the handle and giving me one last chance at redemption.

Her hands drop to her sides. She doesn't face me. She doesn't turn her head over her shoulder. "I want you to admit you have a problem," she says into the old, faded door before finally turning toward me.

"That's what I want. If you can say the words, if you can look me in the eyes and say you have a gambling problem, we can talk about fixing this."

She stares at me with perfect ocean-colored eyes that are magnified behind the tears that flow over them. I bite my bottom lip and shove my hands deep in my pockets.

"I can't do that, Kelly. It was a mistake, a bad call. But I can stop anytime I want. It's not a problem."

She shakes her head in a back-and-forth motion that is seemingly slowed by disbelief and disappointment before she opens the door. She steps through it and closes it between us.

* * * *

My guitar sits across my lap, in the same spot it has been in for hours, waiting to be played. The times when I screw up, when I'm hurt, down or I'm alone usually causes an eruption of musical ideas and potential song lyrics, but here I am, a trifecta of fucked, frustrated and forsaken and *nothing* comes to mind.

My door opens and Xander strolls in, closing the door behind him. He takes a seat next to me and pats his flat palm against my shoulder hard two times then grips his fingers tight into my collarbone.

He says nothing and everything all at the same time, and for all the minutes that pass by, he doesn't talk, but he doesn't let go either.

My phone slides off the couch and crashes to the floor, leaving an impressive thud as the device hits the hardwood and I jolt awake. I don't even remember falling asleep there. More so than that, I don't really remember the last time I slept at all.

It's well into the after midnight-early-morning hours, yet there's a loud knock on my door. I scratch my head, weighing how dumb of an idea it is to answer at this hour to an unknown party. If they're here to rob me at gunpoint for any large amount of money, they're going to be supremely disappointed.

I take the risk and open the door because, hell, I've got nothing to lose.

My jaw clenches when I see it's my mother standing opposite me. I would've preferred the armed robbers.

"Do you have a second?"

"Nope." I start to close the door.

"I'm confident you are going to want to hear me out, Blake."

"You would lose that bet."

She drops her head to the side a bit and I wonder what she sees. Does she look at me and feel proud that I became something despite her constant setbacks, that I grew up to be successful? Or does she see through all that bullshit and realize I grew up to be *her*?

"I can help you get that money back."

"What's in it for you?" I ask, knowing the strings she attaches to this will better than likely be worse than the loss in the first place.

"I am no stranger to losing everything because of these life choices, Blake. You lost money. I lost you. Maybe we can both recoup some of those losses."

• • • •

Then

Our album is actually starting to resemble an album. It's a surreal feeling, creating something from nothing.

Our single is soaring and we're getting on new stages and growing our fan base. Things are almost perfect.

The problem is that almost everything I've contributed comes directly from the prom night fallout. I'd trade the entire damn album for a redo of that night.

"Blake, can I talk to you?" Cooper says. I swallow hard. Who knows what I've done now. I follow him down the hall, running through every scenario I can think of. He sits at a messy, paper-cluttered desk and I stand across from him. "I received a phone call from the University of Minnesota, Department of Music Studies."

My palms drip sweat. His tone and expression give me no indication of what type of news comes next.

"I didn't even know you applied, Blake. That's great. You should be proud of yourself."

"Thank you," I whisper in a tiny voice that's the antonym of proud. I don't feel good about it.

"You know, Blake, if you want to go out to Minneapolis, branch out on your own and see what options are out there, you can."

"I can't," I say, staring at a hole in the knee of my jeans. "I can't leave Xander behind—and you, and the guys."

"You have earned the right to put yourself first, Mathews. Don't say no to this yet. Sleep on it. Decide what's best for you."

"I don't need to sleep on it. I want to be part of this band. I love what we're doing and where we're going. I might hate Minnesota, and I'm not much of a risk-taker."

He nods his head and smiles. "You're sure?"

"You trying to get rid of me, Coop?" We both laugh.

No, no. I just want you to put yourself first for once."

"I am," I say, knowing for the first time, with confidence, that I belong somewhere. I turn to the door to rejoin the band and Cooper adds one follow-up question.

"Why'd you apply if you didn't want to go?"

"I just wanted some kind of solid, concrete evidence that I'm good enough to make it. I don't need college to tell me that. You tell me every damn day."

Cooper's words sink in slowly over the days following our conversation. Looking back on it, though I don't plan to take the spot offered to me, I am proud of myself. I just didn't recognize it at the time because the feeling was foreign. I've never really had anything to be proud of. Now that I've had time to sleep on it, I recognize that applying for college and getting accepted are both accomplishments I deserve to reflect on and feel good about.

I sit on the front steps of the school thinking back on it all. Xander and I used to sit here by ourselves before we knew anyone else. I dreaded moving here and starting at this school. Just when I finally started to think I couldn't possibly miss this place, I realized how much I will.

"Hey," Xander says, shuffling his feet as he walks toward our old spot on the stairs. "Minnesota, eh?" he says, shoving his hands in his pockets.

I look up at him, trying to read his expression. I hadn't told him and I didn't plan to. "Cooper?"

"No" — he shakes his head — "this came in the mail for you." He pulls out a large folded envelope and hands it to me. "If you want to go, you should. Just because I'm not going anywhere doesn't mean you should get stuck here."

"You're going somewhere, Xander. We both are — and we're going to do it together. We started this together and we're going to finish it the same way, whether that means we make it to the top or burn it to the ground."

"Knowing us, it will be the latter."

"Probably true." We both laugh an echoing sound through the stairway. Xander clears his throat and nods his head past me. I turn to see Kelly leaving through the main doors.

I stand and walk toward her with my hands in my pocket and my heart on my sleeve. I have no other choice. If I keep hiding myself from her, I'm never going to know what kind of hand fate holds for us.

"Blake," she says as I approach.

"Kelly," I respond, my voice matching hers. "What are you doing this weekend?"

"Really?" She crosses her arms and leans all her weight into one hip. "We graduate in two weeks and *now* you're going to ask me out?"

"I guess so, yeah." I scratch my hairline.

"I can't, Blake."

"Okay, the following weekend then."

"No, Blake," she snaps. "No weekend. You and I have been doing this dance around each other for years. If it was meant to be, it would have been."

"It's never too late to try." My voice was smaller and less confident than I needed it to be.

"Blake, I just… I just don't think you're what I need right now." She shakes her head and starts to walk away.

I will be." I muster up any sliver of confidence I can find. "Someday, Kelly, I'll be what you need. You'll see."

Her tight lips break into a sliver of a smile – a shimmer of hope, but we both turn away and go our separate directions.

Chapter Twenty

Now

There have been times she's crossed my mind. Where has she been? What is she doing now? Has she seen me play?

Does she think about me too?

Now she sits here in front of me, and I can't think of anything to say. There's more than a decade time-lapse between our reunions, and as far as I can tell, the only thing we have in common is a desire to sit at expensive tables.

"She did a good job with you," mother says, tapping her fingernails against the ceramic coffee cup in her hands. "Debbie, I mean. She gave you so much."

I push my hair back off my forehead and sink into the chair. *Debbie.* I wonder if Xander has told her what I've done.

She did." I nod my head, keeping my eyes fixed on the blank wall. "I couldn't have asked for a better mom."

The words hurt her. I know they do. I just don't care.

"You didn't even say goodbye," I add, my vocal cords strained. "I've gone over it time and time again. How could you just drop off my guitar at Xander's door and tell Debbie you weren't coming back?"

"I don't know what I can say or do to make you realize how sorry I am." She thinks about each word as she speaks, their heaviness weighing on her tongue. "I'm sorry I wasn't a good mother. I'm sorry you had to do so much growing up alone. I'm sorry we moved around so much. I'm sorry we never made it as a family, but I am *not* sorry you ended up with Debbie to raise you. Leaving you behind, under her care... It was the only right choice I ever made."

"I don't understand how it was so easy for you to just leave and never look back." I don't want to be vulnerable with her, but I can't help it. Years of unanswered questions rush through me like water over a broken dam.

She's quiet for a moment, taking deep breaths every few seconds like she's going to talk but doesn't know how to speak the words she wants to say.

"Blake, ninety percent of who you are as a person came from the life Debbie provided for you. The lessons you learned from her and the characteristics you developed were because of who *she* is as a person." She folds her hands in her lap and looks away from me, the painful words she's trying to say cutting her from the inside out on their way out of her mouth. "The other ten percent you got from me and look what it's done to you. I stayed away for years and still managed to pass the worst parts of me on to you. Think of how you feel today, right now and imagine if I *hadn't* left you behind. Think of how much worse off you'd be."

Her words make sense but she's a stranger to me now. I have no idea if she's being sincere or manipulative, but either way, I don't want to talk about it anymore. These aren't parts of my past I want to relive, especially when my future is so uncertain — and I can only change one of them.

"So, you came here to tell me something. Let's hear your big plan."

She takes the last sip of her coffee, looking at me over the mug as she pulls it from her lips and places it on the counter.

"Do you have any plans tonight?" she asks, crossing one leg over the other.

"Yeah, actually — "

"Cancel them," she says. "We're going to the penthouse."

My attempts at rejecting her offer failed. As much as I didn't want to go anywhere with her, never mind the penthouse, I didn't have much of a choice.

When we arrive, the penthouse is quiet and unoccupied apart from my mother, Victor and myself. No Isabella. No JX. No players or tables. I sit in a single armchair while my mother sits to my left in the matching seat to the set. Victor walks back and forth, sipping amber liquor from a crystal glass and looking out over the mile-long view from the penthouse window.

"That does sound like a problem," Victor says at the conclusion of saga — losing the money, losing the girl, losing the dream...not necessarily in that order. "It just doesn't sound like *my* problem."

"Victor," my mother says in a casual, friendly voice as if they've been friends for years. Perhaps they have been. "Be reasonable."

"I am being reasonable, Sharon." Victor speaks to his reflection in the window but directs the statement at my mother.

"Surely there has to be something you want more than the money. I think it is clear that finances aren't something that burden you." Mother taps her toe against the white tile as she speaks.

He turns and looks at her in this deep, hypnotic trance, right in her eyes in a way that makes it so I actually find myself worrying about her. She doesn't need to get tangled up with someone like him just because I screwed up.

"I think there is something you can help me with, Blake. If you can do it, I'll return the money I won. If you can't, you get nothing."

I nod, knowing full well that I'm digging this hole deeper than it already was but I'm curious to hear his ideas. "What did you have in mind?"

He paces back and forth, shrugging his shoulders as he decides on what instructions to provide.

"Your upcoming track release," he says, rubbing at his jaw line. "It's the one Stasia Marquette is on?"

"Yeah." My stomach turns. I don't like where this is going.

"When is the single set to release?"

"Not for more than a month. Why?" I sit at the edge of my seat.

"I want it." His voice is matter of fact, unwavering. He knows what he wants.

"Why?" I ask, but he doesn't answer right away.

"It doesn't matter why. Get me a copy of the singles, Mathews. That's your task. Get me the new material and I will direct your loss back to your bank account."

My gaze finds my mother's and she looks away. I stare at my shoes, knowing if I hand over those tracks, they will be released and leaked before Cooper ever gets to do his usual hype-up and sales will be a problem. I find myself wondering how much money he thinks he can make off the sale of the single. There is a lot of buzz in the music world about our new sound and everyone is eagerly awaiting the release. Ever since our show in Miami, we've topped the charts again. Our fans are on the edge of their seats for those tracks. I could do it. I could turn the music over to him and let him sell it to whomever he wanted. We'd only lose one song, but my debt would be cleared. The thought crosses my mind for one minute — and it's sixty seconds too long.

"I can't do that." I slouch in the chair. "I won't do that to Stasia or the guys. There has to be something else. Anything else." My voice is pleading, setting what little pride I had left aside.

He paces again, then stops, walking toward me and sitting on the coffee table in front of me. "There is one other thing."

"Anything," I say. There's almost nothing I wouldn't do to fix this.

He takes the last sip of his drink and stares into my eyes until he speaks again.

"I want you to leave Consistently Inconsistent."

* * * *

The cold air hurts my chest as I inhale it while walking the city streets from the penthouse to my own address. It's not a walk I would usually make, but the miles might do me some good. He's given me twenty-four hours to give him a final answer on his offer before any attempt at re-earning my losses expires. My thoughts clutter my head. I don't necessarily understand what Victor would gain by my departure from Consistently Inconsistent, but he seems like a man who craves power more than anything. In the end, his win could be just knowing that he is the master and I am the puppet. He might feel all powerful by knowing that if he says quit, I do. Then I think, *Is it the worst idea?* I think back on Kelly's words. *"This was the dream, Blake."* Maybe only one of us was meant to have what we dreamed of. If giving up my dream means she can have hers, how do I walk away from that?

The thing is I *could* buy The Rock Room property, but at this point I've already set myself back so far it would be hard to recoup — and *now* is the time I start to think logically. *Too little too late, I guess.* What if it doesn't do well? What if Ethan is selling it because it's going downhill? Now I see the other side... Now I engage in smart thinking where I assess the drawbacks or potential losses of a deal of that magnitude. It's true what they say. Hindsight is twenty-twenty.

Now, an investment like that is doable — but maybe not logical. That account didn't get the way it was overnight, and putting a large dent in my main bank account at this stage would be an even worse gamble than I've already made. Music is an interesting thing. Current hits become throwbacks, hot tracks become oldies, newer bands come in and knock the popular musicians from number one to not making an appearance on the charts at all. There is no guarantee in this business. I have no idea what tomorrow would bring or where that next dollar is coming from. Pending an unforeseen miracle, I don't see ever being able to save up that kind of money again in the time my career has left.

Small stones roll off my toe as I shuffle my feet across the sidewalk leading to my house, and when I look up, Kelly's SUV is in the driveway. I sprint through the lawn, leap up the stairs and turn the knob, swinging the door open in a swift burst of excitement. The enthusiasm fades as I step into the room, put two and two together and figure out why she's here.

It's not just her.

It's all of them.

Kelly, Xander, Natalie, Dom, Theo, Cooper, Stasia...*Debbie.*

I let out an aggressive sigh and turn to the door, but Xander moves to block it.

"Sit down, Blake." His voice takes a commanding tone I've never heard him use before.

"You need to get the hell out of my way." I crack my knuckles more out of a nervous habit than intimidation—but hey, whatever works.

"No, I won't do that. We all should've stepped in a long time ago and we didn't. Pick a chair, sit down and stop talking."

It's not surprising that Xander has the tough love routine down, since as far back as I can remember, it's always been him we had to use it on.

"Blake," a soft voice says to me and there is a gentle touch at my upper arms. I turn into Debbie and she wraps her arms around me in an embrace that I didn't even know I needed. "Please just come talk with us," she whispers into my shoulder. It was a cruel tactic to bring her into this. I can't say no to her.

I sit in a chair at the side of the room, surrounded by the most important people in my life, and instantly feel like I'm on trial, unprepared for whatever is going to be thrown my way.

"So, what? This is like my intervention or whatever?"

"Call it what you want, Mathews," Cooper says. "We are —"

"Just here because you care about me?" I snap, leaning forward in my chair. "You just want what's best for me? You can all save the cliches. I've seen the movies too."

"Blake," Kelly interjects, her face falling into an expression that's filled with both worry and sadness, "don't be like that. We do want to help. We wouldn't be here if we didn't."

I slouch back into the chair and push my hair off my forehead.

"I know it's hard to hear, man, but your issues are real and they're trickling down, affecting everyone else too," Dom says, his voice calm and quiet.

I rock my head back and forth in a sharp *no* — partly disbelief, but also disagreement. Other than Kelly, this hasn't impacted anyone else. Kelly reads me like an open book, realizing I don't see how anyone else is affected by what I'm doing.

"Would anyone care to share an example of how Blake's gambling problem —"

"It's not a problem." I interrupt her sentence.

"How Blake's *gambling problem*," she continues with more emphasis, "has affected them?"

I'm shocked — actual, genuine surprise — when it's Stasia who talks first.

"You missed my video interview," she says. "I tried to be a good friend and let it go, but it's still bothering me. We have really clicked. You've quickly become one of my best friends, and I've tried to be there for you and support you. Then, when I could've used your support, you weren't there for me."

I nod but can't speak. The walls seem to be closing in. The room gets smaller with each person who talks.

"That show in Vegas was a real problem," Theo adds. "You're tremendously lucky Cooper got people working on shutting your mic down and the stage crew found a way to manipulate the sound, because you were a wreck. If the media had gotten a hold of that, they would have torn you apart."

But they didn't, so who cares?

"Blake," Kelly says, "I love you, but right now, you're not the person I fell in love with. You're distant—here, but not really. Your mind is always elsewhere, always thinking about where you will go next or what lie you will tell me, and I don't like that version of you."

This isn't a new comment for Kelly. She has been telling me that for months. I barely hear the comments everyone else offers, shutting them out, mentally playing my favorite album in my head on full blast.

"You haven't called." Debbie's voice brings me back to the room. "We had virtual Saturday morning coffee together on video call every Saturday morning at eight a.m. my time like clockwork for years. No matter what country the band was touring in, no matter how late you were out the night before, you never missed a call, and I looked forward to it."

This catches my attention. When was the last time I'd called her?

It's been fifteen Saturdays, Blake. Fifteen Saturdays that have come and gone with no call, no attempt. Fifteen Saturdays after years and years of consistency."

My focus shifts to the ceiling. I blink back the tears that press behind them. If they were trying to break me, that might do it. I look at Xander, waiting for him to speak. I might as well get the most painful parts over with at once.

"What do you have for me, Xander? Bad shows, missed band practices?" I ask, keeping my emotions as in check as possible.

He shakes his head and shrugs. "I just want my brother back, Blake. We were a team. We went out for dinner together, met up for drinks or even just had a good conversation. We used to laugh and hang out. You say no every time I invite you somewhere. You have an excuse every time we have a chance to just spend time together outside of a tour or studio time. I just want my brother back."

No one has pulled their punches. There wasn't a gentle comment in the room. If they wanted me to see the error of my ways, they'd succeeded, but I come to the same conclusion I have always come to my entire life. I'm nothing more than a heavy burden.

"So, if the public berating portion of the party is over, what do we do next?" I ask, leaning forward with my elbows on my knees. "The consequences, right? This is the part where you say 'Blake Mathews, if you don't get your shit together, we will send you to a program for rehabilitation, blah, blah, blah...' Am I right?"

Cooper narrows his eyes at the sound of my mocking tone and he finally speaks.

"Do you know how much money studio time actually costs, Mathews?" he says, and I think on it. I don't. I've never really thought about it. "You've missed three recording sessions that we had blocked for laying the new music with Stasia. Three groups of prepaid hours in a studio in addition to the interview. This band has had their fair share of mess-ups but none of them have cost us as much money as you have."

That can't be true. There's no way I've missed that much...have I?

"You're right, though," Cooper continues, scratching his chin. "There has to be consequences. We need you in the studio this week for every block we have, since we're behind now. And I mean rested, ready to go, full commitment. No absences, no screwups."

"And if I don't?" I ask, genuinely curious what he thinks he can scare me with. I'm not saying I can't do it, but what is he going to do about it if I don't?

"You will be—" Xander interjects and Cooper holds up one hand toward him. Cooper's expression is a marriage of angry and disappointed.

"Then you're out," he says—and he's serious. "You won't be a member of this band anymore."

His words go right under my skin. He's got to be freakin' kidding me. The last person we did this with was Julian, and he was exponentially worse off than I am. And what about Xander? But *of course* the band can't exist without Xander Varro. He's the front man, he's the voice. Cooper needs him more than he needs me, so when Xander screws up, we coddle and support him, because without him we all fail, but me? I get tossed. Anger churns in my stomach, and a livid heat rises to my chest.

"Then I'm out." I clap my hands together and rise from my seat. "I quit."

I don't look back as I storm out of the apartment. The impact of my stomps against the floor shake the picture frames on the shelves and I slam the door behind me, unsure of where to go from here.

This is not the place I had envisioned ending up. I'm not even sure when I made the decision to come here, but eventually I took all the correct streets to end up in front of the olive green door at the top of the concrete stairs.

If I take the steps and knock on the door, it's all real. The things they said about me and the depth of this dilemma. Ascending this staircase corroborates their accusations and I know coming here can surely only make things worse. I leave the sidewalk and take the first step, figuratively and literally, because I know, standing in this spot, it's verified now.

I have a problem.

I take the second step, then the third. Three steps that somehow feel like the direct stairway to hell and I'm knocking on its door.

Chapter Twenty-One

Kelly

Blake walked out more than an hour ago. No one chased after him. No one made him stay. It was like we were frozen in time while he kept moving, his unexpected words casting a spell on each of us that rendered us motionless.

"Threatening to kick him out was *not* part of the plan, Cooper." I pace back and forth behind the couch. "Brilliant idea, really." I clap my hands in applause while making it obvious the sentiment isn't sincere.

"Kelly"—Xander takes my hands in his in an attempt to calm me down—"it wasn't his idea." I slowly look up at him and narrow my eyes as he speaks. "It was mine," he adds.

I automatically look to Natalie, though I'm not sure why. She lets her eyes fall downcast, picking at a thread on the end of her sweater as she avoids my eye contact.

She knew.

I drop my hands so they hit my legs with a smack. I think of some choice words to say but I'm outnumbered on this one, so I retreat to my room...our room. Blake's room, I suppose, since I've left. Natalie follows, closing the door behind her and sitting next to me at the edge of the bed.

"You know it had to be this way," she signs, her eyes and lips set in a sympathetic expression.

"You should have told me," I argue, signing and speaking at the same time.

"No, we couldn't." She continues, "You never would have let us do it. He needed to know there is something real on the line."

I nod. Tears fill my eyes and overflow, running down my cheeks. I use the back of my hand to wipe under my eyes. She returns to the living room, leaving me by myself in the bedroom. I fall backward, crash into the bed and stare at the ceiling, wondering where we go from here.

There must be something I'm missing or some information I'm not privy to. Blake is no quitter — clearly. It's what got us into this mess.

But quitting the band? That's not Blake.

He's easily the most persistent person I know.

* * * *

Then

Everyone's enthusiasm leaves our classroom noisy with *almost graduation* excitement. Studying and preparing for exams has gone completely out of the window.

At the other side of the room, a blond-haired boy sits on his desk with his feet on his chair talking his long haired, loud-mouthed best friend.

My heart breaks a bit knowing this is the last classroom Blake Mathews and I will ever share. For years we've done this back and forth routine where he wants to be with me and I say no and when I'm ready for him, he asks someone else to prom.

It hurt more than I'd like to admit. He and I just always seemed to be in different places, going different directions. I suppose it's not worth overthinking now. We're graduating soon.

That and his band is about to make it big. I can feel it. He will be somebody, on the road, in a million cities where people know his name and I'll be here, tied to this town.

His best friend, Xander, got a head start on his heart breaking. Xander dumped my best friend Rina as soon as caps and gowns were ready for pick up. It's just another sign that things wouldn't work for me and Blake either. The bell rings and Blake jumps down from his desk, exiting through the doorway without even looking back at me.

Blake and I don't have the next class together but Xander and I do. We've never been friends necessarily, but I know exactly who he is. We've been in the same class since preschool. I still remember a time when Xander was *Alexander.* He had braces and glasses and a face full of acne. Somewhere along the way he grew out his hair, changed his style and found his voice.

"Kelly." Xander takes the seat behind me, though it's not his usual one. "I need to talk to you."

Georgy Harris runs down the row of desks with his overstuffed backpack swinging back and forth, hitting other students as he passes through.

"That's *my* seat," he says to Xander. Xander leans back into the chair and looks at Georgy.

"See that chair right there?" Xander points across the room.

"Yeah," Georgy says, hesitation in his voice.

"That's your seat now." Xander turns back to me and I stifle a laugh. "Anyway...as I was saying," he continues as Georgie finds his way to his new home, "you need to go out with Blake."

"No, thank you." My answer is stern and steadfast, my eyes are fixed on the doodles I'm drawing on my notebook cover. "That ship left the port months ago."

"Why?"

I can't answer him. The idea of Blake scares me. Their music is so good and they are growing so fast that I am sure I would just be setting myself up to be let down.

"Is this still because of prom?" Xander presses.

"Yes." Because it's easier than admitting I'm too afraid to take a chance on him. "Did he send you to talk to me?"

"No. Yes. Maybe. Just give the boy a chance, Kel." I don't answer him. I just continue to scribble in my notebook.

Blake and I still have one class left together, and it's the last period of the day. We sit in groups to quiz each other on the study guides for our upcoming finals, but most people are talking and socializing rather than being productive. The desks are turned in groups of four and Blake sits two makeshift tables away from me. I stare at the back of his head for most of the class, rather than focus on the study material in my hand. I consider Xander's words. Maybe he's right. What would be the worst that could happen if I just walk up to him, tell him how I feel—and have felt all these years—and finally take a chance on him? It takes all of the courage I have to get up from this chair, but just as its legs screech against the tile floor, the bell rings. Blake gathers his belongings and exits through the door without so much of a glance over his shoulder as he leaves me behind. The day is over—and so is the one fleeting moment of confidence I had.

I don't even stop at my locker as I stomp toward the main exit, beyond ready for this day to be finished. *One day closer to graduation* I think as I place my hands against the metal bar of the door.

"Miss Montoy," someone says as they join me in the foyer.

"What?" I snap, more aggressively than I'd intended. I turn to find Principal Wheeler standing at the top of the stairs. "Oh, I'm sorry, Principal Wheeler. Yes, sir?"

"I just thought you might like to know the yearbooks came in today." He hands me a maroon leatherbound book with gold writing on the cover that gleams in the lights overhead. "I know how much work you put into these. I thought you might like to get the first copy."

"Thank you so much." I smile as I assess the cover. "I appreciate it."

"You deserve it." He winks and turns away before I exit through the doors and start my walk home, yearbook in hand. I head to my house and meet Natalie there to show it to her.

Later, Natalie sits on my bed, flipping the pages in the finalized yearbook. No one else has seen them yet. I'm the only one who had broken the binding on one of these highly anticipated books. Joining the yearbook staff wasn't initially part of my high school plans but it turned out to be something I loved and exceled at.

She turns a page and looks up at me, rolling her eyes dramatically. I smile, knowing exactly what she's thinking. She looks at me again, one eyebrow raised then tosses the book my direction like a frisbee.

"Hey!" I squeal as the yearbook falls open in front of me. "What?" I sign, all smiles and laughter.

"Could you have taken any more pictures of him?" Natalie signs, her sarcasm evident in the way she shakes her head and draws out the speed of the signs for emphasis.

"I missed my chance with him," I sign back to her, sad.

"Why don't you just tell him how you feel?" Her eyebrow arches in a curious form.

I shrug. "Every time I try to, I freeze. I can't say the words."

"So, write them," she suggests, leaning forward and pushing the yearbook closer to me.

• • • •

The cafeteria is alive with excited classmates waiting to get their yearbook. Dozens of boxes of the final product are being unloaded onto the table around me while I sort through and check names off on a list.

"Hey, Kel," Blake says. My gaze shoots upward at the sound of his voice. His hair is a bit longer, an unkempt style that I almost grin at but shut the smile down before it starts.

"Blake." I keep the conversation short. We haven't spoken since the day he told me there would be a someday for us. He'd said "Someday, you'll see" and it's all I have thought of since. I want to tell him he was right, that even after years of pushing him aside, he was the one I needed.

"About your yearbook…" I start, my palms sweating as I speak. His yearbook seems to weigh more than anyone else's as it holds all the words that I haven't been able to say over the last six years. I find my courage somewhere buried deep inside and drag it to the surface. Just when I'm finally ready to tell him I wrote something in his yearbook I'd like him to read, we're joined at the table by someone else.

"There you are," she says, wrapping her arms around Blake's waist, and he drapes his arm over her shoulder.

Carissa Kennedy.

He looks…*happy* with her there, hanging off him. He deserves that. I had my chances, many of them, and I kept pushing them off, sending him away. I didn't trust that we could make something work after the moment we tossed our graduation caps into the air.

"You were saying something about my yearbook?" Blake says, finally tearing his gaze off Carissa and letting his gaze fall to me. That's when I realize that he doesn't look at me the way he did that day in front of the school.

"Someday, Kelly, I'll be what you need. You'll see." Apparently, it's not someday yet — and now I'm forced to wait my turn.

"Umm, yeah." I kick his yearbook with my confession written in its pages further under the table. "It doesn't look like you ordered one."

He scratches his head. "Are you sure? I swear I brought a check and order form in. For me and Xander. Is he on the list?"

I use my finger to run down the rows of names, though I already know Xander's is on there. "Yeah, looks like he already picked his up."

"...have mine." "I know I ordered one," Carissa says, chewing her gum in a dramatic way between gum chews.

"...names A–K are at that table." I point and Carissa skips away.

"...all anyway. It doesn't look like we have one for you anyways. Sometimes we order extras. If there's one left over I'll let you know." The toe of my sneaker is on the box under the table, holding it down as if it's going to jump up and out me at any moment.

"...okay, sure then," Blake says. "Well, I guess that's that. It just sucks. Someday down the line I'm going to miss certain things, certain people, and I won't have anything to remember them by."

His velvet voice, so much deeper and stronger now than it used to be, melts me into the cafeteria floor.

"Any plans for the summer?" he asks. I wish he wouldn't make small talk. I just want him to go away so I can mope in peace and get rid of this damn yearbook that's burning a hole through the bottom of my shoe.

"Not really. I got a job at The Rock Room. That should be pretty fun." I smile because, as much as the Blake and Carissa scene is depressing, The Rock Room is exactly where I want to be. Music. Lights. Crowds. People. I have no idea what I want to be when I grow up, or where my life is going, but I know all my favorite things under one roof is a good start.

"The Rock Room?" A genuine flash of excitement and support shines in his kind eyes. "Maybe if this music thing doesn't work out, you can convince them to hire me."

"The music thing will work out," I whisper, not meaning to have said the words out loud.

"How do you know?" One corner of his lip turns upward.

"I just know." I shrug and give my very best Blake Mathews impression. "Someday, Blake. You'll see."

High school had dragged by and taken its sweet time year after year up until the last three weeks of our final senior semester, when the hands of the clock became unhinged and the days passed in the blink of an eye.

"Is that him?" Natalie signs. I turn over my shoulder to peek without making it obvious. I nod, turning away from Blake. He doesn't even look like himself in his black button-up shirt and dark gray dress pants. His hair is semi-styled. Clean cut almost looks odd on him but he's as striking as ever. He talks to Xander and Xander's mother at the corner of the room. Leave it to Xander to wear ripped jeans and sunglasses to graduation, though I suppose they will be covered by a gown in just a few minute's time.

"He's cute," Natalie signs, "and they're coming this way." She's hurrying off before I can say otherwise. I turn and tuck a loose strand of hair behind my ear.

"Congratulations, Kelly," Xander says. "Didn't think we'd ever make it this far, eh?"

"I didn't think *you'd* make it this far," I joke. Blake lets out an enthusiastic 'oooooohhhh' at the jab.

"Last in class both in grades and alphabetically, but I'm here," he says with a laugh. "I'll see you guys after we graduate." He claps his hands on Blake's shoulders, gives him a good shake and heads up the stairs where we are set to graduate in front of all our friends and family.

"Don't forget about us little people when you go do whatever great thing it is you're going to do," Blake says. He's always had more confidence in me than I've had in myself.

I should be saying that to you, I think." Then again, I've always had more confidence in him than he has had in himself too.

"Mr. Mathews, Miss Montoy, it's time to go upstairs." Principal Wheeler says. Blake nods in agreement.

We take the stairs together, just the two of us, walking toward the event that will close the door on this part of our life and send us down paths that will most likely never lead to each other.

Chapter Twenty-Two

Now

"Kelly?" Debbie says with a double tap on the door. I sit up too quickly and the room spins. "Is he back? Did Blake come home?"

"No, sweetie, he's not back yet."

I drop my head to my hand. I don't know what I was expecting. Surely sitting down with all of us wasn't going to just magically change his situation, but I wasn't expecting him to quit and walk out either.

"He's one of the good ones, you know." Debbie enters the room and sits next to me, occupying the spot Natalie had been in. "He's loved you as long as I've known him. He's a little mixed up right now, but he'll come back around. He always does."

"I hope you're right." She places her hand on mine. "I just wish I'd done things differently."

"I'm sure he does too," she says. "Everyone is still here, and we ordered pizza."

She keeps my hand in hers as she guides me back to my closest friends – my family – but I'm not hungry.

I walk to the front door with my arms crossed as I lean into the doorframe, looking out to the street as if Blake will walk up it at any moment and tell us he changed his mind. He takes it back. He'll get help.

But he won't. When he said the words, when he stood in that room in front of the bandmates he has played beside for somewhere in the ballpark of fifteen years and declared he was out, he'd meant it.

As long as I've known him, he has been part of that band. It's how we met, it's how we continued to grow. It kept us together even when we were apart. So many of our memories circulate around Consistently Inconsistent, and now I'm realizing we will never have the chance to make new ones.

Xander joins me in the entryway and places his hands on my shoulders. He is equally the last person I want to see and the only person I want to see. I turn into him and he wraps me in his arms. I collapse there into his chest and sob wet tears into his T-shirt. My chest rises and falls against his abdomen and he rubs my back, offering a quiet 'shhh' and 'we'll figure all this out' every few seconds – and though he tries to hide it, I swear he's crying too.

* * * *

Then

The winter after graduation I walk home from The Rock Room and pass a small event space. The music that blares through the walls sounds familiar, a song I've heard a million times. It's either Xander Varro or a damn good cover. A flyer with familiar faces on it catches my attention at the doorway. The advertisement says Consistently Inconsistent is set to take the stage in a battle of young stars, a music competition to help teen musicians get to the top.

I push open the door, walk in and hang out in the back of room. Xander is as good as he's ever been, whirling around the stage and teasing the crowd in a way that makes it impossible to not want more.

Blake continues to strum his guitar as he moves toward Xander on the stage. Everyone else cuts out and Blake creates an impressive few chords in a solo he once referred to as a 'lick' – I remember it specifically because *yuck* – but damn it if it isn't a thing of perfection. As if that's not enough, he leans into the microphone, and as Xander sings the words I've come to know and love in this song, Blake adds a background piece, a secondary lyric I had never heard before.

The harder I tried to make you part of my past, the faster you became my future.

After their set, I push through the crowd and locate Blake by the stage.

"Hey," I yell, but he doesn't hear me over the music. I reach forward and place my hand between his shoulders. His T-shirt is slick with sweat, sticking to his skin in all the right places.

He turns and looks at me in a way that says he's excited to see me but it's not the way he used to look at me. Now, I'm just another classmate he hasn't seen in a while.

"Kelly!" He pulls me in for a hug. "How the hell have you been?"

"I'm doing okay," I say, competing with the loud music. "You were great up there. I told you Consistently Inconsistent would do well."

We're done, actually," he says, and I'm surprised. This was it. Kelly. This is the last show for us."

What? No! That's crazy."

We had a small summer tour set to go but it didn't work out. We lost a lot of buzz from the singles and we're not keeping up enough to keep the money coming in to record new ones. I'm taking that spot in Minnesota next semester. Dom and Theo both have school offers, and Julian wants to play football. That's just the hand we were dealt."

You can't walk away. You're too talented! You can't just quit, Blake." But what's my opinion worth? Nothing.

Hey." He places his hands on my shoulders. "It was good to see you. I have to go." He leans in and hugs me, pausing to give me a light kiss on the cheek, barely there, so soft I could have imagined it.

For the days that follow, I hope to see him again. It's a small town, after all. Every time I drive by the local gas station, take the train into the city or walk past a group of people, I secretly hope he is one of them. Even now at work, in the city, miles from our tiny hometown, every time a door opens, I hold my breath and hope it's Blake — but it's not.

In many ways, The Rock Room makes me miss high school. I wanted to graduate, wanted to be on my own and be out of school hallways but this is much harder than I thought. Almost everyone I work around is older than me, and they're always in a rush or bad mood. I wash a lot of glasses for the bartenders and clean up after fans but I also get to run errands for the bands and those moments make it worth it. Being backstage is so exciting, even if I am only delivering coffees or whatever trivial thing they *must* have before they can take the stage.

"Kelly," my boss says to me, shoving a large box into my hands. "You saw the guy the band came in with earlier, yeah? He's their manager. Get these to him, will ya?"

That's it. It's the only instruction I get, which is typical. I've gotten fairly good at this though. The band managers, the booking agents, the publicists... I can usually spot them from a mile away.

"Are you fucking kidding me?" An older man in jeans and a button-down shirt knocks a chair over as he tears through the back-stage area. He screams the question, profanities and all, repeatedly, but nobody answers. Hypothetical, I guess. He's clearly having a bad night and I'd bet anything that these berries won't fix the problem, so I just set them down on a table near the dressing rooms.

Another man in a suit flies through the backstage area. He's The Rock Room booking manager. I know him, but he wouldn't know me from any other bottom-of-the-totem-pole employee or intern in this place.

"What seems to be the problem, Mr. Harrington?" he says, obviously mentally preparing to give the angry band manager whatever he needs as fast as he can.

"We don't have an opener. The band that was supposed to open for us was on a plane that had to make an emergency landing, and now we don't have anyone opening," Mr. Harrington snarls.

"Let's see what we can work out," the owner adds in, but the sweat at his brow indicates he has no idea how to handle this particular situation.

"Unless you have a band on standby, you're going to have a crowd full of people with no entertainment, Steven. Help me out here. Figure something out."

Steven nods his empty head. He has no idea what he's going to do. I pick up a nearby broom and sweep unnecessarily, just to give myself a reason to stay backstage and continue eavesdropping. Steven walks toward me – well, I assume he intends to walk past me, but I take a deep breath and decide if I'm ever going to take a wild chance in my lifetime that this was the moment to do it.

"Steven… Uhh, I mean, Mr. – "

"Steven is fine," he says, turning toward me.

"I know it's not my place…and I'm sure you have things under control – "

"Do you have something for me or not?" he snaps. I don't blame him. I know he's strapped for time.

"I can have Consistently Inconsistent on stage in thirty minutes," I offer, and he thinks about it for a minute.

"Do you have something of theirs?" He rubs his jaw.

"MP3, stream, video? Anything I can take Mr. Harrington?"

"Yes, sir." I pull my iPod from my pocket.

"And… who are you?" he asks, though he starts walking and I follow.

"Whoever you need me to be. I just go where everyone tells me to."

"Okay." He picks up the pace as I trot to keep up. "Then right now you're an intern with the Music Promotion team. Got it?"

"Yes, sir."

Mr. Harrington swings at the pitch, and suddenly I'm dialing a number with a shaky hand and a hopeful heart that I wasn't sure I'd ever dial again, because now I must follow through on a promise that I made I'm not sure I can keep.

"Hello?" Blake says and there is laughter in the background.

"What are you doing?" I ask.

"Kelly?" There is surprise in his voice. "Nothing really. Playing video games with the guys."

"You can't quit music, Blake. None of you can. You have too much going for you. It's all going to fall into place, but you can't give up on it. Not yet."

"Kelly, everything okay?" My heart beats so loud it almost drowns out his voice.

"Blake."

"Yes?"

"You guys have a slot on stage in thirty minutes at The Rock Room tonight, opening for Regrets Only in front of a sold-out crowd. All you have to do is say yes and get here."

* * * *

Now

We're nearing the end of day four since our failed intervention. Everyone has found their way home.

Except for Blake.

Xander, Natalie and Debbie stayed overnight a few times before finally heading back to Xander and Natalie's apartment, and everyone else comes and checks in every once in a while, but for the most part, I'm alone.

Where the hell are you, Blake?

My stomach turns every time I think about him. There have been no phone calls, no texts — no indication that he's even okay. I don't know what to think, so I sit here and imagine the worst.

I've stopped responding to the sound of the door opening. For a while the door would click, I'd jump up, run across the room and it wouldn't be him.

It's tiring and painful.

"Come in," I say without enthusiasm as the door opens. Stasia enters the kitchen with coffee from Charlie's.

"Nothing yet?"

I have to fight to contain my eyeroll. I'm so tired of people asking that damn question. *Oh, actually, yeah! Forgot to tell you — He came home!* Come on, people. Honestly. If I heard from him, everyone would know.

"Nothing yet." I force myself to keep my harsher thoughts to myself.

"I tried to call him." She shrugs. "I know everyone else did too, but I don't know. It's all I could think to do."

"I appreciate it, Stasia, but it's useless." Fatigue weighs down my words. "His phone is here. Xander called it the other day and I heard it ringing. It was arguably the most deflating part of all of this. I couldn't call him, even if he would answer."

I keep my head in my hands, thinking about drinking the coffee in front of me but too tired to make myself reach for it.

"His phone is here?" she asks, oddly excited about the fact. "Did you look through it?"

"It's mostly just text messages and missed calls from all of us looking for him." I didn't dive too deep into it, to be honest. I had so much on mind, and with all of us trying to call it and text him, the damn thing wouldn't stop ringing. It taunted me, reminding me that it was here and he was not, so I shut it down.

"Can I see it?" she asks and I can't see how it would hurt. I walk to the hutch in the hallway and take the phone from the drawer. I hand it to her, and she powers it on. I watch her sort through the phone like one of these detectives on TV with her forehead furrowed and offering a *hmmm* or *huh* every once in a while, but not revealing any comments worth getting excited about.

"Oh, Blake." She covers her mouth and worry flows through the words. She runs her hand through her short hair, pushing it so it flops to the opposite side.

"Do you know where he is?" I allow myself the smallest taste of the hope I've been avoiding for days.

"No, no," she says, "but, Kelly, he's mixed up with the worst people."

"What do you mean?" My voice cracks as I speak.

She hands me the phone, which is open to a screen with a text message from an Isabella.

Victor would like to remind you that the clock is ticking.

"I read that," I admit. "I just didn't know what it meant or who the hell Victor is."

"I don't know what it means specifically but making *any* kind of deal with Victor is a really dangerous move."

"What?" The anxiety of where Blake is and what he's up to falls heavy against my heart again. "How do you know this Victor guy?"

"He's my father."

I can tell by the way the conflicted words roll off her tongue that she's not proud to admit it.

Chapter Twenty-Three

This penthouse is like nothing I've ever seen before. Xander and Natalie have a gorgeous apartment in a desirable location with a picturesque view, and this place makes their home look like a neglected hovel.

Goosebumps cover my skin as a shiver runs down the length of my back. It's pristine and flawless, yet it gives off the same vibe as an abandoned warehouse or hospital would, screaming warnings about trespassing where we don't belong.

Stasia hasn't offered much information regarding her father, but I get the feeling that my uneasiness is warranted. He doesn't sound like the nurturing type.

"Stasia," a tanned goddess of a woman says as she walks down the stairs in impossibly high heels. "It's so good to see you."

Stasia ignores the woman's greeting, pushing her wildly cut hair off her face and pursing her purple-painted lips. "Can I see my father, please?" she asks, as the woman takes the last step and waltzes toward us.

"Hi there" — she holds her hand out toward me — "I'm Isabella."

Isabella, of course. The name in Blake's phone. It didn't bother me before. It does now. *Damn*, she's lightyears beyond attractive.

"My father, *please*." Stasia snaps her fingers.

"Yes, of course. This way then."

I still can't keep my eyes off her heels. She walks the curving steps of the spiral staircase in those shoes more fluidly than I can do it barefoot, and I'm relatively good in heels.

Isabella leads us into an office-type area with a fireplace burning under a gorgeous granite mantel. The hardwood under our feet is a deep red cherry color that runs across the room and halfway up the walls. It meets an electric white paint that flows into crown molding so intricately crafted that there's no need to hang décor, as the walls themselves are art enough.

"Stasia," a man says as he joins us in the study, "my beautiful daughter. You've reconsidered my offer?"

"No, I'm not here to talk about me."

"Then you have no reason to stay. Isabella can show you out." He takes a seat in a chair behind the desk.

"I want to know what it is you have on Blake Mathews." Stasia's voice is firm and demanding.

Victor laughs. A genuine smile grows across his lips. Whatever it was he wanted from Blake, he has likely already won.

"Mr. Mathews is none of your concern, Stasia."

"That may be," I interject, trying to steady my nerves, "but it is *mine*."

Victor looks up, scratches at his chin then rises from his chair. I instinctively take a step back. He comes to the front of the desk then sits on its edge.

So, you're Kelly then, I presume. Yes, Mr. Mathews has told me all about you."

I swallow hard. The way he looks at me is a tranced stare, the way a snake fixates on its prey before striking. He pushes off the desk and walks toward me, looking me over head to toe then leans in and whispers in my ear

"If you'd kept the boy on a shorter leash, you wouldn't have to go around cleaning up his messes."

"Let's go, Kelly." Stasia wraps her hand around mine, pulling me away from her father and I follow willingly, relieved to be distanced from him.

"Don't be so hasty, ladies." His footsteps echo as he returns to the desk. He turns around and sits on the edge of the desk once more, pulling a cigar from his suit pocket

"Blake got cocky—bold and over-confident. I'll be honest I liked that about him. He gets that from his mother. We're old friends, you see, Sharon and me. We go way, way back." Stasia and I find each other's eyes at the same time, surprised at the mention of Blake's mother. "Anyway, I digress. Blake made a bad call. He raised the stakes when he should have folded, so to speak

Victor paces the area in front of the desk, only pausing his monologue to light his cigar.

"This is my favorite part of the story," Victor says, winking at me as he takes a puff of the cigar, smoke billowing around him. "He *lost.*"

Now Victor is just wasting my time. His intimidation is wearing off, anger setting in where fear had once lived

"We — I start to argue but he holds up one broad finger cutting me off before I can argue.

"He came to me a few days later. He told me all about your business venture. Or, well, what would have been your business venture had he not squandered that for you. But, I'm a sucker for a good love story. So, me being the generous person I am, I made him an offer." Victor takes his eyes off me and returns his attention to Stasia. "Are you listening, sweetie? This is the part where you come in."

Stasia's lip curls into a teeth-bearing snarl.

"I told Blake he could have his losses back — every single cent." Victor is silent for a moment then leans into Stasia, his face just inches from hers, whispering to her. "This is the part where you ask 'what did he have to do in return?'

Stasia's eyes narrow, her shoulders tense. I feel sorry for her. She shouldn't have to deal with a father like this. No one should. The devil himself possesses more paternal qualities than Victor.

"Ask the question, Stasia." Victor wraps his hand at her upper arm.

She rips her arm from his grasp. "What did he have to do in return?" she snaps, her nostrils flaring as her chest rises and falls with heated breaths.

"I asked him to hand over your new singles, dear. The tracks you're recording with Consistently Inconsistent. I wanted them. I told him that was his mission to settle his debts."

"He would never do that," I say too quickly, interjecting where I wasn't invited to speak.

"You're right," Victor says, returning to the desk and placing his cigar on a crystal ash tray. "He wouldn't. So, I instructed him to leave Consistently Inconsistent instead."

Stasia's and my expressions are mirror images of each other. He didn't just leave on his own accord. He felt like he had to. When Cooper threatened to kick him out anyway, it was the perfect opportunity for him to walk with no questions asked.

"What are you going to do, Dad? What's your plan? Pull Blake from the band, sign him to the label? Blow him up with a solo act?" Stasia's body shakes with rage.

"Don't be ridiculous, Stasia," Victor says, spitting as he speaks.

"Oh my..." Stasia's words come slow and drawn out as she puts together pieces of a puzzle that only she can see. "You're not doing anything for him at all. You're not even signing him to MLA."

Victor chuckles again, letting out that full-bodied laugh that comes at the end of a joke only he understands.

"If Mathews walks away from Consistently Inconsistent, they are *done*. Face it, Stasia. If one of them goes down, the rest will quickly follow and you will come crawling back to me, begging me to help you put out an album and get your career off the ground."

"You were never trying to ruin Blake's career. You were trying to ruin mine."

"I am trying to *save* yours!" Victor bellows. He throws his hand aside, hitting the ash tray and causing it to fly to the floor in a crash of ash and sparks. "*I* made you. *I* trained you. *I* gave you every musical skill you have. I gave you everything you are, Stasia, and I can take it away. You will record with MLA or you won't record at all."

Stasia swallows so hard that I can see the lump travel down her throat. She taps her foot with her arms crossed as she holds herself together. Whatever she's about to say, it's causing her pain as it works its way through her. Tears form on her lower lids. Maybe he's a monster, but I can't imagine the internal struggle that comes with finding the words to tell your own father off or to walk away and never look back at a person you share a bloodline with.

"Okay." She takes a deep breath and wipes her hands on her torn jeans. "You always said there is something everyone wants more than the money. If I'm what you want, if that's what you want more than what you've gotten from Blake, I'll do it. Let Blake out of this, let him go back to Consistently Inconsistent *and* return what he lost—and I'll work for you. I'll do whatever you want, just let Blake start over."

"No, Stasia!" I cry, my surprise causing my voice to come out in broken tones. That is not at all what I expected her next move to be. "Absolutely not. You can't work for him."

If she stays, Victor wins. Again. In the end he ends up with exactly what he wanted.

"This is the best way," Stasia says, "the only way. Find Blake. And tell the band I'm sorry."

* * * *

Xander is at Blake's house when I arrive back. I tie my hair into a bun at the top of my head and collapse into the couch next to him. He moves closer to me, stretching one arm over my shoulder. I cover my face with both hands then run them under both eyes, surely smearing whatever makeup remains. I'm this tangled mess of confused, worried, stressed and other emotions I can't define. My heart beats hard against my chest, surely my inner walls must be close to crumbling altogether. With a deep breath and heavy sigh I run through every detail with Xander, knowing full well this is a rehearsal for the many times I'm going to have to repeat the story.

I just want to know where he is. I need to know that he's okay." I wipe tears from my swollen lids.

"I know, Kel. I do too." He rubs his calloused palm at my shoulder.

I turn to face him, preparing myself to ask a question that I've asked myself a million times but despise every answer I've arrived at. "You don't think he'd... He wouldn't... You don't think he would have hurt himself... or worse? Right?" I'm mentally pleading that Xander says the words I *want* to hear and not the logical answer but unfortunately, Xander tends to be a logical guy these days.

"I don't know, Kelly." His eyes pull away from mine and find the floor. "I want to say he's not that guy, that he's not the type but unfortunately, especially in this business, it's usually the people who seem like they're doing fine that are hurting in a way everyone else misses."

"I need him to be okay." I sob in a way I can't control.

"We will find him." His usual deep, gruff tone is replaced with a calm voice much like the one he sings with. "I promise..." he adds with the words trailing off in a whisper like he second guessed the sentence as he spoke it.

Chapter Twenty-Four

Blake

An overwhelming feeling of regret washes over me as soon as I knock on the olive door. For a moment, I hope no one answers. Just when I'm about to change my mind, to turn on my heel and walk away with no plan of where to go next, the door swings open and a familiar face stands at the other side.

She's as beautiful as she has ever been, exactly the way I remember her from when we were all close before everything fell apart.

"This is a surprise," she says in a voice that's a mix of shock and sarcasm. "Whatever you've done, it must be really bad."

"How do you figure?" I'm annoyed but she's not wrong.

"You wouldn't have come here if you had any other option. It's good to see you, though, Blake. I wish it was on better terms."

"You too, Mariah. Is Julian here?"

Julian leans over a toy chest, tossing scattered blocks and stuffed animals into the box as I step into the living room. "Who was at the door, babe?" he yells to Mariah, not realizing I'm standing there too. Being a father looks good on him—not the way I would've preferred he'd earned the role but I'll admit he does it well.

"Oh, Blake." His face turns from calm to confused to curious all in a matter of seconds. "What is it? Everyone okay? Are the guys okay?"

His question is genuine. It's a real worry regarding Xander, Theo or Dom causing him to put his feelings aside as his concern for the band he helped build surfaces and takes priority.

"Yeah, yeah, everyone's fine." I run my hand through the tips of my hair and take a deep breath. "I just wanted to talk, if that's okay."

He walks toward me, tossing the remaining plastic toy in his hands to the couch and wraps his arms around me, patting hard between my shoulder blades.

"Yeah, of course. It's good to see you man. It's been a long time. Come on downstairs."

We sit on a large sectional in a basement decorated with some of the coolest music memorabilia I've ever seen. One wall at the back corner is dedicated entirely to Consistently Inconsistent. Awards and vinyl albums cover the area. Most of the pieces are from the time when he was with us but, to my surprise, there are a few selections from after his departure.

"How's Xander?" He walks over to a refrigerator at the corner of the room. "I know it's been a while since his accident but everything with that went well? And he's married now, yeah?"

He walks back across the room and hands me a can of diet soda. At first, I'm surprised. I haven't seen Julian drink anything except hard liquor since high school but then I put it all together.

He's sober.

"Yeah, Xander is doing great. He and Natalie are happy. His injuries were scary but he's healing fine." My face freezes in a confused twist that I tried to hide but failed.

"What?" He cracks the tab on his can.

"I'm surprised you care, honestly. I thought you and Xander hated each other."

"He hates me, and I don't blame him." He shrugs and investigates the soda can — anything to not have to look at me. "He's earned that right, I think. What I did to him...man, I'd hate me too. I did, for a long time. Hated what I had become. I can't hate Xander, though, even if I wanted to. This was my fault."

"You seem to be doing well, though." I tap my fingers against the can. "You never tried to get back into music?"

"I still play — mostly for fun or for my son but never anything professional. Sobriety is something I have to work at every single day and I just don't know that I'm ready to put myself back into that lifestyle. Too much room to make mistakes and not enough people holding me accountable."

"I feel you there." I nod as I say the words.

"Jeez, Blake." Julian connects some dots, just the wrong ones. "Tell me you're not fucking using —"

"No, no." I rush the words, but then think twice on it. "I got caught up in gambling issues that spun out of control, and I can't seem to find my way out of this hole I'm digging. You don't owe me a damn thing, but here I find myself with everything crashing down around me, not in the band and I didn't know where else to go."

"What the *hell* do you mean 'not in the band'?"

"I quit." There's this spot in my stomach that hurts every time I think of my exit, a sharp pain where I figuratively twist the handle of the knife I stabbed myself in the gut with.

"All right then, Mathews." He tosses his empty can into a nearby bin. "Take it from the top. I want to know everything."

* * * *

Then

Looking back on it, our days of touring as an opener went by in a blink. Or, more accurately, a blur of excellent performances and drunken post show parties. Before long, we were the headliner and had openers of our own.

It's true what they say. Time flies when you're having fun.

"What's with the candle?" Xander is kicked back in a hotel lobby chair with his feet on the table and his sunglasses over his eyes. A cake sits in front of us, a large number eight aglow at its center.

"That's the number eight," Cooper says in a voice that gives me *Sesame Street* flashbacks. Xander rolls his eyes.

"I know what it is. Why is it there?"

"You guys are the least fun people I've ever worked with." Cooper doesn't hide his annoyance that he's not getting the enthusiastic response he'd hoped for.

"We're the only people you've ever worked with," Xander says. Cooper pushes Xander's boots off the table.

"It's been eight years to the night since Kelly got us on stage with Regrets Only." My heart clenches at the thought of her. How long has it been since I had seen her? And then I realize, the candle on the cake says it all.

Eight years. Eight years since I left town—and apart from shows there, I never looked back. I left it all in the rearview…including her.

"Thank you, Mathews. You get the first piece," Cooper says, but Xander reaches forward and intercepts the plate before I can get it. The guys laugh and Cooper continues to cut. "Anyone seen Julian? He should be here." He counts out pieces and plates.

Everyone knows the phrase 'sex, drugs and rock and roll'. For us, it's not comprehensive—not one size fits all. Xander, Julian and I quickly fell into one category or another, personifying each one of the words. Xander is the rock and roll. He's all performance, all the time, even off stage—*especially* off stage. He's edgy from the outside in and confidence drips from his pores. Anyone or anything could be his at any time and he knows it, but it's mostly alcohol he chooses to keep for company.

For me? It's sex. I know the kind of reputation I've developed, and I understand the risk. But something about going from the boy who couldn't even get the attention of *one* girl to the man who can have any number of them is alluring in a way that leaves me calling numbers I swore I'd never call and falling into hotel beds I had no intention of sleeping in.

And there's Julian. He's the 'drugs' of the equation. It wasn't always this way and I'm not sure what changed. But somewhere down the line he took a ride and enjoyed the destination too much.

I go off looking for Julian so he can be a part of Cooper's celebration, more for Cooper's benefit than Julian's. A loud laugh echoes from behind the backstage doors, exactly where we left him *hours* ago.

He looks at me as I enter and gives me a hard nod to acknowledge my presence among the strangers he sits between, but my walking in isn't enough to deter him from leaning forward and snorting a line off the filthy backroom table.

"Julian." I instinctively wipe my nose. Just watching him do that makes my nostrils itch. "Let's go."

"Why don't you come join us, Blake? Come on. It's all in good fun." Julian leans back into the couch.

"I'm good, thanks. We need to go," I say, my best Cooper impression in full effect.

"I'll meet you at the hotel." His voice is an eternity away, saying anything he can to get rid of me.

And I leave. My stomach flips relentlessly the entire walk back to the hotel. I tear myself apart for leaving him there, for not fighting harder—but what was I supposed to do?

I cover for him, though my conscience suggests otherwise. Even though I head back to the celebration and am in the hotel lobby with Cooper and the guys, my head is still backstage and I'm kicking myself for letting Julian stay behind. Even once I'm in the room, I pace back and forth, waiting for him to make a safe return.

"Where have you been?" I snap at him when he finally makes it back to our room in the early morning hours. I'm exhausted, having waited for him to come back or for Cooper to come looking for him. He, on the other hand, looks ready to go, like he could run a marathon if I challenged him to it.

"You need to relax." He's as chipper as he ever has been. "I'm here. I'm ready to go."

"I'm not coming to look for you next time. If you stay out all night and the bus leaves without you, you're on your own." I do want to help him, but I can't help someone who doesn't want to be helped.

I shove my few belongings into a duffel bag and throw it over my shoulder.

"Mathews," he says, "look at me." I turn toward him and he puts his hands on my shoulders and positions his face only a few inches from my own. "I'm good, okay? It's called *recreational* for a reason. If it makes you feel any better, tonight after the show we will hang out. Sober. Don't make this a bigger thing than it needs to be."

There was a long while—years, even—since that night backstage with the cocaine where he mastered living two different lives. He showed up to rehearsals and media stints. He was never late and never missed a show. But I knew that behind closed doors he was giving in to an addiction he thought he was hiding from us. 'Recreational' became every night, every night became twice a day, twice a day became every few hours and so on and so forth until his habit grew too big for the cage he was keeping it in. The eight on the candle turned to a ten, but one of us celebrated that milestone harder than the rest of us did.

I couldn't find him anywhere. I looked at the venue, backstage, the bus and the hotel room. He wasn't answering his phone and he didn't show up to the post-show meeting, dinner or Cooper's ten-year toast. He didn't even come on stage for the encore with us. His need for a hit of whatever narcotic was pumping through his system had taken over his ability to play even one more song.

I check a local bar, scanning the area and looking down the row of bar stools to see if he's on one but he's not. At the end of the bar, a hat rests on the bar top over an empty stool. The hat belongs to Julian and I gather the stool does too.

Jogging toward the men's room, I push past a few groups of people and make my way there then throw the door open, but the area is vacant. I turn around, leaning against the jamb, and run a hand through my hair. That's when I notice a group of girls leaning into the women's room, giggling at each other and taking pictures with a small digital camera.

As casually as I can muster, I walk by and say, "Everything okay?"

The girl closest to me turns around and laughs. "Just some guy passed out in the women's room," she says. "They can only see his legs sticking out from the stall. They didn't get close enough to recognize him.

"Why don't you go get a drink and I'll take care of him." The girls agree and step aside.

"Some guys just can't hold their liquor," one of the girls adds as the door swings shut.

Fortunately for them, they missed the tourniquet at his biceps and the needle sticking out of his arm.

Over the years that made up my lifetime I had seen some harrowing things, but none that slapped me in the face quite like that event did. In those seconds where time stood still, having to make decisions on how best to help him and who to call next, I realized that life is short and this career is shorter. If we didn't start making better decisions, we wouldn't have either.

They were words we should all live by, but especially Julian. He learned and he understood. He stopped doing drugs.

For about two and a half months.

* * * *

Now

Julian walks down the stairs to the basement and knocks lightly on the wall. I sit up and rub the sleep from my eyes as he takes the seat next to me, moving the large comforter aside. He hands me a steaming cup of coffee.

"Thanks again for letting me crash here," I say through a yawn.

"You don't have to keep thanking me. I told you that yesterday and the day before and the day before that..." he says, but I do. I stopped corresponding with Julian the moment I figured out Mariah had been cheating on Xander with him, then rolled in here like I owned the place. That was not exactly fair to Julian or Mariah.

"But, Blake, man, you *have* to find a way back to the music. Honestly, fuck Victor—and fuck you too for putting the guys through this. C'mon... You're supposed to be the good one."

"I think that's a title reserved for Dom and Theo. They've never made waves, not even once."

"You know what I mean. You were the closest person to my addiction other than me. You were there every step of the way—the first person to know about it, the first person to try to get me help. Now this? I don't have a chance at getting back to where I was because of decisions I made when I let the problem take a hold of me instead of taking a hold of it. But you do. Take it from me, Blake. You don't want to spend your life in a basement looking at pictures of what might have been. You want to be *in* the pictures."

Mariah walks down the stairs as he talks to me with their son, Gabriel, on her hip.

"How did you finally stop? What was it that finally turned you around and set you back on track?"

"Hitting rock bottom, believe it or not, wasn't enough for me." Mariah sits next to him and he takes Gabriel from her then smiles as he looks at him. "Then I found out I was going to be a dad. Losing everything wasn't what made me realize I needed to change but gaining everything? That was a game changer. Instead of fixating on everything I had lost, I realized what I could have. These two weren't worth losing."

There's a loud knock on the door upstairs, reminding me there is still a world outside of this one.

"Come in," Mariah yells and I sip my coffee. Footsteps hit the top step then the next one, all the way until the owner of the heavy, uneven steps comes into view and Xander stands at the bottom of the stairs.

"You called him?" I look at Julian, feeling somewhat betrayed but mostly grateful. Julian shakes his head.

"I did," Mariah says. "It's time for you to go home, Blake. You are always welcome to visit, but you can't hide here. Time to face the music."

I stand and toss the corner of the blanket aside, leaving my coffee cup on the table and make the walk toward Xander. He opens his arms and I wrap mine around him. He slaps me hard on the back then grabs a fistful of my shirt in his hand. "I could kill you for what you've put us through these last few days, you know that?"

"I know." I slap him on the back twice as hard.

Julian and Mariah join us at the center of the room.

"Thank you both," Xander says as we part, and to my surprise — everyone's surprise — sticks out a hand and Julian takes it in a hard shake. Whatever troubled waters used to flow between them, it seems their current happiness has bridged it.

In the end, regardless of how we all got here, they both got everything they ever wanted — and that's all that really matters.

Chapter Twenty-Five

Xander and I take the sidewalks from Julian's house to nowhere in particular. We walk in silence. He doesn't ask how I am, what my plan is or what I'm thinking. He doesn't ask about Julian or Mariah. He doesn't lecture or berate me. Truthfully, I think he just doesn't want to leave me alone long enough for me to take off again.

I'm grateful that he's not making me talk, but in a distant mind, I have to wonder what he thinks of me right now — what they all think of me right now.

"How's Kelly?" I finally say, chipping away at the ice between Xander and me.

"Worried sick about you." Smoke leaves his mouth and nostrils as he speaks through a draw of a cigarette. "Literally sick. Natalie's been staying with her at your place because Kelly's in rough shape. She doesn't know what to make of all this."

"Neither do I. I should get back, go see her." I'm mostly thinking out loud.

"Have you thought about what your next step is, Blake? I mean, there are programs for this kind of stuff. You can take a break from the band, take some time off and come back when you've got your shit together."

"I'm not part of the band anymore, Xander. Remember?"

"Yeah, but you—"

"No, I can't," I cut him off. My thoughts come spraying out like a broken hydrant, finally able to burst out some of the thoughts I've had capped off. "I didn't leave because of what Cooper said. I was thinking on it anyway. I screwed up. I gambled away a dollar amount I'm not proud of, but I can get it back if I walk away from Consistently Inconsistent. That's my penalty. I have to do that to make everything else right and to restore what I've lost to get Kelly The Rock Room..." I'm spiraling. Despite the abundance of fresh air, I find it hard to breathe.

His gaze finds mine and he scratches his jaw. "Blake." He closes his eyes for a second, deciding how he's going to deliver whatever blow rests in his hands. "Victor told Stasia if she signed with MLA records that all your losses would be restored. Your spot in the band would still be yours, if you want it."

"Wh-why did he do that?" I stutter through the words. None of this made sense before, and it certainly doesn't now. "Why would Victor agree to that?"

"Victor owns MLA records." His words hit me like I'm standing in the middle of a road and a semi crashes into me.

"But Stasia... Her father..." And I see it. The entire picture. I remember the day she came into the studio and the guys recognized her last name right away. She said her father owned it. She has told me countless times that her father tried to keep her to himself, to his label only, and that she avoided it. She's been very forthcoming about her father's power and that his weakness was gambling. Me? I never put any of it together. I was so focused on the money and the game that I never once thought to investigate who I was playing with. My stomach rolls. I feel sick. The earth spins for a second as I forget how to breathe.

I inhale deeply and realize that every time I take one step forward, I take so many more back. I admitted I have a problem. I sought out help. I am on my way back to my house. And yet, somehow, I just set myself back. More importantly, I set Stasia back.

"This is what he wanted all along, Blake. In the end, he just wanted her to sign under him."

"We have to go there." My voice echoes through the open city air. "We can't let her do that." I step past him and he grabs my arm.

"Blake." His voice falls into a sympathetic whisper. "It's already done. She already signed with MLA."

• • • •

Then

Boxes are scattered over every square inch of Xander's and my room in his mom's house. Our mom, I guess since I've officially started to call Debbie 'Mom' without hesitation.

Xander sits on the end of his bed with his head in his hand. "It's going to be weird, us not living together. We've been under the same roof for so many years."

"Xander, we are going to record together. We are going to tour together. We are going to be together so often that we don't need to live together."

The truth is, we haven't spent a night in this house in… I don't know how long. We found a small condo to rent as soon as we could afford one. All five of us, together under one roof. This time, though, things are more official, Debbie is selling the house. I put a down payment on a smaller house outside the city, but I have plans for it. I'm going to make it exactly the home I had always dreamed of. I don't need a mansion. Anything with four walls and a solid roof is a dream-come-true to me.

Xander went the opposite way. He bought out an apartment with a helluva view and top-of-the-line everything in a stupid-expensive area. That was what he wanted, though.

"We did good, man." He puts one foot on one of my already-secured boxes. It's just weird to really be leaving this time. Moving out all this old stuff we haven't thought about in years makes it real."

I nod, thinking back on all the memories, good and bad, that we had here. Climbing through the windows, the home-cooked meals, my test papers on the refrigerator and my mother showing up at Christmas one year.

Having a family — having a sibling — was something I always dreamed of. As a kid, family is what I wanted more than anything and now I have it. Plenty of it. The guys, Debbie and Cooper. I'm blessed, and I do appreciate everything they've done, but now I want to find out who Blake Mathews can be when he's not being supported by someone else.

"This just feels right, Xander," I say, "places to call our own, our own spaces."

"Actually, Julian is moving into the apartment." He rubs his hand at the back of his neck.

"Oh," I whisper. I don't care what Julian and Xander do. They are more than welcome to share a living space if that's what they please. I just worry about them together. Xander is impressionable, whether he will admit it or not. I worry about what kinds of things Julian will put him up to and what kind of trouble they will get themselves in. On the other hand, when Julian is maintaining his sobriety, Xander is not the person I want him around. The times when Julian is doing good, his worst vice is caffeine. He doesn't even smoke cigarettes. Xander's whiskey-with-every-meal state of mind is sure to give Julian plenty of opportunity to misstep.

Maybe, somewhere deep down, there's a little bit of jealousy too. I fear missing out or being replaced. I know living by myself is a good move for me, but I wonder if the bond they create will overpower the ones I've made with either of them.

Xander and I have become brothers in every sense of the word, but Julian and I on any given performance night share an on-stage bond, a mid-show magic that can't be reproduced. It's electric, the show we put on behind Xander as he unwinds at the front of the stage. After the show, Julian and I can be found making plans together in whatever city we are in at the time.

Xander thinks it's because of this special bond he doesn't understand. He doesn't know I have personally sworn myself to babysitting Julian around the clock. I've known every time he's slipped up, I've sat through meetings and I've talked him down when he's been about to break. The whole band doesn't need to know. Cooper doesn't need to know. But someone needed to constantly be in his corner. It was me.

Now I guess it's Xander's turn.

* * * *

Now

The penthouse is almost silent. The footsteps overhead sound close, then far, then close again, the beat of the sounds matching the distinct path of someone pacing. Otherwise, nothing — no music, no conversation. When I knocked on the door, it opened, not fully closed by the last person to use it. Isabella didn't meet me in the usual way she does — like she has nothing better to do but sit at that door like a welcome mat, waiting to greet the people who walk all over it.

My steps feel loud and uneven against the spiral staircase. The harder I try to quiet them, the louder I am. I'm smart enough to know I shouldn't have come here uninvited, but there has to be a way to get Stasia away from her father. This is the last thing she wanted. MLA was never part of her plan. She took so many steps to get out from under Victor's watchful eye and now, thanks to me, she's in his grasp.

Voices carry down the hall from behind the study's large doors, Victor's first then a woman's. Maybe Isabella's, but it's too hushed to tell.

"All is well that ends well. Am I right?" A haughty brag laces his words.

"No. This is not what we discussed at *all*," the woman says.

She's out of view but I can see Victor from where I stand. His body is perfectly visible through the opening in the door.

"I don't know what your goal was, dear" — he flicks open a triple-jet lighter and burns the end of his cigar — "but mine was to get Stasia back on the label she was born to be on. This was about Stasia and only Stasia. I did what I had to do to bring her home." His cigar aroma fills the hallway as he speaks.

"And what about Blake?" she snaps in a low whisper, but there is bite in her words. My heart beats so hard it makes their words hard to hear.

"What *about* Blake? Blake was a pawn. He played the part perfectly, and he didn't even know he was doing it."

There's a long pause with no rebuttal from the other person. *A pawn?* Now that I've heard my name, I inch closer, back against the wall, tip toeing toward the lion's den rather than running from it. Victor sighs loudly. He leans into his desk, and his head falls forward in frustration.

"Stasia sought out Varro and Mathews in that bar. They performed together. The video went viral. I *know* Gary Cooper. I've known him since before he snaked Consistently Inconsistent from MLA the first time around. I knew his next play would be to get her on the track. He's been wanting to replace Julian Young for years and he thought she was his ticket. But Stasia is nobody's ticket but mine." Victor speaks in slow, dramatic speech, allowing the person he converses with to start putting pieces together. He doesn't know I'm standing here putting them together too.

"Ruining Blake's life was not part of the plan," she says and he laughs. She starts to lose her courteous demeanor, a fire starting under her words. "You know no one has even *heard* from him in days?"

I will myself to walk away, to not listen to anymore, but the weight of their words paired with my stupidity and regret restrains me in place.

"Blake was never in danger of any *real* harm," Victor says, and my mouth goes dry. I can't move, can't swallow, can't think. Because I just figured out who the other voice belongs to.

"This, if you recall, was *your* idea, Sharon. You sent Isabella to him, and you instructed her to extend an invitation to my tables. You keep that in mind the next time you come in here and talk to me like this."

Victor walks around the desk and she steps into view. He places his hands on her arms and my stomach knots, threatening to empty its contents all over Victor's hardwood hallways. "Everything he lost has been returned. Stasia is in a recording studio where she belongs. Blake's debts have been settled and so have yours. Can't we just be happy? Why don't you pour us a glass of something expensive and we will toast to a job well done?"

My mind is on every planet except this one, stretched too thin over spiraling thoughts of my mother, Victor, their deal, Stasia and how I somehow tied it all together. Making every necessary turn to complete the walk from the penthouse to my own home, I arrive in my driveway at the end of a journey I don't remember taking.

Leaving the penthouse had been a painful decision. In a way I wanted to bust through those doors and demand answers to the questions that I have. But was it true? Had the reset button been pushed? If I have a chance at a clean slate then there's no place I'd rather be than right here, all questions aside.

My feet are planted firmly in the grass at the edge of the driveway. From where I stand, I can see Kelly pacing back and forth in the kitchen. She dries a dish and opens a cabinet, takes a sip of coffee and tucks a loose strand of hair behind her ear. She's *absolute* — always where I need her to be and always the light in the darkest places.

She stands in front of sink, the window above it framing her like a picture. For a second she pauses, stares into the drain and cries. Tears drip down her face and into the sink. I lean forward, take a tiny pebble from the driveway and lob it at the window. She looks up at the sound of the ping and her eyes meet mine.

I smile and wave a light flick of the wrist. She presses her hand over her mouth and sobs into it. My feet sink into the dirt beneath the grass as I start the walk toward the house. She slams the porch door open and runs outside, jumping up and wrapping her arms and legs around me until we're both falling into the grass in a heap of limbs and tears and relief.

Chapter Twenty-Six

At the very deepest layer of myself, I know that I am in love with her and I always have been. She is brilliant, resilient, patient, beautiful and a perfect combination of sassy and sweet. When I look at her, everything in me unravels. I let go of all my insecurities and the history I carry around and melt into her. She's the only one who can make me feel like everything is going to be okay.

I am in love with her. And that's apparently enough for her.

But it shouldn't be.

We talked for hours — about Victor, about Stasia, about the band and Julian, about her. Me. Us. If there still even is an *us.*

We sit across from each other at the kitchen table. She has one hand laced in mine while using the other to wipe the tears that won't stop falling. We both took the chance to say our selected versions of 'I missed you' and 'I'm so glad your safe' then we brought all the catching up and stories to a close.

Including ours.

* * * *

"Where do you think you'll go this time?" I ask, sitting on the bed with my head in my hands as she throws a few belongings in a bag.

"My parents, just for a few days. It's been a while. I'll visit with them and give Natalie and Xander a break from me then I don't know." She mumbles her words and keeps her eyes fixed on the bag in front of her.

"Come here." My voice is quiet. She steps toward me and sits on the bed. I press my lips to her hairline and wrap my arms around her. "I made you a promise once a lot of years ago. Do you remember what it was?"

She looks up at me, her lashes sprinkled with tears like dew on grass, and she thinks back.

"I do." Her lips break into a hint of a smile with that same shimmer of hope from that day in front of the school. "I told you that you weren't what I needed, and you said you would be."

"I will be." I repeat. "Someday, Kelly. I'll be what you need. You'll see."

She bites her bottom lip as tears stream down her face. "Whatever it is you're looking for, Blake, I hope you find it."

"Just me, mostly. Just trying to figure out who I am and who I'm going to be. I need to get myself back together and be a person I can be proud of so I can be someone you can be proud of too."

It's agonizing, separating from each other, and I do intend to find my way back to her, but she deserves to float through her life and not be weighed down by mine. For me, there is work to be done. I have to take care of myself now if there is ever a hope of taking care of her in the future.

She reaches the doorway and turns around to give me one last, longing look over her shoulder. "Hey, Blake?" My gaze glides up to find hers.

"I'm giving you space because I think it's what you need, and I understand why you are doing what you are doing. But if you need someone, if you need support or strength, I'm still in your corner. I'm going to help you find that hidden piece of you that you're searching for."

"I know." I nod. Half of me wishes she would drop her bags and run to me, but the other half wishes she would go and not look back. I just want a quick exit so as not to prolong the pain.

The latter wish is granted.

* * * *

There isn't one other patron in the small hole-in-the-wall bar down the street from my house. I like it that way—just me and Bartender Terry one-on-one like a therapy session but with hard liquor and outdated jukebox selections.

"Where's your better-looking half tonight?" Terry wipes a glass with a towel. I'm assuming he means Kelly, but, knowing Terry, there's a chance he means Xander.

Either way I shrug my shoulders and take the last sip of my drink. Terry refills it as soon as it hits the bar top. Just another benefit of being the only customer in here.

The door opens and a gust of cold air fills the bar area. Looks like I'll have some competition for Terry's attention and the jukebox selection after all.

"Good evening." I don't have to look up to know who the voice belongs to. "I'll have what he's having — and keep them coming. I have a feeling we're going to need them."

There are dozens of empty stools but she takes the one next to me.

"Blake." She shimmies out of her coat.

"Sharon." I stare ahead and a swell of pride rises in me at my response. She lost her title of anything resembling 'mom' or 'mother' years ago.

She beams a smile at Terry as he slides filled glasses across the bar.

"Of all the gin joints in all the towns..." I scoff into my drink and shake my head.

"Not a coincidence," she admits. "I wanted to talk to you. I need a moment to explain something...a few things."

"I don't have that kind of time," I mumble.

There's a long while where we say nothing. We sit in the same bar on neighboring barstools, but we're miles apart.

Eventually, the song on the jukebox fades out and she fills the void.

"There's almost nothing more diminishing than realizing your son hates you." She rotates the glass on the bar top. "Not just anger or resentment but real, passionate hatred."

My gaze finds the dart board at the opposite wall. I stare at the red of the bullseye, focusing my eyes on the center of the board but I stay tuned in to what she's saying.

"For me it was the first time I saw you perform. You were so brilliant, so much talent. Of course, you didn't know I was there. We hadn't spoken in years. Then you said it. *'This one is for my mother'.* My heart swelled, Blake. For a few seconds there was hope for us. Then you and Xander took turns singing a song that was meant to tear me apart—and you succeeded. That was the moment I knew you truly didn't want anything to do with me."

For years I have wondered if she has ever seen my shows—and now I know. I'm surprised.

"So, since you can't possibly hate me more than you already do, I'd like to come clean about something."

I signal to Terry for my next drink and he nods in response. She can talk all night. There is almost nothing she could say that would interest me.

"I borrowed a large sum of money from Victor. I was struggling, and I had nowhere else to turn. When I couldn't repay it on time or by my first extension or even my second, Victor told me to get creative, to find a way to get him his money. He didn't care where it came from. I was in the same bar as you a few months back—the night Isabella brought you to the penthouse."

This captures my ear, though I do my best to keep my attention elsewhere, not letting her know she has any part of me interested in her stories and lies.

"I watched as you kept pouring more and more money into that cup. I watched the sweat bead across your brow when you thought about saying no. That's when I figured out that you were more like me than I thought. I knew you couldn't walk away. You put more money in than the initial pot was even worth, and you didn't even know it."

My neck grows hot. My stomach twists in disgust, both at her and myself.

"I couldn't very well just ask you for the money, Blake. I mean, c'mon. A guy that writes that harsh of a song about his own mother isn't going to loan her anything. Victor told me to invite you to his table. But that's where things got sticky. He was only supposed to run up your losses to equal mine, Blake. What he won from you was supposed to offset what he'd loaned me. It was a sure thing. It's not like you were going to beat him."

"I did beat him." I flick my now-empty glass away from me.

"Please, Blake, don't be silly. He let you win. He built up your confidence playing with smaller sums so you'd feel like you could keep up with the higher amounts. You won because he allowed you to. You never beat him. He played you over and over again."

I turn toward her, my eyes on hers, and completely invested myself in where she is going at this point.

"I didn't know he had a second agenda, Blake. That's the truth. I didn't know he was going to cut deals with you the way he did. You see, he never actually wanted you to leave the band—"

"He wanted Stasia to leave the band," I say with a nod. Her eyes widen in shock that I already knew the ending to her saga. "Yeah, I was at the penthouse for your little heart-to-heart with Victor. He got what he wanted. Stasia signed. I'm trying to piece my own damn life back together now, so why the *hell* are you here?"

"I think there is a way to get Stasia out of her contract with MLA and back with Consistently

Inconsistent." Her voice is adamant, steadfast — like she means it this time.

My muscles tense at the sound of Stasia's name coming off her tongue. I don't want her meddling with any of my friends' lives — Stasia's, Xander's, Kelly's. The farther away from them she stays, the better. My shoulders rise and fall with each inhale and exhale. My voice grows loud enough that Terry doesn't have to strain to eavesdrop anymore.

"Why do you care what happens to Stasia? Is this your good deed that's going to make me change my mind about you? Your grasp at redemption? Your last-ditch effort at having a relationship with your child?"

She looks at me intently — almost *through* me — before she speaks again.

"It's my last effort to have a relationship with both of my children."

It doesn't make sense at first, but all at once her words send me back in time to where I'm sitting on the top of the stairs listening to an argument I didn't understand at the time, but it makes all the sense in the world now.

At the time I was so young — maybe five or six — and the memories are hazy, but there is something about hearing your mother's voice after a year without it that you don't forget. I had adjusted to life with my father when it had been just the two of us. I thought I'd never see her again. When I heard the sound of her voice, I thought things were changing. To me, her return could only be good. We could be a family. There was no reason for me to search for the bad side of having my mother back. I was naïve. I got to the top of the stairs, prepared to fly down them and into her arms, but her voice turned from the one I remembered to a harrowed shout. My father yelled in return. He'd never raised his voice. He wasn't that kind of man.

"You can't possibly think things can just go back to the way they were now, Sharon?" he had screamed. I still believe that he yelled so he wouldn't cry. He loved her. He loved me. "You've destroyed this family. I gave you everything."

"I know. I know that. And I know I've already asked for too much –" she cried, but he cut her off.

"No. Nothing more. I did my part. I took you in when you had nowhere else to go. I gave you plenty of chances to turn your life around and you went back to him. Again. So go be with him then. Obviously, that's what you want." His voice was quiet, serious. She fell silent, torn between two men who couldn't be any more opposite of each other, but my mother? Well, she can't admit defeat. She can't lose a fight.

"If you kick me out, my son is coming with me." My mother's voice had echoed from their room up the stairs where I sat and listened to my life fall apart. We'd spent an entire year just us and years as a family before that and he let me go without saying a word.

I've wondered for twenty-five years why he didn't fight for me and why he didn't want to keep me with him instead of sending me away with her.

I was never his to fight for.

The realization sends me out of my head and tumbling back into the bar, but I still don't know what to make of it or what to say. I stand and exit the bar leaving my mother behind me.

"Blake." She grabs my arm but I shake free of her grasp and stomp to the door, throwing it open with my body. I scream into the open outside air. My frustration echoes through the street and draws attention from bystanders outside the neighboring establishments. The bar door opens and she joins me on the sidewalk. I have so many questions and she is the only one who knows the answers. I want to leave her behind — for real, this time. I want to walk away and never look back, but I can't. I'm still tied to her in the worst way, held captive by the loose-end-ridden saga that is my life.

"He doesn't know, does he?" My voice quiets. "Victor doesn't know he's my father?"

"No, he doesn't," she says. "I was already pregnant when I met Campbell. He was so kind, so sweet. He knew I was pregnant but he didn't care. He loved us both — me and you — from the start. I tried to give you a better life. I tried to keep you away from this area and Victor because I knew this wasn't a life for you. At the time I was making good choices, the best choices I could for you. Fast forward, a few years later, I was messing up again. I was chasing an adrenaline rush I couldn't find anywhere else. I came back to Victor. I left you behind because, at the time, I cared more about catering to Victor and being the girl on his arm than I cared about you." Her voice doesn't waver, and she doesn't try to sugarcoat it.

"Victor knew I had a son but not for so many years that he ever did the math — or didn't care to. I tried to have both worlds. I tried to go back for you and be here for Stasia and in trying to have both I ended up with neither, digging a hole I couldn't get out of. It was only recently that I started reconnecting with Victor, but he's made it clear that Stasia isn't to know who I am. That's fine. He has his secrets, and I have mine."

"I don't want him to know." I swallow hard. "I don't want anything to do with him."

I know I want you to take my advice." Her voice is low, serious. Her teeth clench as she gives her warning. "Stay as far away from him as you can, Blake."

"So" — I run my hand through my hair — "how do we get Stasia away from him?"

"You stay out of that, Blake. I'll take care of it. It's about time I do something right for you and your sister."

My sister.

The words sound odd being spoken out loud. Stasia and I get along so well that I've kind of thought of her like a sister all along, but the reality of it is that I have something I've always wanted — someone in my life related to me by blood.

"Promise me, Blake," My mother says. "Let me get some things sorted out and don't do anything involving Victor or Stasia until I say so."

"I promise." I'm hopeful that this is the time she chooses to stay true to her word.

Chapter Twenty-Seven

Xander and I sit on his balcony, screwing around with old acoustic guitars in between sips of an even older whiskey. They're throwback times like nothing has changed, only everything has changed.

"Where'd she go?" Xander asks with his pick between his teeth while turning the pegs on the guitar to tune it.

"Her parents', I think." I pluck a few notes and shrug. "I don't know. Trying not to think about it."

"Doesn't sound like you did too much *thinking about it* in the first place." His words are snappy, mixed with sarcasm and wit.

"Space was a good move, Xander. I have a lot to figure out. Honestly, she deserves so much better than what I have to offer right now. I just want her to be happy."

"She would be happy if you would talk to her. Let her help you. That's what she wants."

I am trying to do right by her. A break from me is a good move."

"For *her*." Xander nods as he draws out the words. "I'm going to say this one time, Blake, then we can move on. Kelly isn't the kind of girl you make decisions for. If she wanted space from you, she would have taken it her damn self. She was at your house when you got home because she realized she *wanted* to be with you and to be there *for* you. If you need space for *you*, then take it. But don't you dare use Kelly as an excuse. She would have stayed if you'd asked her."

Xander Varro ladies and gentlemen. Always with the logical approach.

"Have you thought about what you're going to say to Cooper yet?" He plucks a few chords on the old six-string then stretches his hand and fingers. He says he's totally healed and that his injuries don't bother him anymore, but I notice the number of times per day he pauses to crack his fingers or roll out his wrist.

"Not particularly." I down the last of my drink. "You'd all probably be better off if I stand my ground and don't crawl back to Cooper."

Xander closes his eyes and drops his head back to the chair. He fake-snores a dramatic sound that echoes through the open air. I laugh and kick his chair.

"Sorry, sorry," he says, "I must have dozed off. I'm just so *tired* of you feeling sorry for yourself *all* the time." He morphs his voice from a fake yawn to an annoyed yell.

"Blake, you came from nothing—actual, literal, nothing. You didn't even have a room in the house you lived in. Your mother's psycho boyfriend used you as a human punching bag. You spent most of your life underfed and underloved, and damn it, Blake, look at this." He throws his arms in the air and looks around. "Look at where we are and where we live. Look at what we became! You didn't do any of this with your mother or Victor or anyone. *You* did this. This band came from *your* mind. I wouldn't have any of this if it weren't for you."

He leans forward and puts both his hands on my shoulders, giving me a gentle shake as he repeats the words over and over. "*You* did this. *You* did this. *You* did this. *You* did this, Blake. For all of us. The sooner you start recognizing how strong and capable you are, the better."

He stares at me with his face only inches from mine, and in those silent moments we have an entire conversation with only our eyes, but the message is loud and clear. He sits back in his chair and tosses his long hair off his face and forehead.

"Blake, here's the deal. If you're done, I'm done. That's it. If you walk away from this band, Consistently Inconsistent is over — a thing of the past." He takes a sip of his drink and places it back on the table.

"That doesn't make any sense, Xander." I slam my glass too hard on to the table.

"It makes every bit of sense, Blake. We started this thing together and we're going to finish it together, whenever that day may be." He looks at me and his dark eyes soften in a way that makes him look like the young, middle-school version of him who I met all those years ago.

"The truth is, Blake, that I *can't* do this without you. More than that, I don't want to."

* * * *

Then

The sky is a pitch dark, that odd blue-black where, when coming out of a deep sleep, you can't quite tell if it's late night or early morning. My phone vibrates against the bedside table. I ignore it and pull the covers over my head. It rings again in a persistent buzz like an angry bee that doesn't care how many times you swat it away.

So I give in.

"*What?*" I snap into the phone without bothering to look at the name or number or time.

"Blake, it's Cooper." His voice is quiet like he's choking on the tears that come with whatever he's about to say. I sit up in my bed and my breathing picks up its pace as my heart slams against my chest. "It's Xander," he says. The tears he was fighting back break through over the line.

He didn't have to say the words. Somehow, I already knew.

I don't remember forcing myself out of bed, getting dressed or making any of the decisions I made to get myself from my house to the hospital, but there I stand at the emergency room doors, telling myself this is nothing but a nightmare and willing myself to wake up, but I don't.

Everything moves in slow motion as I make my way down the tile hallways of the hospital. My feet won't move any faster, no matter how hard I will them to. The people around me are blacked out of my peripheral vision. I pay attention to nothing except my destination. Nothing or nobody around me matters.

As I turn the corner a tear-stained Jana runs at me, into me in a tackle of a hug. She collapses against my chest and sobs into it. I run my hand down the back of her head, my fingers dragging through her blanket of red-brown hair. Cooper walks up behind us with his head down and his hands in his pockets. Jana steps away, wiping under her eyes.

"How bad is it, Coop?" I swallow hard and try to maintain something resembling composure. "Is he going to be okay?"

"He totaled his motorcycle. He had his helmet on, thankfully, but his body is…ruined. I don't know. There was so much information so fast I'm not really sure what we're looking at. They said one of his hands is pretty much crushed, so I'm not sure what that means for his music —"

"I don't give a shit about the music, Cooper. I just need to know that he's going to be okay."

"Honestly, Blake, I can't answer that. I don't know. No one knows. They're taking him in for surgery now. We will know how bad this is if he makes it through that. It's touch and go." Cooper grabs my shoulder, which I'm thankful for. The force of all this information is enough to knock me to the floor.

Hours later — the longest, most excruciating minutes of our lives — the doctors tell us that surgery was successful, but the following twenty-four hours would be crucial to what happens next. For a while it was just Jana, Cooper and me, but eventually Theo and Dom join us. To try to break up the answerless hours, I wander around the hospital until I find coffee to bring back to the group. When I return, I realize I'm one cup short. To my surprise, Natalie sits by herself across the room on a couch-type seat near the windows. I hand out the steaming cups to each person then walk the length of the waiting room, handing her the one I had poured for myself.

Black makeup stains the area under her reddened eyes. She nods and reaches forward for my hand. Her grip on my palm tightens and her hand shakes with each sob. She is falling apart at the seams. I take the cup from her and place it on the table. Coffee isn't the type of comfort she's looking for. I take the open seat next to her and pull her in close to my chest and stay there with her until the black sky awakens into a pink-and-purple painting.

"I need to see him." I push my hair back off my forehead and head toward the room he's in.

"They asked us to wait," Cooper says. "You can't go in there yet."

"Watch me." I place my hand on the door handle and tiptoe into the room. The door clicks as I close it behind me. At the sight of him bandaged, bruised and hardly recognizable, I clap my hand over my mouth and take a few deep, steadying breaths. I can't lose it — not here, not now. In this moment I have to be strong enough for us both, no matter how much that is to ask of myself.

Moving the chair from the corner of the room to his bedside, I sit at the head of the bed and lean toward him, but I don't dare make any physical contact. The machines around him beep and tubes and wires flow from multiple places on his body.

"Man, Alexander." I talk only to myself but I hope — I know — he can hear me. "I need you to fight like hell because we started this together, you know? These lives we're living, we did this — and we're not done yet." I lean in close to him and keep my head inches from his ear. "You hear me, Varro? We are not done yet."

I need you, brother. I can't do any of this without you. I *won't* do it without you."

* * * *

Now

The bells on the handle ring as I push the door to Chance's open. Stasia faces away from me and Jana sits across from her. Jana smiles a wide-mouthed, teeth-showing grin and laughs at something Stasia said. I missed the joke, since the only part of Stasia I can see is her recently shaved undercut at the back of her head.

"Good morning, Blake." Jana waves to me. "Want me to get you a coffee?"

"No, you sit and relax. I'll get it myself," I say, then pick up my pace and head toward the entrance behind the counter. "It's black coffee. I mean, how hard can it be?"

"Don't you dare, Mathews!" She scoots the chair back and runs toward me, putting herself between me and the opening in the counter. She laughs as I try to fight my way through, and when we look over, Stasia is laughing too. "Go sit down," Jana adds. "I don't need you messing with my stuff."

I do as I'm told and sit across from Stasia, unsure of what to say to her or how much information I should share.

"Seems like you're feeling a little bit more yourself today." Stasia looks at me with eyes that are a mix of pissed and sympathetic. She seemingly wants to be mad at me for all my downfalls but she can't.

"Xander got through to me, I think. His methods are…relentless but successful."

She nods her head and looks out of the window at Charlie's. Jana sets my coffee down and I discretely hold up one finger. She nods, giving me some space with Stasia for a few moments.

"I wanted to talk to you about a few things." I take a sip of my coffee.

"I can't go back, Blake. I know that it sucks for you guys, and it sucks for the tracks we've already recorded. It sucks we did that Miami show and now it's all over. But I don't regret what I did. Consistently Inconsistent will be fine without me, but it won't be the same without you."

"You don't have to be on that label, Stasia. There's still a hand we haven't shown yet. I don't want you working anywhere near that monster if we can help it."

Her eyes narrow as they find mine, her argument at the ready to fire from her tongue.

"He's still my father —"

"He's my father too," I snap, cutting off her words and seemingly her thoughts. Her expression falls blank. I'd rehearsed this differently. "He doesn't know it," I add, while trying to read her expression. "Say something." I'm unsure of what to do or say next. She's silent for a long time as she processes. Neither of us know what the proper response is here.

"So I found this picture once." Her voice becomes quiet and unsteady. She reaches into her purse, digs around for a minute and hands me an old, torn photo. In it a woman in a hospital bed holds a tiny pink bundled child while a man in a suit has his hand on her shoulder. The most noticeable thing is that he doesn't look like fathers usually look in these instances. His hand isn't placed on her shoulder in support or excitement. The way his fingers grip the new mother's shoulders and his gaze falls over the two of them is like he's claiming them—like he owns them.

"Anyway, I kept it. I had a stepmother. She got tired of my father's shit and had the good sense to leave him, but I knew she wasn't my mother. My father always said my birth mother took off and never came back. I looked at this picture and I wondered about her. For years, I wondered. Until the other day I was at the penthouse and she came in with him. I knew instantly she was the woman in this picture."

I didn't realize it before. The color of our hair and eyes, the curve of our nose. The three of us share so many features that I missed until Stasia handed me this photo.

"So that's her then?" she asks. "That's our mother?"

"That's her." I feel sorry in this moment because I have nothing good to say. I would love to tell Stasia that her mother fought for her, that she missed her and wondered about her—that it was an accident, even, or that her mother spent years searching for her without success.

But it would be a lie.

"I'm sorry." I reach out and put my hand on her forearm. "I'm sorry that finding out who your real family is isn't what you probably had envisioned. I wish you could have gotten something wonderful out of all this."

"I did." She tucks her hair behind her ear. I raise an eyebrow at her. "You're not going to make me say it, are you?"

A smile grows across my mouth as I finally understand where she's going with this.

"I did get something wonderful. I got you."

In that second, I feel a bit more whole, more complete than I have in a long time.

"So, what's your next play? You going back to Consistently Inconsistent?" She takes another sip of her coffee and raises an eyebrow over the cup.

"I'll go back if you will," I challenge her, trying to get her to see all her options.

"I can't go back. I signed a contract. You've made it perfectly clear that you disagree. At the time I thought I was doing what was right."

The indifference is evident in her voice. The love of music she once had is gone, and the light behind her eyes had dimmed.

"At the time?" I ask. "So, it's not the right move now?"

"Let me tell you a little something about our loving father." Her eyes narrow into a twisted glare. "For years he told me I would never make it. He said I just didn't have what it takes to make it big."

"You have the most raw talent of anyone I've ever worked with." My voice cuts through hers in a pointed interruption. "None of that is true."

"That's the point, Blake. He filled my head with that stuff so I couldn't see past MLA. He made it so that I thought my only real chance was getting on his label, that I didn't have a shot to explore other options. He put me in a box my *entire* life."

She takes another sip of coffee then taps her fingers on the tabletop.

"You remember the music video I showed you?"

"Yes, of course. It was incredible."

"It was." Confidence oozes out of her. "It was the best I had ever felt—about myself, about my music. I could have truly done something. That video, that single could have launched a very successful career for me. It was a small label, but they believed in me. They poured all of their resources into making sure I was seen."

"So what happened? You never told me why you didn't stay with them." I remember the video well. The whole production was unreal. She looked and sounded like a seasoned professional rather than a debut artist. Other than her showing me the video, though, I had never seen it. It doesn't seem like it made the splash it had the potential to.

"My father *bought* the label. He made them an offer they couldn't refuse and purchased the label then absorbed all its artists into MLA. The other artists on the label, of course, were thrilled. They thought they had just hit the lottery, while their best day ever was easily my worst."

"How did you get out of that?" I scratch my head and wonder how she got around her contract.

"I got lucky on that one. I was kind of...*seeing* a lawyer at the time, and he went through my contract word by word all the way down to the punctuation. He found a clause in the wording that said the artist's contracts were nontransferable with the sale of the company. They said we couldn't be transferred as a group. The way our contracts were written was that if the label was to fold or sell, we would have the opportunity to leave or re-sign with the new label."

"And you walked." I couldn't be prouder of her. This is a tough business. Many people would let the sure thing be their final decision. She had always stayed true to herself and never settled.

"I was the only one. Every other artist signed and allowed MLA to take over their contracts."

It's an odd feeling, realizing that as the parentless boy, I was the luckier one.

"The thing of it all is," she says, her voice fading into a distant curiosity, "with the availability of technology, accessible outlets and social media to build your own platforms the bigger labels are fading. It's part of the reason I didn't want to sign there. I've seen the numbers I thought for sure that the label would be done by now. I have no idea how he's still in that penthouse and throwing all that money around."

She shrugs and the gears in my head work overtime.

"Maybe there's something in that, Stasia. That money has to be coming from somewhere." I repeatedly place the information together but fail to come up with a whole picture.

"So," she says, "if I were to agree to following your lead on getting out of this contract, what's the master plan?"

"You'd have to ask our mother."

She smiles but hesitantly, torn between excitement and disdain.

Chapter Twenty-Eight

The rain falls hard, the drops hitting the roof of the porch in a perfectly rhythmic percussion that matches the tempo of the song I strum on my guitar. This weather tends to be my favorite. It's not something I can explain, but for years I've found myself outside on my porch anytime the sky opens up.

My guitar rests across my lap, my fingers positioned at the neck over the frets while the other strums an inconsistent pattern. The sound of tires over asphalt in the distance holds my attention for a moment, and as I listen, the sound seems to be getting closer. Kelly pulls her SUV into my driveway. Surprising, considering I didn't even know she was back in town. She pulls into her usual spot, her tires disturbing the forming puddles. She slams the door behind her as she exits. Running through the pouring rain, she comes toward me, holding her jacket wrapped tightly around her.

"Kel?" I say as she takes the stairs to the porch. "Everything okay?"

"No." Her hair is soaked and her clothing sticks to her. "Everything is *not* okay." Her voice is sharp yet broken. "I want to know something, Blake."

My mind reels, trying to figure out what I did now.

"This break...this 'taking space' thing... Are you doing this for me or for you?" She looks up at me. The tracks running down her cheeks are a mix of both rain and teardrops. "Because if it's for me, I don't want it. I don't *accept* it."

Damn it Xander

"Kelly." —I place both my hands at her upper arms and look into her eyes— "I just wanted what's best for you."

"No, you didn't. You *are* what's best for me. I love you, Blake. I loved you when we were kids and I love you now. I love who you were, and I love who you are going to be. I was recently reminded of who you and I used to be, Blake Mathews—who we were then and who we are now. I want to know who we are *going* to be. I refuse to believe this is where our story ends."

I swallow hard, unsure what to say. I didn't plan for this moment. In my lifetime, I've been used to ending up alone. I'm more accustomed to people leaving me behind than people coming back.

"I have something for you." She pulls her hand out of her coat to reveal a maroon leather-bound-type book.

Our yearbook

"I know you said you needed to find who you used to be. Maybe this is a good place to start."

"Is this yours?" I run my finger across the emblazoned cover.

"No." Her eyes find the ground for a moment, then her gaze flickers back to me. "It's yours."

"I...I thought I didn't order one or mine got lost or something."

"That's what I wanted you to think." She smiles a light grin. "But that wasn't true. I stole it. All those years ago, Blake, I felt the same way you did. I put it all in that book and then I hid it away because I was scared. I hid how I truly felt about you and hid from myself every single day for all these years...until today."

It's all here in these pages. Our whole story. The biggest parts of my life documented. And there's pictures – so many pictures. There was me playing guitar in front of the school with Xander when he was still Alexander and my name didn't matter. And later, the talent show – pictures of our nameless band, like none of the other acts even performed. Following that are photos from the guys sitting in the bleachers watching Julian's football games, us at prom, during our biography projects. Enough evidence that all the time I was noticing her, she had noticed me too.

I pull back the binding to the final page and her large, curvy handwriting covers the paper.

Blake,

I can't believe it's finally over and yet, in some ways, just beginning.

You told me that someday you'd be what I needed, but the truth is that I don't want to wait for someday. You've been what I've needed all along.

My own insecurities have gotten in the way of four years of somedays, but, better late than never, right?

I've known every side of you. I knew who you were before the band started to pick up, and I know who you are after. I've known you at your worst and at your best, and I've been swept away by both. You are two different sides to the same coin and I love them equally – two completely different versions of yourself at any given moment and both sides of you know me better than I know myself.

Someday is here. Someday is now.

Kelly

I look up over the binding of the book that has her heart pressed permanently into its faded pages.

"You really believe that?" My voice struggles under the weight of the pressure. "You really believe I can be what you need?"

"You've always been what I need. I believe that. But you need to believe it too."

I step toward her. Our bodies are so close that our hearts find each other and beat at the same pace, the same time. I rest my palms against her cheeks, wiping away the tears under her eyes with my thumbs. She pushes to her tiptoes and presses her lips to mine. The rain pours down around us, pounding against the roof above our heads – and yet it's the brightest day I've seen in weeks.

The answers aren't something I've always had, but today more and more of them are surfacing. Julian had said that, for him, losing everything wasn't enough but gaining everything pushed him to fix the parts of him that were broken.

But here with her in my arms, knowing that she's all in and there's no turning back, I understand what he means. Everything I've ever wanted has been within reach, as far back as I can remember. Gaining everything made it so that I had something meaningful to lose, but I know better than to take any chances this time.

The road ahead isn't going to be easy. There is work to be done and obstacles to shatter, but they'll be faced with support in my corner that I didn't know I had – in love, in family and in music.

For the first time in my life, I can have all three.

As we stand together weathering the storm, a second SUV pulls up. We turn to see one door open then the other and two bodies exit the back.

"Who's that Stasia is with?" Kelly whispers as they approach us with the hired car still idling at the sidewalk.

"Our mother." I look down at her as the hundreds of questions she has swirl behind her eyes. I nod my head in agreement with her astonished expression. "It's a long story."

"You must be Kelly," my mother says. "I've heard a ton about you." Kelly places her hand into my mother's outstretched palm.

"What's going on?" I hold Kelly as close to me as she will allow.

"Come with us," Stasia says as her normal, chipper self starts to resurface through all the pain and confusion of the last few days.

"Where are we going?" I say, looking at my mother for answers.

"Shut up and get in the car, Mathews!" Stasia skips through the rain back toward the hired vehicle. "You too, Kelly. It's going to be fun!"

We do as we're told and follow suit, throwing caution to the wind as we climb into the SUV set for a mystery destination led by one ally and one nemesis but hopeful for a good outcome. Or, as Stasia says, some *fun*. The tone of her words and mischief in her eyes say less fun, more revenge. I'm oddly comfortable with either outcome.

When the car pulls up to the building where Victor's penthouse is, I freeze to my seat. Going back in there is not an option for me. Kelly squeezes my hand tight and nods in an attempt to encourage me to trust the family I barely know.

We make it to the penthouse door and knock. Isabella opens the door. Her perfectly gleaming smile morphs to a mix of surprise and annoyance.

"Victor isn't here." she says, before we even ask.

"You're a liar—and you're bad at it." Stasia pushes past her.

"Isabella, darling." My mother's tone is intimidating and unwavering. "You're going to want to get as far away from this penthouse and that man as possible. Things are about to get a little complicated here, and you are not going to want to be associated with Victor Marquette when they do."

"You don't know anything about me." Isabella keeps her composure.

"Oh, sweetie, I used to *be* you. I was the *original* you. The difference is you're being given the option to walk out right now and never look back."

Isabella looks as if she will counter or strike back but comes to her senses and nods. She grabs a few belongings off the table and scurries away like prey narrowly escaping the hunter's reach.

"Isabella, where's that drink?" Victor's voice bellows from the other room as his harsh footsteps get closer. He appears in the room we're standing in and fixes his cufflinks as he walks. When he looks up to find us, his expressions match the ones Isabella wore, only his surprise turns to a third emotion...anger.

"Isn't this great, Daddy?" Stasia's voice is a dramatic mix of sarcasm and feigned excitement. "It's a family reunion!"

Victor lifts his lip in a snarl. "What have you done?" he snaps at my mother. She doesn't flinch.

"I didn't do anything, Victor. Our daughter is smart—more so than you know. She figured it out on her own. She figured all this out on her own."

"Well, Blake helped." Stasia wraps her arm in mine at the elbow. "Intelligence runs in the family."

"Right up there with music and gambling. Am I right, *Dad?*" I try to play into the script, though no one has clued me in on what we're actually doing.

His aggressive gaze flickers from me to my mother and back again. In that second, I find myself worrying about her. I said I didn't want him to know for my own protection, but in many ways, it was for her protection too.

"What is it that you people want?" Victor sits on one of the arms of the couch, folding his hands in his lap. "I can have security remove you in a matter of minutes." He spins a large gold ring around one finger.

"Oh, you wouldn't do that to me, would you?" Stasia lays the angelic act on thick. "Your little girl. Your pride and joy. Your…what was it you called me? Your *solution*."

Sweat beads on Victor's brow. He's nervous. For the first time since I'd met him, he's unable to hide behind his practiced poker face.

"Yes, that was it," she says. "You said I had what it takes to sell a record that would recoup some of MLA's losses. I thought you meant in general—less business coming in, less artists going toward traditional production on a label. But that's not what you meant, was it?"

He opens his mouth to speak but the doors burst open. Men and women in dark suits enter the penthouse and surround him.

"Victor Marquette," one of the suits says in a commanding tone. Everything happens in a blur from there. One FBI officer recites Victor's rights. Handcuffs are placed at his wrists. It almost doesn't seem real.

Words like 'criminal' and 'illegal' are thrown around, but I only catch bits and pieces as they run down the list of charges until they get to one.

Embezzlement

We follow outside and watch as they place a resentful Victor into the back of the police cruiser. Red and blue lights flash into the sky like fireworks set off at the end of a beautiful victory.

I wrap one arm around Kelly's waist and the other around Stasia's shoulder. She, admittedly, seems torn. He was terrible to her for her whole life, but he was the only parent she ever had. I'm too familiar with what it's like to be left without both—and now she has a taste too.

Chapter Twenty-Nine

Cooper sits in a chair with his feet up on the desk between us. Coming here, apologizing, asking for my spot back and promising change has left me feeling so small that I can barely see over the desk—but at the same time, I feel lighter, like I've unloaded some of the burden I have been carrying around. Painful seconds have ticked by since I strung together enough words to ask to be back in the band. My best attempt to take it all back came in mumbled apologies and long pauses as I fought myself over what to say next.

"No," Cooper says, the words cutting me down a few more inches. The world spins and my mouth falls open, but the word *no* echoes so loudly in my head that no other thought can overpower it. "You're not ready, Mathews."

"I'm making strides." My voice comes out a quieter version of its usual self.

Cooper stands and walks around the desk, sits on the front of it and crosses his arms.

Have you thought about attending meetings?" He looks at me for the first time since I walked into the room.

"Not particularly." I shrug and scratch the back of my neck.

"Sit down." Cooper turns a chair and leans over his desk, retrieving his laptop and handing it to me as I sit. Loaded on the screen is a twenty-question survey. 'Has gambling introduced problems at home?' 'Has gambling gotten in the way of work?' 'Have you gambled until the money is gone?'

I don't have to take the survey to know what the outcome will be, but I answer each question as honestly as I can and hand the computer back to Cooper. He glances over the screen and shuts it before returning it to its spot on the desk.

"Find a meeting, Mathews. Then we'll talk." He pushes himself from the desk and starts to walk away. His back is still toward me when I scrape up what's left of my courage and toss it his direction.

"You really think that's a good idea? That a meeting or group will solve more problems than it will create?" I lean forward and rest my elbows on my knees. He doesn't turn around and I don't take my eyes off the floor. Neither of us wants to see the other's eyes in these strained moments. "It only takes one person to open their mouth that I'm in that group and the media will blast it anywhere they can."

"It's supposed to be anonymous, Blake." His voice projects away from me. He takes another step forward and continues his echoing steps down the hallway.

"Supposed to be." My voice is a whisper, talking to no one else but myself.

* * * *

Performing has never bothered me. Stage fright wasn't an issue I had ever faced.

Until now.

Every eye is on me. My heart pounds in my ears.

"Just introduce yourself and tell us why you're here. We're all in this together," the leader of the group says in a calm, hypnotic voice.

"I'm Blake." That seems like a wasted effort. They all knew that already. I heard the whispers when I walked in the door. I saw the shock leave their lips. Everyone else in this room has a safety net of knowing that even if they didn't remain anonymous, for the most part, it wouldn't matter if their name was uttered in public instances. Unfortunately, that same net won't catch my name if it falls. "I have a gambling problem." The words grate over my dried throat. I look into the group and find Julian's eyes. *"Just keep your eyes on me, bud. You and me. Pretend it's a conversation with just me and you. We're the only ones here."* That's what he'd said and he's right. It's easier to talk to one person than a crowd. But it's the person directly behind him that breaks my concentration. Just past his head, my mother sits, and for just one brief moment, our eyes meet. She dips her chin and lifts it again in an encouraging nod.

The remaining attendees take turns detailing devastating stories of their own tragedies and triumphs, both in battling this addiction and overcoming it. I do my best to learn from and listen to each person, until it's my mother's turn. She is the last person to speak, and as she does, I can feel her eyes on me, but I distract myself with anything within reason — the clasp on my watch, the threads from the frays in my jeans, my loose shoelace. I close my eyes and replay my own story. Had I said too much? Had I said enough? I came here to fix myself, and though I know the time will come when I have to confront the issues between my mother and me, listening to her side of the story is not a luxury I feel she deserves at this point. I'm not there yet. Like the brochure says, *one day at a time.* Today is not that day.

"Does it get easier?" I ask Julian at the end of the meeting. My shirt sticks to my chest, slick with nervous sweat.

"Every time." He hands me a bottle of water. "You have to allow it to work for you, though. You can't show up here just because Cooper is holding your spot in the band over your head. You have to want to be here."

"Cooper's an ass." I wipe the moisture from my hands on my jeans.

"Cooper wants what's best for you." Julian shoves his hands into his pockets. "I was given the same option. Narcotics Anonymous or leave the band. I left the band and still ended up in a program. In the end, it was the best thing for me." He nods, weighing his word choice. "I just wish I'd seen it sooner."

"Thank you for being here. The last couple of weeks? Well, you made all this much more tolerable." I clap my hand at his shoulder. "You don't owe me anything. I haven't been a great friend to you, and you put all that aside to help me when I needed it. I think we've all come a long way, but your willingness to help when I didn't deserve it says a lot about where you are now verses where you have been."

It's the best I've got. My allegiance has always and will always lie with Xander. Julian broke all the unwritten band rules when he went behind Xander's back the way he did, but I suspect the sober version of Julian – the Julian we met and knew – wouldn't have done such a thing. The vices change who we are and make us unrecognizable to everyone else but mostly to ourselves.

The Julian standing in front of me is a portal to the version of him we knew pre-fame.

"You were there for me plenty, Blake. You took care of me too. You ended up in a position you didn't ask to be in time and time again. It's about time I return the favor, I think."

We stand together for a while in silence, unsure what to say. What would be too much? What wouldn't be enough? My mother approaches us at the table at the back of the room.

"Blake," she says, an oddity to her tone that indicates acquaintances but not friends – and definitely not family. We haven't worked out who we're going to be in all this or what it means for me and Stasia. At the end of the day, Debbie is my mother, and the reemergence of my birth mother isn't going to change that, but perhaps we can work toward something considered civil. "Hi, I'm Sharon." She holds a hand out to Julian and he takes it, introducing himself.

"Sharon is my mother." His eyes widen and hers light up. Amazing how six syllables can warrant so many different responses.

After some small talk, we exit the building and my mother and I stand outside. She lights a cigarette and offers me one. I take it and she lights both.

"So Stasia is meeting with MLA's lawyers today." Smoke exits her mouth and nostrils as she speaks.

"Is that so?" I hadn't thought about what would happen to MLA next. Those artists still have a home there and those employees still need work. Just because the owner is going away for a long time doesn't mean the label dissolves. "What even happened? I never really asked how we got to this point."

"Stasia was hesitant from the beginning about MLA's ability to stay afloat with the availability of technology and other options to record and market songs without the need for a major label. She felt stuck with MLA after she signed the contract. I felt stuck with Victor because I feared him. I made poor decisions—I'm not a stranger to those—but it was easier to live on his arm with money at my disposal than to owe him money and be scared of what he would do to get it."

Her voice changes from pride while talking about Stasia's intelligence to genuine hesitancy talking about Victor. A shiver runs down my spine when I think about the kind of life they had together and the things she'd endured while living under his thumb.

"Anyway, Stasia knew the money wasn't coming in as fast as it was going out—the purchases, the penthouse, the gambling. Then, you told her that money had to be coming from somewhere, and she and I put our heads together to see what we could do to find out where the cash was coming from."

The cigarette I hold burns away between my fingers, never finding its way to my lips.

He was taking that money from the MLA artists, Blake. For years and years, he was finding ways to distribute their earnings while pocketing extra percentages here and there—extra expenditures, moving money that didn't belong to him long enough that it started being profitable. The money that he gambled away, the money he initially lost to you wasn't his to gamble with. He was stealing it from people who trusted him to grow their careers, not ruin them."

I remember the day we sat at a restaurant and heard a young, determined female promise us the world and we believed her. Her pitch was so consuming, so promising. If someone hadn't stepped in and changed our direction in that moment, we would have been personally funding Victor's lavish lifestyle as well. But someone did step in. Someone had put us back on track.

Cooper.

Cooper had stepped in and changed the course of our life for the better before we had the ability to make the wrong choice. And in this second, I get it. Cooper isn't giving me a hard time to ruin my life. He's saving it...again. He's taking away my ability to make the wrong decision by making the decision for me but allowing it to seem like I'm making it for myself. Go to a program or leave the band. He knew there was only ever one option. And once again my life is headed toward the better of two options because Cooper stepped in at the right place at the right time.

"So, what happens now? Why the lawyers?" I lean my shoulder into the building and drag the lit portion of the cigarette down the bricks.

"Most of the executive people jumped shipped. No one wants to be associated with the name while it's under fire, and the rebuilding process will be strenuous. So the decisions right now lie with the family of the owner — and Stasia is all he has. He always intended for her to take it over and everyone who would have taken it over has relinquished their rights to her, whether she wants to run the company or not. She's going to take it over or it's going to sell or dissolve."

My mind tries to wrap itself around all the possible options and outcomes. Stasia is a musician. She doesn't want anything to do with the business side or logistics. She wants to make her own music, not control someone else's.

"So, we will see what she decides, I guess." My mother shrugs and flicks her dead cigarette into the bushes.

• • • •

I'll never get tired of seeing Kelly's SUV parked in the driveway when I come home. After so many weeks without it, it's a welcome sight. I open the door and kick off my boots. I'm about to call out to her but I hear voices in the dining room. I shuffle toward the sound and turn the corner to see Xander and Natalie holding hands at one side of the table, Stasia sitting at the head of the table with mountains of papers in front of her and Kelly sitting beside her, leaning in over the documents. Cooper stands behind both of them.

"What's going on?" I think back to the last time a similar group of people crowded my house as part of a disastrous intervention.

"We're figuring out the best way to keep MLA going, despite the negative spotlight it's currently in," Stasia says.

"These artists still need someone running their production and marketing," Cooper says, pushing his glasses up to his hairline.

"You're going to run MLA?" I ask Stasia with my voice stuck somewhere between confused and impressed. But at the back of my mind, I wonder if this means she won't be recording with us after all.

"Hell no." She shakes her head so drastically that her hair shifts wildly out of place. "I was never meant to be a CEO," she adds, "but I know someone who is."

I look over at Kelly and she shrugs. "This was the dream, Blake. You were going to be the famous musician. I was going to be the CEO."

"Of a huge company," I add, thinking back to our high school days where these words were just a hollow dream written on paper to help us pass a class. She pushes her chair back and walks toward me, placing her hands in mine.

"What do you think?" she asks, but her eyes say she wants this. Her heart is in it, regardless of what I say. "Cooper, Stasia and I have been going through a lot of this. We think we have the knowledge and experience to get MLA back on track — maybe even better than before."

"I know, I know." I squeeze her hands tight in mine. "But what about The Rock Room?" Kelly's home is The Rock Room. It's what she knows, and it's where she grew up. I can't imagine her letting The Rock Room fall into someone else's hands just because MLA fell into hers.

Her head falls over her shoulder to look at Xander and Natalie.

"We figured we'd keep it in the family." Xander signs as he speaks, then wraps his arm around Natalie's shoulder.

Kelly looks at me with a playful grin, her eyebrow arched, her lips curled to a proud 'we have it all figured out' expression.

"There's still a problem with your plan." I turn Kelly so I'm hugging her from behind. "I can't be a rock star if I'm not *in* the band."

My words are pointed at Cooper—but with a dull blade. He laughs as we all stare at him. Kelly presents her signature pouting lip.

"You better uphold your end of what we talked about, Mathews." Cooper shakes a finger at me. I nod and Kelly spins in my arms. She lets out a shriek before pressing her lips hard into mine. She pulls away but leaves her forehead pressed against mine, her lashes tickling the bridge of my nose.

"This was the dream." A happy tear streams down her cheek.

"I come bearing gifts," Jana's voice cuts in. She steps toward the table with a round of coffees for all. "What did I miss?" Jana walks around the table and passes out the much-needed caffeine.

"Nothing, really." Stasia chews on a pen. "Just working out some business plans. Looks like Kelly's going to run the label and Natalie's going to run The Rock Room."

"I thought you were going to stay home with the baby," Jana says and signs simultaneously, looking at Natalie. Every eye in the room darts between Natalie and Xander and Jana. Natalie laughs. Xander wipes his brow but then he laughs too.

"We hadn't actually gotten that far yet." He clears his throat.

"You're pregnant?" Kelly signs and squeals and Natalie shakes her head no, signing something back.

"Adopting." Xander signs and speaks. "We just got the call a few days ago that we've been approved to be potential parents."

"Of course you got approved," Kelly says through tears. "How could they not approve you?" She walks across the room and throws her arms around Natalie.

"We are still pretty shocked ourselves," Xander says and there's not a dry eye in the room. He looks at me, pushes his chair back and walks toward me.

I open my arms, and he steps into them. I pat between his shoulder blades. He steps back but keeps his hands on my shoulders.

"Think you can keep your shit together long enough to be a godfather someday?" Eloquently worded as always.

"One day at a time," I say, not as a cliché but truly meaning every word. These are all steps in the direction toward the lives we envisioned for ourselves, and now the only things that can get in our way are us — and only if we let ourselves.

Step by step, taking things one day at a time. The tiny, fractional progress forward to the end goal of not being my own worst enemy.

Chapter Thirty

Consistently Inconsistent hasn't topped the charts this many consecutive weeks since we started touring. Something about adding Stasia to the album brought a new sound, a brilliant dynamic that our fans can't stop listening to and keep asking for more of. As a band, we haven't worked this hard or laughed this much in a lot of years. Adding a new voice isn't necessarily an easy task, as we learn each other's styles and try to intertwine all our talents, both new and old, into something that sounds fresh, while maintaining the identity we're known for.

After months of laying tracks with Stasia, putting together new songs and rehearsing old ones to get her concert-ready, this tour was much-welcomed and highly needed.

It's been months since the last time I gambled in any form. I'm seeing more clearly these days and loving the music the way I used to, if not more so. My time is spent making new music and kicking old habits. Maybe I'll have to put in a conscious effort every single day, but the fight is worth it.

The lights stay low and Xander makes his way to the front of the stage.

"Hello, Nevada," he sings to a rambunctious crowd. "It is *hot* in Vegas!" He lifts part of his shirt and wipes his brow, and the crowd continues their wild exchange. "How about you guys start us off? Let's go, just like this." He claps an even tempo and the fans match his pace. Dom and Theo jump in, starting off a song from our second album.

Stasia, just for a moment, jumps into Xander's microphone at the front and center spot. He steps back, watching as she sings and steals his spotlight. He shakes his head then turns to the front of the stage, jumps off it and high fives the fans closest to the stage barriers. They go crazy thinking Stasia kicked Xander out of his own song. They don't need to know that it was rehearsed that way.

It's fun, the back-and-forth – *dare I say it* – sibling-style relationship we all share. I tear up the set list, just for kicks, and we allow the crowd to yell out requests, playing what we can and allowing Stasia to put her own twists on old songs we hadn't yet rehearsed with her. There are times that to us, it's a bit messy, but the crowd doesn't notice. They're too busy having a damn good time. Toward the end of performance, Xander and I do something we haven't done in ages. We sit at the front of the stage, just us two, singing slower stripped versions of our songs on acoustic guitars. I look out over the crowd and think back to our first tour, and every tour since then, and I know this is what I want to be doing for as long as fate will allow. For as long as the music is still there, I won't do anything to jeopardize it ever again.

"Great show, gentlemen," Cooper says as we exit the stage, "and lady." He claps his hands and lets everyone pass except me.

"Where are you going tonight?" He keeps his firm grip at my upper arm.

"Hotel. Pool. I don't know. I'll be fine, though, Coop. I promise."

"I think Xander mentioned they were headed to the bar and casino next door. I know this is a tough city to ask you to play in. I don't want to be setting you up for a challenge." His eyes soften to a worry.

"He'll be fine, Coop!" Stasia yells from the other side of the curtain. Cooper nods and lets me go.

The lights flash at the top of each machine. Rows and rows of sparkling icons and pictures dance at the top of the slots they're adhered to. The machines come alive, buzzing and singing each time someone wins or presses the button throwing more and more money at the machine they sit at. I stand in the hallway where the walkway around the casino meets the gambling floor. Beyond the slot machines, tables hosting Black Jack and Roulette fill the area.

For what seems like miles, it's just lights and sounds and temptation. Cooper suggested we take Vegas off the tour list, but just because I have struggled doesn't mean the Vegas fans should suffer. Besides, everyone is here. This is the last tour before Xander and Natalie open their home to a child, so we are taking full advantage. Kelly, Natalie and Jana flew in to Vegas this morning to join us for this leg of the journey. I lean into the wall and sip my drink when Kelly joins me.

"What're you doing, Mr. Mathews?" She pulls my arm over her shoulders and leans into me.

"Looking for Xander. I thought Cooper said they were coming over here after our show. Haven't seen them since."

She looks out over the machines and tables then back at me. "How are you feeling?"

"Like my luck has finally changed." I pull her into me and kiss her hairline.

"Do you want to get out of here?" She wraps her hands in mine.

"Yes," I say, not because I can't be here but because anything she has planned is a much more tempting offer.

We walk to the hotel, hand in hand, heart in heart and head to the outside area by the pool. A waterfall pours down an elaborate rock feature and joins the deep end of the water.

"Give me your phone." She positions us in front of the waterfall and takes our picture. She kisses my cheek, and I grin like a moron. It's a perfect picture.

"One more." She steps in front of me. Just when I think she'll snap the picture, she shoves me hard into the water behind us.

I pop up through the surface, laughing but feigning a threatening expression as I lunge toward the edge of the pool, ready to take her in with me. My soaked clothes weigh me down as I run up the steps from the pool to the patio. She tries to run, throwing the phone onto a nearby chair. I wrap my arms around her waist and pick her up into a cradle. She screams through her laugh and I jump in, taking her down with me. She emerges, wipes her hair away from her face and runs her hands under her eyes. Kelly reaches forward in a pounce and grabs the hem of my shirt, pulling it over my head and tossing it to the edge of the pool. I reach forward to follow suit, but as my hands find the hem of her shirt, she stops me and presses her palm against my chest.

"When... when did you do this?"

"What?" I play the ignorance card, looking down to where her fingers trace the space over where my heart beats to pretend I don't know what she's talking about.

"You filled in the Queen card." Her eyes brighten to a crystal clarity, and in them I can see my reflection and our future.

"Blake?" She looks up at me with a smile that shines brighter than all the Vegas lights combined. "Do you want to get married?"

"Right now?" I'm unsure if she's baiting me or if she's truly ready to commit to me, right here, right now, for the rest of her life.

"Right now." Her lips grow into a blinding smile.

"Yes." I've never been more sure of anything in my lifetime. She tosses her head back in an excited laugh and I wrap my arms around her, lifting her out of the water. She wraps her legs around my hips. The hotel doors open and Xander, Natalie, Jana and Stasia walk to the edge of the pool.

"Xander!" I yell, turning quickly with Kelly still against me. She laughs and clutches me tighter like I'll drop her with any too-quick motion. "I need you to come be my best man!" Every head turns toward us. Kelly loosens her grip on my neck and signs to Natalie, whose eyes immediately drip with tears of excitement.

"Let's go make this weird, makeshift family official." I bring Kelly back to her two feet against the pool floor.

"One moment, please." Xander leaves for a few moments and returns with two bottles of champagne.

"Where the hell did you get those?" I ask as he loosens the fasteners.

"It's Vegas, man," he says as if that answers the question. He shakes both bottles and tosses me one. We pop the tops at the same time, a spray of foam and champagne raining through the air over us and meeting the water. I kiss Kelly and she takes the bottle from me, drinking directly from it. Xander takes a running start and cannon balls into the pool next to us, fully clothed. Stasia, Jana and Natalie follow.

We splash and dance in the water, passing bottles back and forth, enjoying this family we have made before heading to whatever chapel we find to make us official. Though, in my eyes, no piece of paper is going to make me more hers than I already am.

We get out of the pool, our clothes dripping across the pool area. I wrap one arm around Kelly, and Natalie takes her hand. Xander and Jana join Natalie, and Stasia links her arm in my free arm. Together we walk as family members linked together for some of us by blood but mostly by choice and happenstance.

And music.

And maybe a little bit of luck.

Want to see more from this author?
Here's a taster for you to enjoy!

Consistently Inconsistent:
Three Beating Hearts
L A Tavares

Coming Spring 2022

Excerpt

Liam

Green signs with white text reflect the names of familiar streets as the tour bus flies underneath them.

Twelve pages. I think to myself as I peek at the last page number of the book I hold. Only a few exits from home and I'm a dozen pages short of finishing the story.

"Did you do it?" Theo sits down in a chair nearby and sips from a beer bottle. "Did you get through all fifty?"

"Almost." I hold up the book but keep my eyes on the text, trying to finish before we reach our destination. "I'm a bit short right now, though."

"What number is this one?" He leans forward and flicks the cover.

"Forty-eight." I shrug. "But unless I can finish this one and two more in the next fifteen minutes, I'd say I'm not reaching my goal."

"Technically." He takes another sip between words. "We've still got the Boston shows. The tour isn't over yet, so you've still got time." He winks as he stands and heads toward the back of the bus. I bury my face in the text.

As the bus pulls into our drop-off spot, my band mates holler and cheer, kicking off the usual welcome home parties they throw themselves upon arrival. They will get off this bus before it even comes to a full stop and hop from bar to bar until last call, then open the doors to their own homes, where they will continue to drink until the sun comes up, sleep the day away and not wake until we're required to be at the venue for our home shows.

We close every tour at home. Sometimes it's one show, sometimes it's three. The number of shows and the Boston venue we play at changes, but our traditions upon returning don't. They will launch our home stretch with their inhibitions off and their 'check liver light' on. Some things never change, no matter how much we've grown. My bandmates always revert back to their wild youth years the moment the tour bus wheels hit Boston's pothole-filled pavement.

"Planning on staying the night?" Xander hits me on the back of the head in an annoying but playful way as he passes me. "We've been parked for a few minutes now."

"I only have a few pages left. I'm surprised it's taken you this long, though. You're usually halfway down Boylston Street by now."

"I forgot my sunglasses. What is that, anyway?"

It's a book, Xander. Ever read one?" He smiles and shakes his head, but I can't tell if the *no* motion is sincere or sarcastic.

"I'm headed out. You sure you don't want to come?"

I'll say 'no' and he will say I'm missing out. The tour bus final scene never changes.

"You ask me that every time." I peek up at him over my glasses and the top of my book. "I'm good. I have somewhere to be."

"You say that every time." He shakes his head and puts his sunglasses on.

"It's true every time."

"You're missing out."

"You say that every time."

"It's true every time."

We laugh a light sound at our exchange. It's not the first time we've had this conversation. For as long as we're touring, it won't be the last. He turns to head off the tour bus.

"Xander?" He turns and looks at me, though his gaze is hidden behind dark lenses. "Be careful. Take care of yourself and the boys. I know I don't partake in the crazy sideshow that you guys put on when we return home, but I do care. Get everyone home in one piece."

Xander pushes his sunglasses into his in-desperate-need-of-a-cut hair. "You say that every time."

"It's true every time."

He slides his sunglasses over his eyes once more and retreats from the bus.

Alone on the silent tour bus, I finish book number forty-eight on my list and I'm not impressed. The story had so much potential. For nearly four hundred pages it was perfectly executed with many memorable parts, then the story crumbled in the last ten. I sink my head back too hard into the headrest. There are few comparable disappointments than investing yourself in a story that has a bad ending. At the same time, there's no stronger parallel to life. It has its ups and downs with good and bad sections along the way. Characters are introduced that we get attached to and some that are forgettable. It's colorful, exciting and every day is like turning a page until there are none left to turn. It ends. It's over. It will happen to every single one of us. For most of us, our final pages will be disappointing. I wish that wasn't the hard truth, but it is. Turning the final pages of one's own story or the story of someone close is always disappointing.

I order a car service on my phone then toss the book and my cell into my bag and carry it off the bus with a goodnight wave to our remaining equipment staff. My ride arrives and the driver gets out of the car to take my bag to the trunk then open the door for me. I slide into the back seat. When the driver returns, he sets his focus on the rear-view mirror.

"Consistently Inconsistent, eh?"

"Yeah," I admit in a small voice, but I'm not exactly sure what he's asking.

"I saw the patch on your bag." He puts the car into drive and pulls away from the curb. "You ever seen them live?

There it is. He's a fan. He used the patch as a gateway to start small talk about something we might have in common, yet failed to recognize he has the drummer of said band in his car. It's not the first time. If I had a dollar for every person who has asked me to take a photo of them with Xander or Blake, I could buy a small island.

It doesn't bother me. When I'm not on stage, I lead an incredibly quiet existence. I am different than my bandmates, and though they are closer than family to me, I've always been the black sheep. We are so close, yet so far apart. We live entirely different lifestyles. One of my biggest joys comes from watching Xander and Blake smile. There were so many years that they didn't. They are so full of life that it's contagious, and I'd confidently say ninety percent of my laughter is caused by them or at their expense. Theo, too—his favorite moments are ones he gets recognized *before* Xander or Blake. He keeps on about it for hours. Even after all these years, the celebrity never gets old for them.

I fade into the background, and nine times out of ten I'm okay with that. I get lost behind walls that I built. Though I don't let it bother me widely or outwardly, it does sting every once in a while, when people know the band but don't know I'm in it. Perhaps, somewhere along the way, I let myself get too quiet.

"You sure this is the address you meant to put in?" he asks with heavy skepticism as we arrive at my destination.

"Positive."

"It's dark out there, you know. And...kind of scary, don't you think?"

I smirk as I open the door. The judgment in his eyes and stillness in his body language makes it clear he's not getting out of the car.

"I'll be okay. Pop the trunk for me, if you don't mind."

I retrieve my bag then slam the trunk closed. "Have a nice night now." I wave as he speeds off. The light his headlights had provided dimmed more and more as he got farther away. The world gets darker—and more silent.

I walk the familiar path through the gate, passing a thick grouping of trees, and continue onward into the perpetual darkness that the cemetery offers. I turn down the dirt pathway that leads to my final destination, and in the distance, I can see the light of a single flickering candle that dances against the headstone. It seems the light winds have extinguished every other candle within a visible distance — but not hers. Hers dances in the dark.

I wonder for a moment who might have lit it and smile at its resilience. She would have liked the symmetry in that — surviving brilliantly, even when the odds were stacked against her, dancing when the time seemed the most inappropriate.

The headstone is heart-shaped — a choice I never agreed with but didn't get a say in. It's made of a brilliant blue-green marble that shines with a topcoat that's so clean it's reflective. Five years of rain and snow haven't taken its toll on the stone outwardly. Just under two thousand days of battling weather day in and day out and it gleams the same way it did when it had been placed. She would've liked that too. She'd also smiled and glistened, though she battled her own elements each day of her life.

Two dates — dates that are not nearly far enough apart — are carved deep into the rock. It's always been odd to me that we focus on two particular days, when the real magic and the true memories were all of the dates in between. The ones not mentioned are the times that made up her legacy and her life. There were so many of them worth publishing throughout her twenty-seven years.

The cold from the ground seeps through my jeans as I sit, but it doesn't bother me. All my memories with her come flooding back, and those mental comforts outweigh the physical discomforts.

Starting from night one, I sit and talk out loud, recapping the tour. My voice echoes as I share everything I can remember in detail, and though I am aware there is no one within ear-shot listening, I know she is

I finished *Among Broken Clocks* today. I wish you'd annotated in the margins or something to prepare me for these garbage endings." I wrap my jacket tighter around me "I would've loved to know your thoughts on every book you left behind."

The sun peeks through the trees, turning the midnight-black canvas to shades of pink and orange. I spent the entire night sitting and talking about the tour and the books – the same way I'd spent each night I'd returned from tour for the last five years that she's been gone and with her in person the ten years before that.

I push myself off the ground and place one hand on her headstone "I miss you, Raya. You told me all this would get easier with time. You were wrong."

Home of Erotic Romance

Sign up for our newsletter and find out about all our romance book releases, eBook sales and promotions, sneak peeks and FREE romance books!

About the Author

When it comes to romance, L A doesn't have a type. Sometimes it's dark and devastating, sometimes it's soft and simple - truly, it just depends what her imaginary friends are doing at the time she starts writing about them.

L A has moved to various parts of the country over the last ten years but her heart has never left Boston.
And no, the "A" does not stand for Anne.

L A Tavares loves to hear from readers. You can find her contact information, website details and author profile page at https://www.totallybound.com

Made in the USA
Middletown, DE
17 October 2023

40996201R00191